MAKE ME WORK

■

MAKE
·
ME
·
WORK

Ralph Lombreglia

FARRAR

STRAUS

GIROUX

NEW YORK

LIBRARY OF CONGRESS CATALOGING-IN-PUBLICATION DATA
Lombreglia, Ralph.
Make me work / Ralph Lombreglia
p.   cm.
Contents: One-woman blues revival—Late early man—A half hour with God's
heroes—Can you dance to it?—Piltdown man—Natural product—
Every good boy—Make me work—Heavy lifting.
I. Title.
PS3562.O483M35   1994   813'.54—dc20   93-26485   CIP

The stories in this collection originally appeared in the
following magazines, sometimes in slightly different form:
"One-Woman Blues Revival," "Late Early Man," "Heavy
Lifting," in *The New Yorker*; "A Half Hour with God's
Heroes," "Make Me Work," "Every Good Boy Deserves
Favor," in *The Atlantic*; "Can You Dance to It?" in *Epoch*;
"Piltdown Man, Later Proved to Be a Hoax," in *The Paris
Review*; "This Is a Natural Product of the Earth," in *The
Little Magazine*.
The author is grateful for permission to reprint.

Kate Bernhardt, one-woman fiction workshop, contributed more to this book than I can begin to acknowledge. She was the first editor of these stories, though she wasn't the last. John Glusman of Farrar, Straus and Giroux, Charles McGrath of *The New Yorker*, and C. Michael Curtis of *The Atlantic* also hover angelically over these pages, along with Liz Darhansoff of Darhansoff & Verrill.

To them, and to friends and family too numerous to name, for inspiration and revelation, whether they knew it or not, love and thanks.

for Kate and Sophia

CONTENTS

■

One-Woman Blues Revival   3

Late Early Man   30

A Half Hour with God's Heroes   60

Can You Dance to It?   88

Piltdown Man, Later Proved to Be a Hoax   103

This Is a Natural Product of the Earth   127

Every Good Boy Deserves Favor   148

Make Me Work   166

Heavy Lifting   189

MAKE ME WORK

■

ONE-WOMAN BLUES

REVIVAL

■

As Lisa drove to the radio station, it started raining again, a cold, prickly rain that made her windshield look like a special effect on TV—the world dissolving into something else, one luminous dot at a time. And not a moment too soon, she thought. Cut. Fade to sunny seashore scene. It had been raining now for more than a week, and this was mud season to begin with, when the snowmelt came down from the mountains. The mantle of the earth was mush. Struggling to open the hood of her quixotic car this morning, she'd stepped on her front lawn, and it sucked the boot off her foot. Water stains were etched on her ceilings, like antique maps of her craggy heart.

She left the wipers off and turned on the radio instead. Milo Puccini, who had the show before hers, was playing a new cover of "Over the Rainbow" by Brain Bandage, a group of cyberpoppers from Secaucus, New Jersey, whose music featured hostile military drumming, phase-shifted guitar fuzz, drugged boys chanting, and —you had to hand it to them—a Chicano trumpet section, which took you by surprise. But Chicano trumpets or not, it was still robot music, reveling in its own soullessness. Lisa didn't get it— kids and their trips these days. When she was in college, she'd taken a cultural-history course with a professor whose favorite phenomenon was the "sunset effect"—the tendency of things to get most garish just before they disappear—and that was how she explained pop music to herself now: a tremulous thing glowing weirdly in the dusk, like phosphorescent lichens on fallen trees.

It was Lisa's job to defy the darkness, to keep the old light shining, however thin and ghostly. She did the classic-rock show on WWHY in Hollyfield, Vermont—ten in the morning to four in the afternoon. She'd done it for seven years. She played all the great stuff on her show, with emphasis on the tunes you would have heard when the station was founded, twenty years before— back when the whole town wore Guatemalan peasant blouses and ate umeboshi plums. She didn't personally go back *that* far. But neither was she a newborn like Milo here, fresh out of Hollyhock College on the hill.

The sopping landscape was disappearing nicely. She shivered and turned up the heat in her old Toyota. It was a homely little stump of a car from the early nineteen-eighties. You still saw a lot of them on the road—never-say-die vehicles, which usually came in blue, orange, or white. Lisa had found one in metallic mocha. She was lucky that way. But hers was saying die. It had taken twenty minutes to get the thing going this morning, and every time she hit a puddle it almost conked out. It didn't like to be wet. Neither did she. She had an image of Mitchell, her husband, somewhere warm and dry, with some little someone, enjoying her misery. It was a thoroughly irrational thought—Mitchell wasn't aware of her misery and, as far as she knew, he wasn't seeing anybody—but at least it was more rational than her sleepless conviction at 3 a.m. that Mitchell was somehow making it rain. It was a strange thing, estrangement. And *she'd* left *him*.

When she couldn't see the painted line on the road, she chickened out and flipped the wipers to high, and something better happened than the mere reappearance of the world. The wipers were exactly in sync with "Over the Rainbow," hitting it right on the backbeat, fitting in fine with the android groove. More than fine: they were the most happening thing on the tune. And when, bit by bit, the wipers went out of phase, Lisa kept time with them and let "Over the Rainbow" deconstruct itself. Brain Bandage would have liked that, and for that reason she arrived in the station parking lot liking them more. But she couldn't account for the drive that got her there. She'd flown the whole trip on autopilot, something she'd been doing more and more these days. So far, nothing bad had happened. Maybe her shrink was right, and it really was her subconscious mind she was supposed to trust, even for the allegedly conscious things.

■

She should have seen the end coming when she started conducting her marriage through the dog. But it began innocently enough; even Mitchell had found it amusing at first. The dog was a black Lab named Jesse, which Lisa had bought two years ago. She'd always wanted a puppy. Mitchell had always opposed getting one. He didn't really care for living things; it was all he could do not to kick her cat. Lisa was suspicious when he finally relented, but she hoped his heart had opened to the concept of family. She didn't deny that Jesse was her surrogate son, and soon she was talking to him that way. When Mitchell came home after work, she'd say, "Look, Jesse, Daddy's home! I wonder if Daddy got those groceries the way I asked him." If Mitchell was in a good mood, he'd say, "Yes, Jesse, I got the groceries. They're in these paper bags your mommy can see perfectly well I'm carrying. And now I wonder if Mommy's planning to cook my dinner for me." They had some yuks doing the communication riff with Jesse. But then Lisa started doing it more and more, for all the stuff that was really pissing her off. "Well, Jesse," she might say, "I thought your daddy could sit and talk to me for a while, but I guess he'd prefer to catalogue his record collection some more." Or, "What do you know, Jesse? Daddy's in another one of his crummy moods." By the end, she wasn't saying anything to Mitchell except by telling it to the hound. It was confusing for Jesse, poor beast, especially when the screaming started.

Mitchell, a mercurial man, owned the record store in Hollyfield. Four months ago, Lisa had left him after eight years of marriage.

He hadn't been abusive, exactly. He was just a self-centered goon whose charm of a decade before had dissolved entirely in his mania for collecting artifacts and memorabilia of the history of rock 'n' roll, in particular anything having to do with the life and career of Elvis Presley. Mitchell had come into this world as a normal Presley fan, but he'd evolved into one of those people who buy black-velvet paintings of Elvis, and bourbon bottles shaped like the King in Vegas, and don't see anything funny about it. He attended rock-nostalgia trade shows. He *corresponded* with other collectors. For eight years, he had pretended to be preparing himself—mentally, financially—for the child Lisa wanted to have, and then he announced that he thought a dog and a cat were sufficient.

When Lisa decided to move out, she got the notion of a cabin in the woods—just she and Jesse and the cat, away from Hollyfield and everyone who knew her and Mitchell together. She would purify herself with a winter alone and then start her life again in the spring, reborn with the bees and the daffodils. It seemed like a good idea at the time. Now, after that winter in the woods, analyzing her life, she was at the edge of the map, where it says "Here be dragons." She should have sampled some other opinions—Milo's maybe. You'd never catch Milo falling for the old bucolic fantasy. Or Brain Bandage. Brain Bandage would have stayed right there in town with the empty mill buildings and the crowded bars.

She found an early-nineteen-sixties ranch-style house for rent five miles into the country—a joyless little box that in any location but the redemptive woods of Vermont would have bummed out the Buddha. The house had a redwood deck overlooking the back yard, and that had clinched it for Lisa—standing on the deck with the realtor, looking into the evergreens. The realtor was a matronly woman named Louise, who said the woods were full of wild pink dogwoods in the spring. A yearning possessed Lisa to see songbirds land in the salmon-colored blossoms. She wanted to sit on the deck with her coffee at dawn and watch bunnies hop in her parcel of lawn. She dismissed the long, cold months she'd have to spend inside the house, which had been rented for years by two old-time hippie couples who'd left the four simple rooms in terrible shape. They'd left other things, too, including a plastic bag full of pennies on the kitchen counter, like an offering to something or someone (the Maharishi, perhaps, whose image adorned a lapel button stuck to a corkboard by the phone), and a note, pushpinned to the basement door, that read, "Peace be on this troubled place."

■

It crushed Lisa's spirit to step through the glass doors of WWHY's one-story bunker, but at least it wasn't raining in there. If she'd been paying attention in the past year, she'd have seen that bad architecture was enveloping her existence like the aura announcing an epileptic attack. For twenty years, the station had been housed in a funky old Victorian on the campus side of town, a former Hollyhock women's dorm that contained the whole essence of WWHY. But six months before Lisa left Mitchell, the struggling station was bought by a speculator named Otto, who also owned this concrete abomination out on Route 100. So far, he'd done nothing to his new acquisition but rip it up by its roots and drag it across town. Lisa doubted he'd ever mess with the programming. Musically, Otto was at the plaid-pants end of the dial, and some other local descendants of Lawrence Welk already had a station up there, wallpapering their assigned frequency with easy-listening goo. If Otto believed in anything, he believed in markets, and everybody knew what WWHY's market was—Hollyhock College and the bands of hippie leftovers living all through these beautiful green hills of Vermont.

Another glass door gave onto the hallway, its cinder-block walls made to resemble nougat candy by a thick coat of pastel-speckled rubberized paint. The whole building belonged under the earth—a genuine bunker, where you could stare at soft-serve concrete till you ran out of water, ate the cat food and then the cats, and finally climbed out to see what was left. We should be breathing through tubes, thought Lisa, walking down the hall. Milo was in the announcer's booth, his Eraserhead haircut partially obscured by the big white headphones adorning his ears like landing lights. Lisa made a face at him through the glass, but he didn't see. Rodney, engineering in the opposite booth, opened his mike and spoke into Milo's phones. Milo turned and saw Lisa, and began slapping his watch. I know, I know, she answered, mouthing the words. She was forty minutes late.

Rodney beamed through his dusty wire rims as she entered his booth. If you needed a techie in your life, a man with a nice wad of keys on his belt, you wanted it to be Rodney. He was the original engineer of WWHY and its chief engineer today—the only member of the staff with an actual license from the FCC. He resembled the young Thomas Edison, right down to the shoes, though he wasn't really young anymore. Nobody was, except Milo.

"How about these great sounds, Rod?" Lisa said, plopping into a chair.

"Milo's music upsets me," Rodney replied.

"Really? Some mindless dolts using a million bucks of studio time to make stupid, pointless ugliness? What's upsetting about that?"

He looked up from the clump of audio cables he was untangling. It seemed as if he'd been untangling them for a while now. "I guess it's just me," he said.

There was a sad story you always heard about Rodney, and if you hadn't heard it he would tell you himself, with the most heartbreaking earnestness. Owing to some boyhood mishap, he had a metal plate in his head. That wasn't the story. The story was that one night in the early seventies, some d.j.s at the station talked Rodney into smoking marijuana with them, something he'd never done before. The pot interacted with his plate in some unprecedented neurometallurgical way, shifting valences or unleashing ion fields in his brain, with the result that he never came back down. The fun-loving d.j.s laughed when he told them the next night. They assured him that he was imagining it. But he wasn't. He waited a few more days, then a week, and nothing changed. He never touched a reefer after that night, and he'd been stoned for two decades now.

"What are you doing here?" Lisa asked. Rodney rarely officiated over particular radio shows—twiddling the knobs and watching the meters. The transmitter itself was his sphere of operations now, out in the hills. Lisa thought of it as a furnace that Rodney stoked, heroically, all by himself.

"We got a bone in our throat around 4 a.m."

"No kidding. Did we die?"

"Briefly."

"Got any bigger bones?"

They laughed. On the other side of the glass, Milo was wearing a pink T-shirt that said "Elvis Came From Mars" below a picture of the young Mr. Presley singing from the side of his horsy, carnal mouth. The T-shirt troubled Lisa out of all proportion to what it said. Quite possibly Elvis *had* come from Mars—she'd had the thought more than once herself, in connection with the King's possession of her estranged husband's soul. But this apprehension went beyond Mitchell and her marriage; she felt it coming from further down. For weeks she'd been this way, plunging into deep anxiety over the slightest things. It was partly the relentless rain. She wheeled her chair over and put her cheek on Rodney's shoulder. He smelled musty—mildewed, in fact—but so did everything these days.

Behind the glass, Milo was scowling at her while some head-banging travesty whacked away on the monitors. "Hello, Lisa," he said, his voice floating over the music like the Wizard of Oz's. "Thank you for coming to do your radio show this morning."

Lisa and Milo agreed on only one thing in life, but it was something so fundamental that it made them friends—the vileness of "mellow." She leaned into Rodney's mike. "Milo, give me a break, will you? My car wouldn't start in the rain, and then it kept conking out all the way over here. I got about two hours' sleep, because my bedroom smells like a landfill and a monster raccoon runs through my floor all night. My dog wakes up and howls at 3 a.m., my cat starts yowling, and my shrink is now pushing survivors' groups and light meds."

"What kind of light meds?" asked Milo.

"Survivors of what?" Rodney asked.

"Marriage and downers," Lisa replied.

Milo stared at her, gnomelike beneath the big phones, while his ravagers of beauty finished their song. Then he opened his mike to the world. "All right, everybody," he announced, "our very own flower child, Miss Lisa, is finally here to do her show. Please be nice to her today. Her car won't run in the rain, so she parked it at the dump and lives in it now with her dog and her cat and her raccoon. They take bad medicine and never go to sleep. If her husband is listening, she's not coming back. It's a sad story. But the old girl can still rock 'n' roll, so let's segue into those classic moldies with the new one from Lizard Euphoria, a little thing they call 'Want Slash Need.' " Then Milo spun the tune, if tune it could be called, and pried the headphones off his head.

Which somehow caused Lisa to figure it out. It wasn't really about Elvis at all. The picture of the King on Milo's shirt was taken in 1957—the year her father threw her bottle in the sea. She'd been thinking about it in the shower this very morning. It happened on a Jersey-shore vacation with her folks when she was three years old. She was playing beside her parents' beach blanket, dropping her bottle in the sand and then crying because it had sand on it. Her mother cleaned it off for her four or five times, and then the next time she dropped it the old man leaped up and flung it into the waves. That was how Lisa was weaned. Thirty-five years later, a T-shirt was making her feel bad about this. So it was true: she was hysterical. All the stray garbage-signals of the world had found their satellite dish, and its name was Lisa. Her father was dead now, meaning he was truly alive. Alive forever. Leaving her husband had brought him back; she thought about him every day.

Milo poked his head into engineering. "I'm playing the long mix of this," he said. "Seven minutes."

"Milo," said Lisa, "promise me something or I'm gonna worry. Don't go in Mitchell's store wearing that shirt, O.K.? He's weird about Elvis."

"Mitchell weird?" Milo said. He looked down to see what shirt he was wearing. "Lisa, I drive all the way to Brattleboro to buy music, just so I won't have to set foot in Mitchell's store, ever, for any reason. No matter what I'm wearing."

Lisa shot him with a gun-shaped hand that meant "Good thinking."

"I don't shop at Mitchell's store, either," said Rodney. "He yelled at me once, and all I was doing was looking through the bins."

"Yeah, but how many hours had you been looking?" Milo asked.

"I don't keep track of things like that, Milo."

Lisa wheeled her chair back to look at Rodney. He was really a very sweet man, she thought, far sweeter than most. But he'd shaved himself badly the day before, leaving a patch of brown-gray stubble under one nostril, and several more on his neck. No, Rodney was not the answer. She stood and kissed his cheek. "You're not the answer, either," she told Milo.

"What's the question?"

"What is Lisa doing for the rest of her life?" she said, and gave herself to the fluorescent hallway, the shining linoleum path to the coffee machine.

"She's doing the classic-rock show on WWHY!"

"Oh, no," she said, not looking back. "No, no, no." Though it was perverse and destructive, she allowed herself the thought that she was old enough to be Milo's mother, simply to enjoy the consolation of the subsequent thought: But I would have had to get started awfully early. And then she recalled that she *had* gotten started awfully early.

She yelped once in the coffee room and poured herself a mug of the black acid bath from the Mr. Coffee carafe. One of Milo's pre-dawn survival tricks was to put three foil bags of ground coffee in the filter instead of one, and then coax the results past his tongue with heavy measures of non-dairy creamer. He had left the morning arrivals to figure this out for themselves.

She had a sip of sludge. She hadn't been on a date since leaving her husband, and now it was the weekend again and she just wanted to go out with somebody, and not somebody she already knew, either, which ruled out everyone. There was a very nice gay man, HIV negative, who donated sperm to lesbian couples in the area. She never thought she'd join the ranks of the turkey-baster moms, but it was starting to look like either that or become Lisa Harrington, Raccoon Lady of Hollyfield, Vermont.

■

It had been a dumb move to feed the raccoon in the first place, she'd be the first to admit it. But he was cute and she was lonely. Recipe for trouble.

Her rented house had a pantry window facing the redwood deck in back. Since the end of the bitter-cold weather, she'd been leaving it open so Sergeant Pepper, her cat, could come and go at will. One evening after dinner, cleaning up at the sink, she sensed Sarge in the corner of her eye. When she turned to look, it wasn't him. It was a mammoth raccoon on the windowsill, looking at her with his broad masked face. He was moving his pointy nose all around, smelling the pantry smells. His long, black claws hung over the edge of the sill.

You couldn't live in Vermont without seeing lots of raccoons, but she'd never seen one this close up, or this big. She'd certainly never seen one sitting in a pantry window, so trusting and calm. She felt, after all these unsatisfactory years of adulthood, that she might finally be in a fairy tale. "Who the hell are you?" she said. "Do you talk?" To her great disappointment, he did not.

Jesse was sleeping on the living-room rug. Lisa stepped into the pantry, and, far from running away, Sparky—she'd already named him Sparky in her mind—came a little farther in. Quietly, she took bowls of dry cat kibble and water out the back door to the deck. Sparky waited on the railing, rising up on his hind legs to sniff the air and flex his slender hands. When Lisa went back in, he hopped down and ate the food, while she watched through the door. She had to keep the window closed from then on; otherwise, Jesse would kill Sparky on her kitchen floor, or Sparky would kill Sergeant Pepper on the redwood deck. Somebody would kill somebody. When Sparky came the following night, he scratched adorably on the glass. Lisa bumped him up to Sarge's canned provisions—Elegant Entrée, Liver in Creamed Gravy, Tuna in Sauce.

Beyond the town limits, they didn't send a garbage truck to your house; Lisa had to take her own trash to the dump once a week. Between trips she kept her bags in the basement against the cool stone wall. A week after Sparky arrived, she went to take another load down, and a stench came up the stairs. She crouched on the steps with the flashlight. Every garbage bag was ripped open. She sent Jesse first and then followed him down, tiptoeing in her flat shoes around the scattered trash. The dog wriggled through the basement like a large black muscle, vacuuming the floor with his snout. Periodically, he stopped to scratch himself, and it made Lisa feel itchy, too. Her ankles bristled. Didn't I shave my legs this morning? she thought, glancing down at the stubble there. She could have sworn she had. The light in the basement was bad, but she seemed to have hair on her feet as well. Then she saw the stubble hopping.

She shrieked and ran upstairs, and washed her legs in the tub, spritzed her rubber boots with flea spray and went back downstairs. Jesse was still on a psychedelic nose trip at the far end of the room. In the yellow light of the bare bulb, Lisa saw the black particles of fleas rush away from her boots like iron filings repelled by magnetism. Thousands of them were flicking around the concrete floor amid piles of white dust and plaster scraps she'd never noticed before. She glanced up at the ceiling. It was all busted—holes punched through it in many places, irregular clumps of white solids dangling by threads.

It took her a second to understand what this was. Sparky, the fat hog, had been running in the space between the ceiling and the floor upstairs, breaking through the plaster wherever it wouldn't hold his weight.

■

Milo's musical parting shot was pure thrashing rudeness, but it gave Lisa four minutes in the record library. She arrived in the booth with a stack of CDs, put on her phones, and cued up a disc. She was supposed to do a station ID followed by spots for a water-bed store and a Chinese takeout place, but they'd wait. She pulled a slider on the console to kill Lizard Euphoria, pushed another slider open, hit the button, and—*wham!*—Jimi Hendrix cracked the gloom with "Still Raining, Still Dreaming," the only song Lisa could possibly play to start a radio show today, because it *was* still raining and she *was* still dreaming, and because if raccoons did talk they'd sound like the amazing wah-wah guitar Hendrix played on this tune.

Lay back and dream on a rainy day. Jimi made her feel so much better that she went on to his version of "Red House," a blues she dedicated to herself because her raccoon- and flea-infested house was red. By the time the great man shook his strings through the first chorus, she had figured out what to do: an all-day blues marathon. Her condition called for the heavy medicine. I'm a one-woman blues revival, she thought, and ran to the record library again.

"How about some B. B. King, everybody?" she said when she was back in her d.j. chair, and the Master riffed on Lucille, his famous guitar. "Now let's hear from the other King," she told radioland, "and I do mean Albert," and Mr. Blues Power ripped into one, followed by Buddy and Freddie and Muddy and Memphis. She did a whole half hour of the Wolf, and calls came in on the listener line. They were liking this out there. She'd struck a nerve with these blues. It must have been the weather, not to mention the economy these days. Vermont was more depressed than Lisa was. Last month, the station had run a news piece on the numbers of people eating road kill to get through the winter.

Maybe she could get someone to eat Sparky, she thought, answering the flashing phone. No, she didn't want Sparky on a spit. She just wanted him out of her house.

The man on the phone was all worked up and couldn't speak English very well. "This is best radio I hear since I come to this country!" he exclaimed.

"Glad you like it," said Lisa.

"I love blues!" he said.

"Great. What's your name?"

"Tommy T.!"

"Tommy T. That's your name?"

"Yes! I grow up with this blues!"

He sounded Eastern European—Czech or Polish or something like that. "And where was that, Tommy? Where you grew up. Gdansk?"

He was silent for a second inside her phones. "You have excellent ear," he said. "My home is near Gdansk."

Lisa laughed. "I was kidding, Tommy. It was a joke, you know? Lech Walesa? Solidarity? Gdansk shipyards?"

"Yes!" he said. "Why is Gdansk joke?"

"It's not. I meant that Gdansk is the only thing people like me know about your country, so I mentioned it."

"Oh."

"Would you like to request a song, Tommy?"

"I know how your car is breaking!"

" 'I Know How Your Heart Is Breaking.' Sounds familiar. Who did it?"

"No! You! Your car!"

"My heart is breaking. As a matter of fact, it is, Tommy. But just how did you happen to know that?"

"The man on radio tell about it. Before."

A man on the radio told him my heart was breaking, thought Lisa. One way you knew you'd plunged to the deep, hidden crux of reality was that the strange people started calling you up. It happened to Lisa periodically—clusters of crazies ringing her phone.

"Tommy, have you ever noticed how other people's license plates contain secret messages meant for you alone?" He fell silent. Lisa recalled that she was strange now herself, and shouldn't be casting stones. She had a James Cotton song going with twenty seconds left to run and there was nothing else cued up. "I have to put you on hold," she said, and hit the button for Rodney's booth. "Rod, talk to this guy for me, will you? I can't figure him out."

She flipped through some discs. The station had a brand-new CD copy of "Layla," by Derek and the Dominos—an immortal creation that contained, as she remembered it, an astounding version of "Have You Ever Loved a Woman." It was a song about a man in love with his best friend's wife, which Eric Clapton actually had been at the time. That was why it was astounding. If you didn't know, you knew the instant you heard his guitar.

She let it roll and punched Rodney again. "So what's the story?"

"He's from Poland."

"I got that."

"His whole life is the blues."

"I sort of got that, too."

"He came to America to play blues guitar. He wants to fix your car."

She unraveled this for a second. "Oh, my car."

"Yeah, what did you think?"

"Never mind." He was a guitar bum who also worked on cars. Why did those things always go together? And here was evidence that it went well beyond America—to Poland, of all places. Didn't that prove it was something in the structure of the male brain? She got back on the phone.

"You play Eric Clapton!" Tommy exclaimed.

"I do that sometimes. But this one's for you, Tommy."

"Thank you!"

"I understand you play the blues."

"Yes! I am blues-guitar player!"

"A guitar player who fixes cars? I've never heard of that."

"I am fixing car for living. You stall in puddle, yes?"

"Yes. Right. But now it won't even start in the rain anymore."

"I know! Vapors! Wires getting wet! Not hard to fix. Great honor to fix blues lady's car. Please come to shop today. I fix for you!"

She did need to do something about the car, and her usual mechanic was Mitchell's best friend. "What's your real name, Tommy?"

He didn't answer right away. "Tomasz," he finally said. "Tomasz Tomaczewski. But is no good for blues."

"I can see that. And where are you fixing cars, exactly?"

She knew the garage he was working at, and said she'd drop by after her show. She had a soft spot for Tommy T., because he reminded her of a feeble old joke she'd loved as a girl at summer camp—the one about a Polish window washer who frightens a woman on the phone. *I am viper. I am coming to you.*

"I am coming to you," she told Tommy T.

"I fix car for blues disc-jockey lady!" he declared.

■

The garage where Tommy T. worked was a place Lisa had seen for years but never visited—a former gas station known now as Al's Car Repair. She sputtered over there in the unending rain. Rodney had gleaned on the phone that Tommy knew someone who knew someone who knew Al, and that was how he'd got this job. He must have been an ace mechanic, but, even so, he was dumb lucky to be working at all; he'd been in the States only three months.

As if her car knew where they were, it hit a puddle in Al's

potholed lot and died right there. She opened her door to the stinging weather. WWHY was playing loud in the shop. She got halfway across the lot when the world wobbled like a bad TV tube. In the dark mouth of the building, beside the stout chrome shaft of a lift, her father was working under a car. Not her father as she knew him last, but a man younger than she was now—the father who threw her bottle in the sea. He was wearing bluejeans and a red plaid shirt, and his straight brown hair fell to his shoulders like the prince in disguise in a story he used to read to her. She stopped in the lot and closed her eyes. In the red darkness, her father-prince emerged from the building with her bottle in his hand. When she opened her eyes, the real guy had come out holding a wrench. It wasn't her father in his late twenties, just a man who looked miraculously like him. "*Blues?*" he cried out.

She smiled and nodded her head. He came running over. He wanted to shake hands, but his were coated with engine grease, so he just waved the wrench around and babbled. He was a good five years younger than Lisa was, and he acted younger than that—the enthusiasm overdose combined with the language barrier, she supposed. But he wasn't the dark, self-involved guitar jock she'd expected. He was a big, cute puppy of a guy.

"I know, Tommy!" she finally got in. "You love the blues. You told me."

Two other guys came out, men in grubby overalls who wanted to see the lady d.j. "We always listen to your show!" one said.

"We didn't think Tommy was really gonna call you," said the other.

"Tommy," Lisa said, "I hope you didn't call me on a dare."

Tommy didn't understand this.

"We didn't dare him to do nothin'," said the second guy. "It was his idea."

"If I close my eyes it's just like the radio!" the first guy said.

People always said this. The guys pushed her car into a bay, where Tommy examined it for a while. It turned out she had bad corrosion of delicate parts, and the supplier was closed for the day.

Tommy would get replacement parts tomorrow, but her car had to stay the night.

"I give you ride home," Tommy said, but first he had to wash his hands and show her his guitar and amp, which he had right there with him at Al's Car Repair. They were precious vintage Fenders, just like the ones the famous bluesmen used. He opened the guitar case and lifted a Stratocaster from the orange plush. It was blue. He held it up like a baby for Lisa to see.

"You bring this stuff to work with you, Tommy?"

"I worry if someone will steal! Also, maybe after working I jam. I must jam, Lisa!"

He had an old beat-up Dodge wagon, not the most confidence-inspiring vehicle for your new mechanic to be driving, but the heat and the wipers worked, and they were the essential things right then. The weather was revolting. Lisa thought, When I get back in my house, I'm not coming out till I see the sun, like a groundhog. Which reminded her. "You know anything about raccoons?"

He looked at her quizzically. "Animal?"

"Yeah, the animal." Tommy T. made her feel afresh the vast possibilities of America, where raccoons might be a brand name of something, or a rock band you'd never heard about. She spread her fingers across her face to mimic the masks of the woodsy creatures who seemed so cute till you discovered they were vermin, vicious and diseased. She had stopped feeding Sparky, but he came to her closed window every night anyway. When she banged on the glass to make him go away, he hissed at her—a frightening, feral hiss. "I think I have one in my basement."

"Not good when animal in house," Tommy said.

"Any animal? I have a dog and a cat."

"Dog is good! Why not dog get raccoon?"

"Because he'll kill it, Tommy."

"Good!"

"I don't want my dog killing things. Besides, raccoons have rabies. That raccoon could bite my dog and my dog could die."

This was hilarious to Tommy. "Raccoon not kill dog! Dog kill raccoon!"

At Lisa's house, he guided his big spongy boat into the horseshoe drive. Lisa was unlocking her front door when she saw him getting his equipment out. "Tommy, it's perfectly safe here," she said, and gestured to the woods around them. "Nobody's gonna steal your stuff."

"Too cold for guitar in car," he said, hauling out the battered luggage of his sacred things.

Her heart sank at the adolescence of it, his obsessiveness about his stuff, but artists were like that, weren't they? It wasn't like being an Elvis fanatic. If you could find a man to love you the way Tommy T. loved his Fender guitar, you'd be all right.

She heard Jesse plop down from the bed when she opened the door. She'd been letting him sleep with her since she'd moved out here—starting him at the foot of the bed, but giving in until now he stretched out full-length, with his head on the pillow. He came down the hall like a cannonball, saw the man in the drive, and flew past Lisa out the door. Tommy had his guitar in one hand and his amp in the other, and no time to set them down. When the dog leaped, Tommy hoisted his knee, and Jesse landed on his back with a squeal Lisa had never heard him make. He got up and tried it again, and got the same thing from Tommy.

"No jump!" Tommy commanded. To Lisa's amazement, Jesse obeyed. "Heel!" Tommy said, and Jesse escorted him up the steps, all eye contact and lolling tongue. He'd met the alpha male Lisa was always hearing about from the obedience-school people.

Tommy taught Jesse to sit while Lisa got the guitarist a beer. She wondered about the signal she was sending, having this stranger in her house, and thought she should get right to the raccoon. Sparky saved her the trouble. They heard the undeniable scrabbling of a sizable mammal in the floor.

"Oh, ho!" Tommy said, crouching to follow the sound to the pantry threshold, where a pipe came up from the basement. "Stay!" he told Jesse, his hand like a cop's. The hole in the floor was larger than the metal tube passing through it, and missing the decorative cuff used to finish such installations. Tommy beckoned Lisa over. In the gap between floorboards and pipe, she saw the eye of a raccoon.

"He watch us!" Tommy whispered.

"Sparky, you devil," Lisa said. "I call him Sparky," she told Tommy.

"You have hammer?"

"You're not going to hit him with a hammer!"

"No! Not hit him! Nails, too?"

She had those things in her junk drawer in the pantry. Tommy swigged his beer and headed for the basement. "Stay," he told Lisa and Jesse both, and closed the door behind him.

"Don't you hurt him!" Lisa said to the door.

Tommy started smacking the basement pipes with the hammer. The clanking shot through the arteries of the house and ended up in the fillings of Lisa's teeth. Suddenly the floor was raccoon pin-ball, Sparky bouncing around like bonus points in five places at once. She heard Tommy yelling, "Ha! Hey! You!" and hammering nails into wood. Was he crucifying the poor thing?

She pulled Jesse out the back door. Sergeant Pepper slipped out, too, and jumped onto the deck's wooden railing. Lisa dragged Jesse down the stairs and hooked him to his wire tether that ran the length of the yard—scene of her dreams of springtime rebirth and renewal. At the moment, it was a slapping, sucking pit of muck.

After a while, Tommy appeared on the deck. "Surprise!" he called down. Through the railing, Lisa could see Sarge nuzzling his ankles. "Sparky not boy!"

"What!"

"Have babies!"

"You're kidding me!" Lisa cried. She ran up the steps. "Then we can't throw them out! Stop! Don't do anything to them!"

Tommy had coffee grounds and scraps of deliquescing salad on his boots, and he was scratching himself all over. "Lisa, you have female emotion."

"Don't you dare tell me that!"

"Sorry!" he said. "I find hole, too!"

"They were coming in a hole?"

"I hammer it up!"

"How many babies?"

"Three? Four?" He pulled down one of his socks and clawed his ankle. "Fleas bite me, little suckers!" He stamped his foot. "Lisa! Sparky must live outside!"

"I guess you're right," she said.

He pointed along the length of the house. "I get them out window! Watch!" he said, and ran back in.

Lisa returned to the muddy yard. It was twilight—the magic time, when the souls of animals took dream forms and wandered through the world, visible only to the shamans of the tribe. Lisa remembered this from some spooky Carlos Castaneda books she'd read in college. The basement window popped inward and Tommy's face appeared in the house's foundation. He propped the window with a stick and disappeared.

"No jump!" she commanded Jesse, but he jumped anyway, choking on his wire. Then his mouth dropped open in a rictus. He flexed the black leather of his nose-wings, tuning in to nature's great radio.

Lisa didn't like being outside alone at night, and now her shaman thoughts were making her feel upset. She heard a flapping sound and looked up: bats were flying against the nacreous sky. Softly, she started to sing: "Heavenly shades of night are falling, it's twilight time . . ."

A loud, weird wail hit the darkening air. Her heart stopped, and she fell to her knees in the mud. She wasn't breathing. She looked for Jesse. He was dead, too; the electrocuting spirit scream had knocked him right into the ground. Then she touched her face. No, she wasn't dead. Jesse wasn't, either. He sprang up like a swamp creature to howl and lunge at the otherworldly sounds emanating from the house. Lisa struggled to her feet. The tops of her boots had filled with mud. She slogged across the yard until she could see into the open basement window.

The bare bulb in the ceiling was on, and Tommy was in the halo of yellow light with his Fender Stratocaster. He'd plugged his amp into the socket above the bulb, and if he didn't have it turned up all the way, Lisa didn't know what all the way could possibly be. It was monstrously loud. She could feel his fingers slither over the strings as though she were the guitar herself. His long brown hair waved around his face as he played one screaming blues lick after another.

It was more than Sparky could take. Her bandit's face appeared in the window. Tommy leaned into his amp for the feedback and fuzz of Hendrix at his most crazed, and smaller raccoon faces popped up next to Sparky's, dazed and confused. One by one they went over the sill like lemmings, pushed from behind by their mother.

Jesse had been woofing at the sky to protest the guitar, but the raccoon activity caught his eye. He ran across the yard on his tether and stood on his hind legs in disbelief, which caused Sparky to see that a large dog occupied the place where she'd pushed her babies. She flew out the window. Lisa dove for Jesse and wrestled him into the mud, and together they watched as Sparky herded her brood across the yard and up the trunk of a leafless maple tree. Their hunched forms stood out against the sky—a mother and three babies in the safe, high branches.

Tommy unpropped the window and slammed it shut. Lisa hadn't realized he'd stopped playing his guitar. She hadn't realized something else: the raccoons were so easy to see because they were bathed in moonlight. The moon was out, inside a big hole in the clouds. It wasn't raining anymore.

Tommy appeared on the lighted deck, squinting into the night. "Raccoons go away!" he called to the back yard, but no one answered. "I play blues for you, Lisa!" No one answered. He came down into the mud. Lisa was sprawled across her Labrador retriever in the foot-deep soup. "Hey, what happen?" Tommy said.

"Tommy T.," said Lisa, wiping mud from her eyes. She unfastened Jesse's tether and let him go. He hit Tommy like a bomb. "My hero."

■

Jesse went back on his wire run, and Tommy T. went in the shower. Lisa gave him her largest, longest robe—a pink terry-cloth one with satin lapels. She made him a plate of cheese and crackers, and left it on the counter with another beer. He'd piled his clothes outside the bathroom door. In her flowered kimono, she took his muddy things and hers to the washer downstairs. The raccoons were gone but not the fleas; they peppered her ankles as she hopped from foot to slippered foot. When she got back upstairs, Tommy had found the food and was eating it in the living room while inspecting her record collection. The pink robe, ankle-length when Lisa wore it, barely covered his knees. "You look ridiculous." She giggled.

Tommy looked down and laughed at himself. "Great records!" he said.

"We get them for free. Your clothes'll be ready in an hour."

She forgot that she couldn't start her washing machine and then hop in the shower. Cold water trickled on her toes. Tommy was not likely to run away without his jeans, but with men you never knew. Paradoxically, she wanted him to leave, so she could call her girlfriend, Sally, in town, and talk about him. When the water came back, she showered and hurried out. Tommy was making no attempt to run away. He was playing an obscure Willie Dixon album and singing along. She watched him from the doorway. He seemed so relaxed and happy. She thought twice about entering the living room in only a kimono, her wet hair combed straight back, but she couldn't very well get dressed and leave a foreign guest stuck in a bathrobe by himself. "You play great guitar," she said.

"Thank you!" he said, and finally shook her hand. Then he kissed her.

"Tommy T.!" she whispered.

"Lisa disc jockey," Tommy whispered back, putting his arms around her.

"Lisa Harrington," she said, putting her arms around him.

Unearthly shrieks erupted from the basement. Tommy gasped and dropped his beer bottle. It hit him on the toe. He hopped to the kitchen with his foot in one hand and the foaming bottle in the other. "What is this?" he cried.

"I don't know!" Lisa said. Jesse began to howl in the yard. The shrieking in the basement was now joined by scraping and banging, and a screeching like innumerable nails on a blackboard. "I've never heard anything like this in my life!"

She looked out the pantry window. In the moonlight, Jesse was flying around on his wire like Peter Pan. She remembered the hippies' note, pinned to the basement door. "Let's just leave and come back in the morning!"

Tommy grabbed her flashlight from a shelf, put his boots on his bare feet, and slipped away, one slow step at a time, into the bedlam below. When he was gone, the telephone rang. Lisa snatched it from the wall. It was Mitchell.

"I can't talk to you now," she said.

"What the hell is going on over there?" he said. "What's that noise?"

"I don't know. I think this house may be haunted or something."

"Really. Well, I just called to tell you I've met someone. I didn't want you to hear it through the grapevine."

It was the most considerate thing Mitchell had done in ages. Had he actually changed? She felt a pang of loss and regret. "Who? Who did you meet?"

"What difference does it make?"

"I'd like to know."

"Her name's Diane. She works in that boutique on Main Street."

"The leotard store?"

"Yeah, I guess that's what it is."

"Not the little blond one."

"Yeah, I guess she's little and blond."

Lisa slammed the wall with her fist. "Mitchell, she's, like, ten years younger than I am! And you're six years older than me! You could be her father!"

"Why do people always focus on that?"

"I'll bet she wants to have a family, right?"

"I don't know, Lisa. I just started seeing her. You left me, remember?"

"Yeah, and this is why, you ass!"

The logic of this stopped him for a second. "Are you O.K. over there, Lisa? Yes or no."

"No. And I found something out for you today. Elvis came from Mars." She slammed the phone down and turned to find Tommy standing there.

"Guess what!" he said. He led Lisa down the deck steps and swung the flashlight on the house. Sparky was on the narrow ledge of the basement window, clinging there with her rear feet and scraping her front paws down the glass with a teeth-shattering screech. Behind the glass, a smaller version of Sparky clawed in a similar fashion, and screamed, while Jesse howled and bucked like a bronco in the moonlit yard. "I close baby inside!" Tommy said sheepishly.

"A *baby* is making that sound?"

"Want his mama!"

"What do we do now?"

He slapped the backs of his hands. "Gloves?"

In a kitchen drawer she found two oven mitts imprinted, for some reason, with maps of Montana, and practically made for raccoon wrangling. Tommy put them on, and Lisa put on her boots, and they went down into the cellar. At the far end, the baby was perched beside the window on a pipe. It stopped shrieking when she shone the flashlight in its eyes. With a deft maneuver, Tommy seized it in the mitts. Lisa moved the light into Sparky's face through the glass and swung the window up. Jesse's barking filled the room.

"I forgot the dog!" she said. "He's blocking their tree."

"Get him away!" said Tommy.

Out in the yard, Lisa leashed Jesse and took him off the wire run. "No pull!" she cried, but he towed her halfway to the house like a water-skier. Lisa stopped him the way you stop in real waterskiing, by falling in. "Bad dog!" she cried, and hauled him back across the yard.

Tommy pushed the screeching baby out the window. It plopped into the soupy ground. Sparky jumped down and nosed it out of the mud, and together, mother and child, they crossed the yard and climbed the tree.

"I love lady mud wrestling," said a voice behind Lisa. "Never saw it with a dog before, though."

She spun around. Mitchell was standing at the edge of the house in his black leather jacket and paratrooper boots. Jesse yelped and bolted away, pulling Lisa off her feet again. She rose from the mud in a rage. "No pull, Jesse!" she screamed. "Mitchell, what the hell are you doing here?"

"Ah, my grateful wife. You were in trouble, so I rushed over to help."

"Thanks, we don't need any."

"Who's we?"

"Me and Jesse. See you, O.K.?"

"Lisa, I don't think so. I'm worried about you. Look at yourself."

She reached a wild pitch of exasperation. "Hear that, Jesse?" she cried. "Your daddy's worried about me! He was never worried about me before!"

The back door opened, and Tommy stepped onto the deck above them. Sergeant Pepper got out again, too; he leaped onto the railing to rub against the corner post and meow at the moon.

"The place is haunted, all right!" said Mitchell. "Here's the ghost! What big teeth you have, my dear!"

Tommy lit their faces with the flashlight. "Ghost?" he said. "Teeth?" He came halfway down the stairs. "What man is this?" he asked Lisa.

"It's my husband," she said.

"You put my leg on, Lisa!"

"This is Tommy," Lisa told Mitchell. "He's from Poland."

"What's he doing here?"

"He's not my boyfriend, Mitchell. He's fixing my car."

"They do things funny in Poland."

"He fell in the mud helping me. I'm washing his clothes."

"You look nice in that robe, Tommy," Mitchell said. "I gave that to Lisa for Valentine's Day once. Why don't you come down here? I don't like talking to people on stairs, especially when they're wearing my wife's underwear."

"He doesn't live here, Tommy," Lisa said. "We're getting divorced."

"Why should Tommy care, Lisa? He's just fixing your car."

Bravely, Tommy came down the stairs and stepped into the mud. Up in the house he'd looked silly in the knee-length pink robe, but now, his long hair brushing the satin collar in the moonlight, he looked like Galahad—transported here with the dress and manners of a more heroic age. Animals obeyed him. "You are man from music store," he said to Mitchell.

"Yeah, that's right. Why? You shop in my store? I don't remember you. I'll have to give you a special deal from now on."

Mitchell's tone of voice upset Jesse. He hunkered in the mud and barked.

"Can't you shut up the goddamn dog?" Mitchell said to Lisa.

"No bark!" Tommy said. Jesse cast his eyes at Tommy's feet and stopped barking. "Come!" Tommy said. When Jesse skulked to him, Tommy took the leash from Lisa and made Jesse heel and sit.

"Wow," said Mitchell. "Look at that. How long you been training my dog, dude?"

"*Your* dog!" Lisa said. "You hate this dog! You never wanted this dog!"

"How long you been seeing this guy?" Mitchell asked her. "You had him in the wings before you left, didn't you? You sent him to spy on me in my store. Maybe this has been going on for years, huh?"

"I met him this afternoon, Mitchell. You know why the dog obeys him? Out of respect, that's why. Think about it."

"You need a new headshrinker, Lisa."

"Headshrinker?" Tommy asked her.

His innocence was exhilarating. "It means a psychiatrist," Lisa said.

"Crazy-people doctor?"

"That's right," Mitchell said. "She's crazy, Tommy."

"*He's* the crazy one!" Lisa said. "*He* thinks Elvis Presley's still alive!"

"There happens to be a lot of evidence he is," said Mitchell.

A bark of laughter burst from Tommy's mouth. "Elvis is dead, mister!"

Mitchell flinched as though he'd been struck. "Don't you ever say that about Elvis, punk!"

"You're sick, Mitchell," Lisa said. "You're not a well man."

"I'm sick? I'll show you how sick I am!" he cried, and raised his hand.

"Stay!" Tommy yelled.

"You're next!" Mitchell screamed.

"He's all talk, Tommy!" said Lisa.

But this was something Tommy had no reason to believe. "Get him, Jesse!" he commanded, and unhooked the leash, and when Jesse left the ground you could tell that Mitchell had not been the daddy he should have been.

LATE EARLY MAN

■

"**I** was talking to your girlfriend this morning," announces Anita, speaking from the carpeted floor of our editing suite, where she's sprawled like a stranded whale, her head cushioned by a coil of video cables, her silky blue harem pants pulled up over her knees. She's buffing her face with an ice cube as though taking a gravestone rubbing. After lunch she lost the ability to sit up in a chair, and I had to take over at the controls. Our suite contains the only air conditioner in all of Paradise Productions, and it broke down last night, and this is the two-week stretch of hell we go through every summer in Boston where you can't buy an air conditioner no matter how much money you're willing to spend. The hardware commando, Marco Tempesto, was supposed to come over and fix the one we have, but apparently he's too busy building one of his laser guns, or simulating reality on a computer somewhere. "She was telling me she wants you to do this to her," Anita says.

I twiddle a knob on the console to stop the videotape. "Wants me to do what?"

"You know. Knock her up. Make her pregnant. I'm supposed to plant that suggestion in your mind."

Anita has been with child now for as long as anyone can remember. The baby was due a week ago and there's still no sign that it plans to throw in the towel and come out. Everybody in the office lost the birth-date lottery; we had to make new guesses and put them in the hat all over again.

"Rebecca told you that?" I say. "When?"

"This morning. She was leaving for work when I came in. You were in the shower."

"And she said she wanted me to knock her up."

"Yup."

I have to say, this amazes me. Rebecca and I had a terrible fight this morning before I got in the shower. She was gone when I got out. Usually, when she sleeps over with me here, she'll at least stay for coffee in the morning. I'll make a big pot and maybe Dwight and Anita will roll in and we'll all have a cup together. That's how I met Rebecca in the first place, by subletting the first floor of this house; Anita liked me so much she fixed me up with her old friend. Then she decided I had the eye for video and she hired me to work upstairs at Paradise Productions. You don't usually think, when you rent an apartment, that you're getting a whole new life, but it happened to me.

"Can I give you some advice?" Anita says. "Do it so she has the kid in the spring. Everybody told me, 'Anita, whatever you do, don't be pregnant in the summertime.' That was the one thing I was supposed to remember. So what do I go and do?" She raises herself on one elbow and counts with her fingers. "In fact, right now would be the perfect time. She'd drop the kid in May."

"Anita? Didn't you kind of get pregnant by accident?"

"Walter! We always thought we might try someday. It crossed our minds. Don't call my baby an accident!"

"I just meant you're not really the family-planning type, you and Dwight."

"You're right. We're more the walk-off-the-edge-of-a-cliff type." She selects a new ice cube from the bucket and burnishes her face some more. Then she stops, lapsing into reflection. "Do you think that's a problem?"

"No, I have a lot of respect for people who walk off cliffs."

"You're nice, Walter," she says. "I'm glad we found you. Now what's going on up there? You're not telling me anything."

"Benny's molecules are attacking the other molecules. Benny's are winning."

"Oh, good. We're up to the molecules. What's after that?"

"The scientist comes on and starts talking."

"Right. Stop it there," she says. "Let's think this through. We have the nice molecules. Why do we need a scientist talking about them?"

"Because Benny said we have to?"

"Yeah, but that can't be the reason. Scientists are boring. People turn off when they see scientists. No offense."

"What do you mean 'no offense'? I'm not a scientist."

"But maybe you played a scientist once. Like that guy in the commercial who says, 'I'm not a doctor, but I play one on TV.' "

"I've never played a scientist."

"Well, forget it, then," she says. "What am I apologizing to you for?"

"I think we should crowbar the scientist in. Benny wants him."

"I know, I know," she sighs, rearranging herself on the floor and resting her arms on the medicine ball her belly has become. "Don't you sometimes wish Benny never found his niche in life?" Then she starts to giggle, but that jostles the baby too much. "Ow. It always kicks me when I laugh. It hates it when I'm happy."

Benny is Benjamin Silk, our client. Anita and Dwight are actually fond of Benny, partly because he's one of their best accounts, but also because he sees the world the way they do, as a collection of bites—verbal ones in Benny's case, the maxims and mottoes by which he manages reality. "Niche in life" is one of his favorites. He found his, and now everybody else had better find theirs. Me in particular. Benny sees me up here, an out-of-work actor writing video scripts, and he pegs me for a guy wandering through life in his boxer shorts, trying to remember what he did with his niche. He would like to save me from this fate. But that's the problem: I think niches are fate. Consider the unlikely people who manage to rendezvous with their niche. I've known a carpenter named Tilt and a tree surgeon named Wilde. Rebecca goes to a dentist named Payne.

And then there's Benny Silk himself. The first time I encountered him I thought he was the most abrasive person I'd ever met. Then I found out his line of work: abrasives. Benny's the marketing director for an abrasives manufacturer. If it can scrape the surface off an object, if it can grind something down to a nub, if it can scour, sand, buff, or polish to a deep luster, Benny's company makes it. But he wasn't always in abrasives. He's done laminates and films, adhesives and coatings. Did a long stretch in lubrication. They all had their rewards, but they weren't his niche. Then Benny entered the realm of grit and found himself. He became an abrasives evangelist. "You gotta be rough to be smooth, son," he barked at me the moment we met, apropos of nothing except perhaps my scratchy chapped hand crushed in his lotion-soft one.

Anita and I have been editing Benny's latest project for two weeks now—an infomercial about a fabulous new line of synthetic sandpaper. That's twice the editing time in the budget, and it's still lying there dead. We can't figure out how to jolt it into life. The sandpaper in question is called Veritas Grit—christened by one of Benny's young marketeers from the Harvard Business School. Benny couldn't be more proud of this new stuff if it came from inside his own body, but he knows he's got a hard sell on his hands. Our tape claims that Veritas Grit works as well on metal as it does on wood, works even better on plastic, works wet or dry, and lasts longer than the competition's best stuff. The problem is, it costs about twice as much. People will see the price in the store and go for the other brand. We have to convince them. To this end, we've cut in testimonials from users in the field, official company demos, Tempesto's computer-animated molecules. Today we spent the morning playing with the idea that Veritas Grit is "the sandpaper of success," before we finally dropped that, out of shame. Still, Benny wants some compelling something, and whenever clients want something and don't know what it is, they go with an authority figure. Benny has forbidden us to remove this scientist.

■

Dwight lurches in, a skinny six-foot-six-inch man in a red T-shirt with a yellow peace symbol on the front, sharkskin slacks, low-slung tasseled loafers, translucent green nylon socks. "How's that old rough cut?" he says. "Getting it smoothed out?"

"It's beginning to grate on us," I say.

"It's grinding us down," Anita says.

"Rubbing you wrong?" says Dwight, smiling brightly and joining his bride on the floor. "Going against your grain? Taking the edge off?"

"Dwight," I say, "do you notice anything about this room?"

He tumbles one of Anita's ice cubes in his mouth for a minute as though polishing a jewel. "Hot in here," he says around the ice.

"We can't work under these conditions, Dwight. Look at poor Anita."

"I told Anita she should be home where it's cool," Dwight says, patting her head. "But Anita's a big girl. She wants to work."

Alongside Dwight's bony frame, Anita seems to have doubled in size in the heat, like bread dough. "I just want to wrap this tape," she says to the ceiling. "I just want to finish this project and go have my baby. And I can. I can. I just have to do it lying down, without moving."

"Dwight, get Tempesto over here to fix this air conditioner."

"Not possible, Walter. Tempesto's working on something else for me right now. Very important."

"More important than finishing this wretched thing?"

"As a matter of fact, that's what he's working on. I've enlisted his help."

"No, Dwight," says Anita. "That can't go in this tape."

"I think it's just what this tape needs," Dwight says. "We need to show Benny's sandpaper in action. Show people the power of Veritas Grit!"

"Benny'll never go for it."

"Anita, don't say that. We haven't even pitched it to him yet."

"Pitched what?" I say.

"What are you doing tonight, Walter?" Dwight asks.

"Busy. Tied up."

"With Rebecca? She's invited."

"To what?"

"I already invited her," Anita says. "She thinks it's stupid."

The intercom beeps and Susie's transistorized voice issues from the speaker. Susie is our new Korean receptionist, discovered by Dwight in the corner store just days after her family arrived in the States. *"Dwight, Tempasta on two,"* Susie says. *"Tempasta for Dwight."*

"Speak of the devil," Dwight says.

I dive for the phone and punch line 2. "Tempesto, we're being roasted alive! You're torturing a pregnant woman! Get over here right now!"

Then Dwight clambers up and we wrestle for the phone. He wins, having the advantage of being on his feet. "What's up?" he asks Tempesto.

"Fix our air conditioner, you bum!" Anita calls out.

"Again?" Dwight says. "For God's sake, Tempesto. Do they have our stuff? Great. O.K., I'll grab Walter and we'll be right over."

"No! You can't take Walter!" Anita cries, waving her arms like an overturned crab.

Dwight hits the intercom button. "Susie to Editing Suite B. Suite B calling Miss Susie."

"Where is Tempesto, anyway?" I ask.

"Encountering some difficulties," Dwight says, fanning Anita with a folded Boston *Globe*. "Anita, you're my pregnant wife. I don't want you to be unhappy."

"Then go work on your own project and leave us alone!"

"I finished my project. I came in around three and wrapped that one up."

"How can you work with no sleep like that?" I say.

"That's when I'm at my best, Walter. If I'm well rested, I think too much. You can really screw yourself up, thinking."

Susie appears in our doorway in a state of excited wonder, her arms and eyelids fluttering like hovering birds. I can never decide if Susie grasps the strangeness of her fate or if she thinks crazy video people await every girl who comes to America.

"Susie," Dwight says. "Anita's uncomfortable."

"Too hot for mothership!" says Susie, fanning her perspiring throat.

Dwight pulls a clump of bills from his pants pocket and extracts a couple of twenties. "Take the rest of the afternoon off, Susie. Take Anita to a nice air-conditioned movie. Eat ice cream."

"Tank you, Dwight!" Susie says.

"It's air-conditioned at home," Anita says. "We could rent *Rosemary's Baby*. Or maybe *The Exorcist*."

"I like romantic," says Susie, following us to the door.

"I've seen all the romantic ones."

"Tempasta have many kidnapping!" Susie adds.

"Kidnapped?" I say. "Again?"

■

The radio in Dwight's air-conditioned 1964 Bonneville says that joggers shouldn't be jogging today—it's ninety-eight degrees, with an air inversion trapping car exhaust like a humidor—but as we cross Storrow Drive they're out in normal numbers, running in place as they wait for the light, poised to inject themselves into Boston's jugular vein. They look like tropical fish schooling outside our windows in their colorful shorts and shoes, gasping for air. Dwight is talking to Benny Silk on his cellular phone, taking the sports-fishing approach to client management—paying out some line, letting Benny run a little. "You're absolutely right, Benny,"

he's saying into the phone. "Yup, yup, I couldn't agree more."
We cross the river and take Memorial Drive, past the Harvard
sunbathers on the banks of the Charles, and by the time we turn
on to River Street toward Central Square, Dwight is reeling Benny
in: he will meet us after work at an industrial building in Somerville, next to Route 93, where Dwight will unveil his secret weapon
of sandpaper salesmanship. Then Dwight hangs up.

"Can I make a call on that? I've never talked to anybody on a
cellular phone."

"What are you, early man? I'm riding in a car with early man?"

I call Rebecca at the TV station where she makes documentary
films. I hate it when we have a fight and then she leaves, and I
can't even remember what the fight was about. If she wants to
have my baby, she must like me O.K., but a few sweet words
would improve my day. "Guess where I am," I say.

"I tried to call you before," she says. "They wouldn't put me
through."

Her trying to call could mean our fight is over. Or it could mean
she wants to fight some more. "Anita made Susie hold our calls.
Because of the crunch we're in."

"Then I left a message on your machine downstairs."

"Dwight wouldn't let me stop there. We're going to rescue
Tempesto."

"Where are you?"

"Driving down River Street."

"I hate that. Why do people have to talk on the phone in their
cars?"

"Would you like to ask Dwight? It's his phone."

"I'm mad at Dwight. That's what I was calling about. Everybody
knows Anita's a nut, but what's his excuse?"

"For what?"

"For letting her work in her condition, and then taking her to
this hippy dippy thing tonight."

"Hippy dippy?"

"You don't think a belt-sander race is hippy dippy? Maybe the

Merry Pranksters'll be there. Maybe we'll all drink some electric Kool-Aid."

"I've been wanting to get a new outlook on things."

"When I'm a week overdue, you better not pull stuff like this on me."

"We're having a baby?"

"I meant if we ever did. Which I doubt we will, since I'm with a man from Mars."

"This is the first I've heard about it."

"Precisely. I've tried to bring it up about a hundred times. But you were on Mars."

"She's mad at you, too," I tell Dwight, holding out the phone. "Belt-sander races, huh? Fascinating."

"I was planning to tell you," he tells me, and then, into the phone, he says, "What did *I* do?" After a good long tongue-lashing, he finally gets a word in. "She insists on working, Rebecca," he says. "I want her to stay home. I am not a slave driver. It's her tape. She's the producer. I'm the executive producer. You went to college with her, you know how she is. I need Walter there tonight. Our client has taken a liking to him. You're coming, right? I was counting on you to bring Anita. You'll love it. Tempesto? He's being held for ransom. Yes, again. Don't ask me. O.K. Bye."

He hangs up. "Are you and Rebecca getting along all right, Walter?"

"I don't know, Dwight. I'm drama. She's documentary. It's a constant struggle."

"I figured you were the real issue. She said I was a negligent husband, a rotten father-to-be, and an example of the Peter Pan syndrome. That just doesn't fit."

"Well, you have to admit. Belt-sander races. It looks pretty bad."

"Walter, you, too? You don't trust me?"

"You don't tell me anything, Dwight."

"You know Veritas Grit is a big deal for Benny's company."

"Right, I know that."

"I'm sure it's great sandpaper and everything, but sandpaper's sandpaper, don't you think? You know the real reason it's such a big deal?"

"This must be the part you didn't tell me."

"Because the guy who named it Veritas Grit is the son of one of the company wigs. Fresh out of B-school, doesn't know a thing, but before long he'll be Benny's boss. He's hot to make his mark. He wants a video that people won't forget when they see it at trade shows. He wants a spot for cable that'll be like MTV for the abrasives world. He's talking about taking this account to an ad agency."

"The ambitious little snot!"

"Right. I tell Benny we can do all this for a fraction of the price, but it's not gonna be Benny's call. The wig's son is gonna call it. Veritas Grit's his baby. I'm giving birth to a human being, this guy's giving birth to a piece of sandpaper. And the question is: Whose kid's getting that money?"

"Our kid is!"

"You bet. So I'm telling all this to Tempesto a few days ago, and he mentions these belt-sander races he goes to sometimes. And, bingo, it hits me. *Winners use Veritas Grit.*"

We arrive at a used-computer store outside Inman Square. Dwight parks, and we step out into the broiler of the world. "I love this place," he says. "They have everything. All the MIT guys get their iron here."

This is the third time Tempesto has been kidnapped this summer. The first time probably shouldn't count since he abducted himself—as a publicity stunt for a holographic light show he was projecting on the Hancock building at night without a license to do so. The second time was by a convention of cyberpunk misfits in upstate New York who fed Tempesto magic mushrooms and made him stir-fry hundreds of pounds of chicken in an old satellite dish over a bonfire. This time it looks for real. The counter clerk takes us to a back warehouse room, where Tempesto is seated at a table with three other guys, surrounded by hulking, extinct computers. He seems positively jolly about the whole deal, but that's the way he always seems. "This is one for *The Journal of Irreproducible Results!*" he calls out as we come in, a chubby man with a bushy black beard and sunspot-flares of shiny black hair firing out all around his head. He's in his customary white jumpsuit despite the heat.

"What do you mean 'irreproducible'?" I say. "You're kidnapped again."

"I meant my cards," he says, laying them down. They're playing poker. "My third full house today!"

One of the men has the bearing of the owner, and a beard like the grandfather of Tempesto's beard. He hands Dwight a computer printout and says, "He stays till we settle that."

The printout appears to be the tab Tempesto has been running at the store. "What have you been doing?" Dwight asks him.

"Art," Tempesto says. "Life."

"Your card. Give." Tempesto extracts his Visa from a jumpsuit breast pocket and flips it through the air, where it flutters like a silver butterfly before alighting on Dwight's outstretched hand. He puts it in his pocket, then hands the clerk his own Visa card.

"Oh, he has a gold one," says a different poker-playing guy.

"I'm the boss," Dwight says. He points at the cards. "Are you ahead at least?"

"Yeah, but we're playing for obsolete memory chips. They wouldn't let me play for my bill."

Out front, Dwight signs the slip and the clerk heaves three identical computer printers onto the counter—big old ones from the dinosaur days of the daisy wheel. Each of us grabs one of the brutish, heavy things and staggers into the parking lot. "Why are we buying these crummy printers?" I ask, on the way to Tempesto's van.

"Because Tempesto has made an amazing discovery," Dwight says. "This particular old crummy printer happens to contain exactly the right gears—"

"With exactly the right spindles and teeth and ratios," adds Tempesto.

"For gearing up a Makita electric belt sander. The kind of belt sander we're racing tonight. No other machine known to man contains those gears."

The most astonishing variety of junk—part electronic, part lumber, part dirty clothes—is tumbled in Tempesto's van. He heaves his printer in with a crash. Dwight and I heave ours in, too.

"I'm starved," Dwight says. "Anything in the fridge?"

"I've got leftovers you wouldn't believe," Tempesto says. "Did a big dinner last night. Had a lot of people over. There's a feast waiting for you guys."

"Tempesto's a great cook, Walter. Wait'll you see."

"You are, Tempesto? Really? What's your cuisine? Tuscan Transistor?"

For a minute, his incredulity grapples with my incredulity. Then I see that his feelings are hurt. "You never came to my house?" he says. "You never ate my food?"

■

Tempesto's apartment is basically Tempesto's van on a grander scale, without wheels and with electricity. A lot of electricity. Things are plugged in at Tempesto's place in a way the early electrifiers of America never intended. Power strips are scattered across the floors in every room, not a single empty socket left for one more computer, or television, or synthesizer, or CD player, or oscilloscope, or neon sculpture to take suck, from this address, at Boston Edison's breast.

Copies of *The Journal of Irreproducible Results* are lying on the counter in the kitchen. "I thought you made this up," I say, leafing through an issue of it.

"I don't make things up," Tempesto says. "There's too much that's real already." He's pulling plastic-wrapped dishes out of the fridge and sliding them onto the counter. He calls out their contents as though announcing the guests at a ball. "Roasted eggplant with herbs and garlic. Veal Marsala, sautéed broccoli rabe. Chicken breasts with red peppers. Marinated mushrooms, mozzarella in brine, sun-dried tomatoes in virgin olive oil. Green beans in tomato sauce." He pulls a big flat bread out of a drawer —"Focaccia," he says lovingly—flips open the microwave, cranks up the conventional oven, gets a double boiler going on the stove. When everything's warmed up, we leave the kitchen for the living room, where the table is covered with circuit boards and schematic diagrams. Tempesto pushes it all aside, and we sit down with plates of food and big goblets of Corvo table white. He is a great cook. These are the best leftovers I've ever had. They're better than most things I've eaten the first time around.

"Drama factoid for you, Walter," Tempesto says, raising his glass. "This serviceable *vino* is exactly what Ben Kingsley and Jeremy Irons drink in the lunch scene of the film version of *Betrayal.*"

"What happens in the lunch scene?" Dwight asks.

"That's where Ben Kingsley has just found out that Jeremy Irons has been sleeping with his wife for, like, years," I say. "But Jeremy Irons, who's his best friend, doesn't *know* he knows."

"They drink a load of this wine in that scene," says Tempesto.

"Whatever happened to free love?" Dwight asks. "I kind of miss it."

"It was just an introductory offer," Tempesto says.

"Speaking of cheating," I say. "Are you guys fixing this race?"

"Cheating?" Dwight says. "Progress is cheating? Early man ties a rock to a stick and he's cheating 'cause he has a hammer?"

"Did you ever consider the seminary?" Tempesto asks me. "You did, didn't you? You know how I know? I did, too. It's the truth. I was gonna be a priest. I never really escaped it—the red lights, the magic. They may get me yet. I can always spot a brother."

"I never knew that about you, Walter," Dwight says. "Maybe you shouldn't be doing corporate video after all."

"I probably shouldn't. It's probably a place I'm passing through."

"On your way to the priesthood," says Tempesto.

Dwight has one rule for eating—stop before it hurts. Failing to observe it, we finish our supper and waddle to Tempesto's workroom. In the middle of his bench is a plastic gallon jug lying on its side, a power cord coming out its spout, machinery dimly visible through its translucence like a ship in a bottle. The words "Veritas Grit" are written along each side in red Magic Marker. Tempesto holds it up for my admiration. The jug's bottom side has been sliced off, and a belt of sandpaper occupies the rectangular opening.

"That's a belt sander? What happened to it?"

"We modified it, Walter," Dwight says. "This is no longer a street machine."

It doesn't look anything like a belt sander. The plastic hood hangs around it like a lady's hoopskirt. "Didn't that used to be a jug of milk?"

"Spring water, actually," Tempesto says merrily. He puts a screwdriver bit in his drill and reverse-engineers one of the old printers until the precious gears are out. Then he removes the sander's pearly housing and puts the gears in there. "Makes it like lightning," he says. "Except that after a few minutes the teeth start to shear off the gears, which is why we need a steady stream of these printers." When he's finished, he hooks it up to some kind of tachometer on his bench. I don't know what's normal for a belt sander, but when he revs this one the needle flies right off the scale. "Yow!" he says.

"You're gonna cream those poor guys," I say. "You're gonna sand their faces off."

"Yes!" says Dwight.

■

The sun is going down on the beautiful city. We're heading east on Memorial Drive—me in Dwight's passenger seat, Tempesto in the back with the sander and video gear and two of his famous lasers. Red-gold light suffuses the Bonneville through its rear window. This is Dwight's favorite stretch of road in Boston, especially at this time of day; the sunset has turned the buildings of Back

Bay and Government Center into fiery pillars blazing in the air—
geometrical solids made of light, pure as Tempesto's holograms or
computer graphics. Their painterly twins shimmer in the silver-
blue river below. The traffic is thick and fast at MIT, then thick
and slow down around Lotus and Lechmere and the optimistic
new structures of East Cambridge. It's a scorching Friday in August,
and the prosperous people are making their break for the Cape.
We escape the throngs by swinging past the Museum of Science,
wherein some of Tempesto's creations are displayed, and on into
the tattered margins of Somerville.

Our destination is a block-square brick building five stories tall,
its entrance shadowed by an elevated piece of Route 93. Dwight
carries the video camera and a black plastic garbage bag with the
Makita inside. Tempesto has the two lasers. I have the tripods
and the cables and the little color TV. We take the freight elevator
to the top, where Tempesto's friends are hosting the belt-sander
races in their custom-cabinetry shop. The shop is the whole fifth
floor of the building, pulsing with loud Chicago blues from the
stereo. There must be a hundred people here, but the shop has
floor-standing fans and cross-draft from every direction, and the
heat's not that bad. Sheets of plywood on sawhorses are covered
with bottles of hooch and bowls of punch, dishes of hummus and
baba ghanouj, salsa, chips, and wheels of cheese. The worktables
have been pushed away, and people are dancing beneath springy
cords for power tools which hang like bright-blue pigs' tails from
the ceiling. The racetrack runs all the way down one side of this
huge warehouse space—a three-foot-wide channel like a boccie
court but longer, framed by upright two-by-fours to keep the sanders inside.

You wouldn't think a two-hundred-pound man in a white jumpsuit with the words CYBER SWINE stitched across the back in large
red letters could disappear into a crowd, but this is what Tempesto
now manages to do. Most of the men here have ponytails and
beards, mesh caps advertising lumber-supply houses, big hanks of
keys snapped to belt loops of their jeans. I see several guys wearing

T-shirts silk-screened with the legend HIPPIE TRASH, and more women in attendance than I would have predicted. Unlike the men, they seem to have ventured outside this building since Wood-stock days. They have actual haircuts, stylish ones, and color on their faces, glittery earrings and hair clips and slinky legwear, and they all look nice, but the most interesting women in the room are the two over by the stereo, holding drinks and nodding their heads at a large middle-aged man in a gray tropical suit two or three shades lighter than his blow-dried hair.

"Benjamin Silk!" Dwight cries out, and then Benny looks up and sees us, and scoops us toward him with his outstretched arm. I detect that he doesn't know who Rebecca is. And that he'd like to find out, the weasel.

She casts me a piercing look. "We're learning some secrets of corporate life," she says.

" 'For every back there is a knife'?" I ask.

"That's what I always say," says Benny.

"Of course it is, Benny. Where else would I have heard it? Who else has been through the wars the way you have?"

"Have you been introduced?" asks Dwight. "This is Walter's sweetheart, Rebecca."

"No!" Benny says. "I didn't realize that! You and Walter! Well, isn't that wonderful. What's a nice girl like you doing with a bum like this?"

"I've always had a thing about bums," Rebecca says.

"You think you can save 'em, right? Lots of women think that. Can I give you some advice? Forget it."

Anita puts her fingertips on her belly like someone testing a melon at the market.

"Dancing?" Dwight asks.

"It's at the Whisky a Go Go in there," Anita says. She's had all the ultrasounds and the amniocentesis, but she and Dwight want the baby's gender to be a surprise.

"It dances?" I say.

"The baby likes music," Dwight says. "I think it's the bass."

"Feel the baby, Walter," Rebecca says, pushing me forward. "I want Walter to learn about babies," she tells the others.

"Watch yourself there, Walter!" Benny says.

I don't know how you feel a pregnant woman. "I've never done this before," I say. I put my palms on Anita's belly through her paisley maternity smock. The first shock is how taut it is. I didn't think it would feel exactly like a drum. The second shock is that somebody's in there, drumming. An up-tempo blues is playing on the speakers out here, and inside Anita the baby is jamming like a veteran of the Muddy Waters band.

"You could have one of your very own," Rebecca says.

"I don't know. It seems like an awfully big decision."

"Or none at all," Anita says.

Diagonally across the room, beneath one of the big industrial windows overlooking Route 93, Tempesto has set up his lasers on the camera tripods. "Streetlamp shooting gallery!" he calls out now over the music. "Three shots for a buck!" he adds, and we join the crowd in front of the window to see his demonstration. It's that sublime moment in a cloudless day when the smoggy yellow horizon dissolves slowly upward through values of blue into an indigo chamber containing Venus and a few airplanes. Most cars aren't using their headlights yet, but the mercury-vapor lamps have begun to glow like giant luminous insects flying in formation over the lanes of 93. The traffic north is moving, but south to the Cape it seems to be backed up for miles. Tempesto trains one of his lasers on the highway and presses the button to shoot. He misses a few times, then hits the photoelectric cell controlling a street-lamp on the northbound side. It goes black, to the amazement and cheers of the flock around him. Dwight pays Tempesto a dollar and aims the other beam. He's done this before; on his third shot he gets a lamp.

"I'm next!" the carpenters shout, waving their dollar bills. "Let me try!" they cry, pushing one another out of the way.

After a few minutes a knocked-out lamp wakes up again, so the underlying game is to see how many you can zap before they come back on. Little by little, patches of Route 93 go dark.

"Do men ever grow up?" Rebecca asks Anita.

"No," Anita says.

Meanwhile, Dwight has led Benny across the room to the race-track behind us, where he stands looking down at the long enclosure on the floor and shaking his head. Dwight moves him toward the drinks. I drift over there around the dancers, and when I arrive at the plywood bar Benny is sipping a gin and tonic while Dwight drizzles hoisin sauce into a plastic cup. "This is the flakiest thing I've ever seen," Benny says as Dwight pours tomato juice and vodka in on top of the hoisin.

"They don't have any Worcestershire," he explains, and then he takes a sip. "Delicious. Walter, help me out. Benny thinks belt-sander races are a stupid idea."

"No," I say. "Really? Ever seen one?"

"I didn't even know there was any such thing."

"Well, don't judge a book by its cover, Benny. Try to imagine yourself as early man. All around early man are sticks and stones. One day it hits him: tie a stone to a stick. What's he got?"

"A hammer!" Benny says.

"Right. And then?"

"Civilization!"

"Now you're getting it," says Dwight. He fetches his plastic garbage bag from beneath the bar, and extracts the modified Makita.

"Well, get a load of this!" Benny says, turning it over in his hands, looking at the name of his new product emblazoned on its sides, the fresh belt of Veritas Grit installed on the machine. "We've got a nag running in this race?"

"Tell Benny our idea, Walter," says Dwight.

"It's simple," I say. "Winners use Veritas Grit."

Benny's smile opens up like a streetlamp coming on in the darkness. "They can't argue with that, can they?" He sips his gin and tonic and thinks. "They just might go for this back at the ranch! They just might! But you gotta show us. We're from Missouri."

"I'm from the Bronx," says Dwight. "Follow me."

At the far end of the room, the contestants have gathered with their precious horses in their hands—Makitas and Milwaukees, Black & Deckers, Skils. The races are held in heats, two sanders at a time, until two finalists remain to race the best three out of five. Yellow extension cords emerge from two knife switches at the beginning of the long, enclosed track. A racer hooks his sander to a cord, waits for the signal, and throws the switch. Anita starts taping the first racers getting ready to run.

"Can you do that?" Rebecca says. "Are you O.K.?"

"It's just a tiny little camera," Anita says. "I'm fine. I love shooting."

Her camera goes through a cable to the small monitor propped on a chair. I watch the proceedings on the screen, through Anita's eye. The racers get into position; the official gives the signal; they throw the switches. The whole thing takes about three seconds—the sanders hurtling down the track so fast I'm surprised Anita can pan to get it. Somehow it's not quite the mythic deed I imagined. But Benny's enjoying it thoroughly. "Way to go, boy!" he calls out to the winner.

Most of the thirty or so contenders have shown up with the sanders they use every day, rugged machines that put bread on the table but don't know the taste of glory. After a half hour of heats, all but ten have been eliminated. Tempesto, known to be fast, has skipped the preliminaries. Now he's up. The guys with the HIPPIE TRASH T-shirts have the hot sander, an expensive-looking Milwaukee, but Tempesto doesn't go against them at first. He has to grind his way up through the ranks. He approaches the track holding Dwight's garbage bag, and with a grand flourish he unveils Veritas Grit.

"What the hell is that!" the other racers cry, laughing at the ugly homebrew thing. "What's Verified Grit?"

"Veritas," Tempesto corrects them. "It's Latin for Harvard."

He plugs the machine in and places it on the track next to a spanking Black & Decker, lots of heavy chrome. The official counts down to the start. When the Makita gets the juice it makes a cracking sound they haven't heard around here since Yastrzemski retired, bucks into the air, hits the floor and zigzags out of control, pinballs against the wooden boundaries, knocks its opponent over, and finally flips right out of the track and across the floor before Tempesto shuts it down.

"What the hell was that!" the carpenters shout.

Dwight and Benny huddle around Tempesto for a conference. Tempesto seems to know what's wrong. He sticks a screwdriver into the machine to adjust some things, installs a new sandpaper belt, and they run again. Whatever he's done is what it needed, because now Veritas Grit just makes the Black & Decker look silly, smoking past the finish line before the poor Decker is halfway there.

The carpenters are mad. They demand to see the Makita. They want to hold it. "It don't weigh nothin'!" one of them exclaims. "Disqualify this thing!"

"No, boys," says Dwight. "No, no. Nobody said this was a stock-sander race. You don't change the rules in the middle of a game."

The carpenters run their knowing thumbs along the belt of Veritas Grit. "Where did you get this?" one of them asks. "I've never seen this anywhere."

"That's our sponsor's new product," says Tempesto, winking at Benny, who is happily florid on the sidelines, gin and tonic coming through the armpits of his suit. "Soon at a store near you."

The carpenters call a time-out to tweak their machines. Rebecca puts Anita in a chair by the window and rubs her with ice while Dwight rewinds the tape to look at it.

"I'm liking this!" Benny says, watching the little screen. "I think I can sell the kid on this! This is the kind of thing he just might like!"

"That's the spirit, Benny!" Dwight says.

"I just had a thought!" Benny says. "A big thought! This could become some kind of craze! We could become the Budweiser of this!" He puts his hands in the air and then draws them apart to form the banner he sees in his mind. "The Veritas Grit World Championship Belt-Sander Races!"

"Think wild!" says Dwight. "Dream, Benny!"

"Hold on!" Benny says, putting his arm around my shoulders. "Wait a minute! We could put Walter here in it! Walter here could talk about being a world-class belt-sander racer, and how he would never race without Veritas Grit."

"Great idea, Benny!"

"Except I'm not a world-class belt-sander racer," I say.

Benny gives me a quizzical look. "Of course you're not," he says. "Nobody is. It's just a fantasy we're having." Then the significance of that hits him—he's seriously considering staking his career on a fantasy—and I watch his face go through a couple of surreal changes while he wrestles with that. "We'd be manufacturing a craze, Walter. We'd be sponsoring a sporting event, the way Budweiser does. Nobody in the abrasives industry has ever done that before. They never had a sport to sponsor!"

"Benjamin meant you'd be in the video as an actor," Dwight says. "You remember—acting? Your niche in life? You'd be acting as though you were a world-class belt-sander racer."

"Oh, acting," I say.

"He gets it now," Dwight says to Benny. Then he lowers his voice and points to his head. "A lot of actors are not really all that—you know."

"We wouldn't need Einstein," Benny says. Then he slaps Dwight in the belly. "I'm liking this! Winners use Veritas Grit!"

When the races resume, a few men have removed parts of their sanders' housings to lighten them up, but these half-naked creatures run very wrong, sucking sawdusty wind and finally choking out altogether. Heat after heat, the rogue Makita narrows the field, Anita memorializing its conquest on videotape. I watch her pan for cutaways of an ecstatic Benny cheering from the sidelines. "Go,

Veritas Grit!" he cries, urging his sander on with thrusts of his arms, and even here in the pandemonium I can see how nicely those shots will work when the tape is cut together, what a pro Anita really is.

In the end it's Hippie Trash versus Veritas Grit, as Dwight and Tempesto always knew it would be. The men put new belts on their sanders for the finals. I go to trackside to catch the action live. Veritas Grit's gears must be wearing down because the first runoff looks like a tie to me. I glance back at Anita to see if she got the photo finish, but she's standing there holding her belly, looking like a person who just ate the entire lump of wasabi from her sushi dinner, thinking it was something else.

Rebecca has seen her, too, and beats me there. "The baby!" she says.

Tempesto calls a time-out and sneaks off to put new gears into Veritas Grit. Dwight hustles over and hugs his wife. "Now look," he says. "Everybody stay cool. There's ten minutes left in this, and I don't see why we can't take care of business and have a baby, too."

"Dwight, you swine," Rebecca says.

"Rebecca, I'm closing an important business deal. We need this business to buy Pampers and strollers and everything, O.K.? Is your car air-conditioned? No? Here, trade keys with me. You and Walter take Anita to the hospital in the Bonneville, and I'll be over in a half hour in your car. You won't even be in labor yet, honey," he tells Anita.

"She's in labor right now!"

"She's just starting, Rebecca. You realize this will probably go on for about twenty-four hours? We went to the Lamaze classes, didn't we, babe?"

"You went to the first one," Anita says, not bitterly, just sticking up for the facts.

"We know what to expect," Dwight tells Rebecca. "You're overreacting."

"I'm overreacting?"

"You're being considerate. But you're a little worked up."

"I'm worked up?"

"Anita's going to the hospital to have a baby. People do it every day. You'll be fine, sweetheart," he says to Anita, though she seems to be going into a trance.

"Walter, you know where Brigham and Women's is, right?"

"It's where all the hospitals are, isn't it? I think so. Do I?" I ask Rebecca.

"Oh, God," she says.

■

The whole concept of a freight elevator takes on new meaning as we transport Anita to ground level in the dark, creaking box. Rushing from the building to open the car for the women, I wonder if Hippie Trash did something psychedelic to the punch upstairs. I'm picking up the world like a satellite dish. I'm hearing everything. I hear the blades of crabgrass rubbing each other in the crummy sand-soil of the concrete planters along the parking lot. I hear the mechanical noises of the belt-sander race. If I had to be up there right now, the sandpaper would shred my brain. As it is, I can distinguish the scrape of every different shoe on the asphalt out here.

"Does anybody else happen to feel like they're on drugs?" I say.

"I do," Anita says.

"Drugs?" says Rebecca. "You're supposed to be driving the car."

"I can drive fine," I say, the way people always say these things.

We get Anita in the back seat of the Bonneville, Rebecca in there with her. Once I get behind the wheel, I understand what's happening to me: I have a friend who has become for the moment a creature, a mammalian creature engaged in the live birth mammals are famous for, and I'm sympathizing with that, resonating with it. I'm an animal now myself.

"Music might help," Anita says. "Could you turn on the radio?"

It's only an AM, and at first all I can find are talk shows—people claiming to have been inside UFOs, telling about having fat vacuumed from their buttocks and bellies. Finally I hit music on an oldies station—Little Eva singing "The Loco-Motion."

"That's good," Anita says. "I like that song."

"Remind me what I do now?" I call to Rebecca in back.

"Go down this access road and make a right at the fork. I'll tell you from there. Don't go up the ramp onto 93."

"Where's that?"

"Right up there."

It's dark down here below the highway and I don't see what she means. My skin is screaming thousands of messages at me, and I'm giving birth to a baby in my brain, and the next thing I know we're rising into the air.

"Walter!" Rebecca cries out. "I just got finished saying don't do this!"

"I got mixed up. I'm sorry. Let's not fight, O.K.? Dwight and Anita never fight. We always fight. Plus, I'm having a mystical experience."

"Well, go back! Back the car back down the ramp and get off!"

But it's too late. We're up there now. The space behind me was the only free slot on this whole merciless highway, and it's been filled by a car which in turn left a space that has been filled by another car, like one of those puzzles of linked plastic numbers sliding around in a frame. One little mistake and we're hopelessly locked in a grid.

Beneath the spectral mercury-vapor light, the traffic is moving in geological time. We need a helicopter right now. I open my door and stand on the frame to look out over the cars. It's just more of the same, forever and ever. The atmosphere is a kiln where thousands of clay vehicles are baking. Anita can't stand it, and I have to get back in. Now that we're not moving at all, the air conditioner is dragging Dwight's old behemoth to the tar pits. The temperature gauge edges into the red as I watch.

"I have this unbelievable urge to push," says Anita.

"Well, don't do it!" I say.

"She must have been in transition at the races," Rebecca says.

"Really? Jesus, Anita, didn't you know the baby was coming? I thought women just sort of, you know, knew things like that."

"I felt a little crampy," she says. "I thought it was the baba ghanouj."

On the theory that action is better than inaction, I pull off the road and make a run for it down the shoulder. This works for about a hundred yards, until the shoulder suddenly stops. I try to pull back into my lane but the people alongside us are getting revenge by not letting me. I'm looking around the car for something to threaten them with when I see Dwight's cellular phone. I'm not used to the idea of phones in cars; I forgot it was there. "I have to make a call," I say, getting out and closing the door gently on the telephone's cord. A woman answers when I dial 911. "We've got somebody having a baby here," I say.

"I'm showing you on a cellular phone," she says. "She's having the baby in a car?"

"Right. We're stuck in traffic on 93 south."

"Where on 93? Between what exits?"

"No idea. We're at the place where the shoulder of the road disappears."

"What can you see right now?"

"The Schrafft's Building."

"In front of you?"

"Right. Affirmative."

"You're in Somerville. Describe the car. Year, model, color, plates."

"1964 Bonneville. White. Four-door. I can't see the plates, the phone won't reach that far. It's the father's car. He's not here. Could you send a helicopter?"

"No, sir. We can't land a helicopter on that part of 93. We'll send an ambulance."

"What if it happens before they get here?"

"Make sure the baby can breathe. Put it on its mother's breast. Don't cut the cord."

"What about germs? The car is filthy."

"An unread newspaper is relatively germ-free. You can deliver the baby on that if you have to. We'll have somebody there as fast as we can." Then she hangs up.

The traffic has moved a little bit. A Lincoln Town Car is alongside us now, the people in it watching me talk on the phone. They remind me of my mom and dad. I knock on their passenger window. The lady lowers it with the electric button. "Hi. Would you folks happen to have a recent newspaper?" I see a crisp copy of today's *Wall Street Journal* right there on their back seat.

"Need the show times for the movies?" the man calls out sarcastically. "Why don't you just call on your phone there, big fella?"

Maybe he is my father, after all. I crouch down to check. No, he isn't. "We're not going to the movies. A woman in our car is having a baby, and in a pinch you can deliver babies on newspapers. That *Wall Street Journal* right there would be fine."

He makes his wife put up the window, and I see them arguing about it without sound, gesturing wildly. I'm about to knock on the next car when the radiator goes on the Bonneville, sheets of white steam spewing from the grille and hood with a horrid hissing sound. The man gets out of the Lincoln with the newspaper and looks in our car. I look in with him. It's like a wolf den in there, one female hunkering on the floor, another one, heavy with young, lying on the seat. They're breathing rapidly through their mouths and staring out with eyes dilated to black disks. The man pushes the newspaper at me and backs away, but his wife is already out of the Lincoln. "Oh, my God!" she cries when she looks in the car.

I get back in with the phone and open the *Journal* to its deep middle sections. "The lady on 911 told me this," I tell Rebecca. "We're supposed to spread these out over the seat. Anita, an ambulance is on the way. Hang in there, O.K.?"

"The women in my family have pretty easy births," she says between gasps of air and pain, as though her job is to comfort us.

"My doctor says I have a pelvis like the Holland Tunnel." She thinks about this for a second and laughs. "Too bad we can't take it to the hospital."

"Anita, I think you're starting to rave a little bit. Try to be calm."

She snorts fiercely like a riled-up horse. I get the number of the cabinetry shop from Information, and ask for Dwight. He's still there. They bring him to the phone.

"I was just leaving," he says. "What's going on?"

I tell him.

"This wasn't the plan, Walter," he says.

"I know it wasn't, Dwight. What can I say? We're stuck in traffic."

"What are you doing on 93 in the first place?"

"I made a mistake and got on it. Here, I'm putting you on with Anita."

"You were supposed to be here to tell me to push," she says to Dwight.

"Don't tell her that!" I say at the phone. I look outside. The woman from the Lincoln has spread the word, and now about thirty people from other cars are staring in through our steamed-up windows like a gathering of spirits.

"Walter thinks you're mad at him," Anita says. "Tell him you're not." She passes the phone back to me.

"Is that you there, where all the people are?" Dwight says. "I think I can see you from here."

"Yeah, we've got a crowd here."

"The Bonneville's overheating, isn't it?"

"Yup."

"It does that when you run the air conditioner without driving."

"I figured that out."

"I'm not mad, Walter. You're doing your best."

"Thanks, Dwight. I called for an ambulance."

"I see it coming on the shoulder right now. Should be there in a couple of minutes."

"Oh, yeah. I hear the sirens."

"You're fine now. I'll meet you at the hospital. Oh, hey! Guess who won the race."

"Us?"

"You bet. Veritas Grit. Benny's going wild. He wants to see a proposal for a big promotion. And, Walter? He says this is your niche. You're gonna be the Veritas Grit spokesperson. You could be looking at national TV with this."

"Gee, that's great, Dwight. Thanks."

The radio starts playing "I Second That Emotion," and then all at once the crowd around the car breaks into cheers and applause. When I look in the back seat I see that the baby has left the mother ship and is now half in Rebecca's hands, half space-walking in its birth fluids across the tiny print of the New York Stock Exchange. It's made of rubber—that's my first thought, seeing it jiggle from behind. But I'm not in my right mind. Rebecca gets a grip and lifts, and the baby's slimy body flips over suddenly in her arms. It's a boy. His two-second-old face meets my thirty-five-year-old one, the eyes puddling darkly beneath the matted hair, looking into mine and saying, *I'm here again? Who am I this time?* And then, unmistakably, he winks at me. For an instant I think I get it, the whole thing, life in all its dimension. Then Rebecca puts him back on his belly, slides him up the front of Anita, and he enters earthly bliss.

"Dwight!" I say. "You're a father! It's a boy!"

"A boy? The baby's born? I have a son?"

"Look at the size of this kid!" I say.

"Where's Anita?" he cries.

"What do you mean, where is she?"

"I mean how is she!"

"She seems fine. She's smiling. She's holding the baby."

"It's a boy!" I hear Dwight shout to the cabinetry shop. "He's big!"

Tempesto's voice comes on. "We're firing a twenty-one-gun salute! Look in the steam!"

Sure enough, red filaments flash like pick-up-sticks tumbling through the white cloud around the car. The streetlamps around us start to go out.

"Walter," says Dwight. "Hold the phone up to the baby." I do that. "Dwight Junior!" he says, his tiny voice coming out of the earpiece. "Son! This is your father speaking!"

"Walter, let's have a baby!" Rebecca says as we gaze upon the strapping boy on his mother's breast, born in a '64 Bonneville broken down on the side of the road while Smokey Robinson sang on the radio and his father spoke to him on a cellular phone. I think: This will be no ordinary child.

"Sure, sweetheart," I say. "Why not?"

And then, just as I kiss Rebecca, our fogged-up car becomes a huge heart attack, throbbing with red light and screaming sounds. Out in the distance, beyond the gaping ghost faces against the steamy glass, the ambulance has pulled to a stop behind the eight or ten cars lined up behind us on the shoulder. I fight through the crowd to meet the men coming toward me with a stretcher and a box of first-aid gear.

"What the hell happened to the lights?" the one is saying to the other.

"It's the laser beams!" I shout, gesturing back to the vapors billowing above the Bonneville. "Men in that building over there are shooting them out with laser beams!"

"Is that right?" the first man says, stopping to look where I'm pointing. "Laser beams, Louie," he says to the other guy, but the red ambulance light cancels out the red lasers so you can't see their flicking tongues in the steam anymore. "Been out here awhile, huh, pal?"

"I'll never rent on the Cape again," the other man says.

"No, we go to Maine now," the first one says. "I couldn't take this. We'd like to help you, bud, but we're here for a lady having a baby."

"It already happened!" I cry. "He's born!"

"The baby we're looking for, or the Baby Jesus? We're looking for a Bonneville with a pregnant lady inside."

"In that crowd of people!" I tell them, so drained by birth I should be on that stretcher myself. "But she's not pregnant anymore. It's a boy named Dwight Junior. Go ahead. You'll see him. A big wrinkly red guy on the phone with his dad."

A HALF HOUR WITH
GOD'S HEROES

■

Josephine assumed she'd find the shrine in a wooded glen down a private road. She expected a quiet place with a statue of the Virgin or a plaque recounting the miraculous event the trees had witnessed decades before, when a girl named Rose felt herself summoned down the path, a little crippled girl known far and wide for her special devotion to Our Lady—something along those lines. A shrine. And the gift shop, Josephine's interest, would be a modest shed-like affair with a nun inside selling beads and figurines. So Josephine imagined; her ex-mother-in-law, Camilla, hadn't described the shrine, and Josephine hadn't asked.

She grossly underestimated the zeal of the faithful in Massachusetts. She was driving along, paying more attention to Camilla's directions than to the snow-banked road, certain she'd missed a turn and looking for a place to pull off, when, coming around a bend, she slammed on her brakes and fishtailed down the mercifully dry pavement, skidding to a halt three feet from the last car in a good half-mile-long line of cars ahead of her. The traffic jam wasn't the reason she'd stopped. She hadn't even seen it till after hitting her brakes, and so the shrine could chalk up another miracle right now—Josephine's being alive. She'd stopped because an incredible rainbow radiance was shimmering in the gray sky behind the skeletons of the trees, as though a saint were materializing that moment in the sunken cow pasture off to the right, or men from outer space—who probably *were* the saints to begin with—were landing their saucer there.

The driver she'd almost rear-ended was cursing Josephine in his mirror. His kids were turned around in the back seat, making faces at her. She straightened her car and got in line, and inched along until she saw that the expanse below the road was not a cow pasture but a huge asphalt lot with hundreds of cars parked in it. The only miracle was the amount of electricity being used for the galaxy of colored lights strung along every tree limb and roof peak and window frame of the sprawling complex of buildings down there. They had a big canvas tent set up alongside the parking lot, next to acres of snow-covered lawns and a frozen duck pond with a promenade stretching into the middle of it. Then she saw the castle. It was up on the hill, the monastery where the brothers lived. It was bigger than some real castles she'd seen on TV, big enough for hundreds of people, and its storybook façade was encrusted, like everything else, with countless Christmas lights.

Josephine didn't see where they got off calling this a shrine. Jesus Land, maybe. God World. It made her upset, but so did religion generally. She'd had plenty of priests and nuns in her life, especially nuns, and she could live just fine without the Church, which had no monopoly on God so far as she was concerned. She wouldn't have been going to a shrine at all except that her house had been on the market for more than a month and she hadn't had a nibble. Nobody had come back for a second look. Granted, it was a sad piece of property, a two-bedroom box with no character whatever, not even shutters—workmen had taken them off years before to install the ugly vinyl siding and had never put them back. The front yard was a joke, the back yard an only slightly larger joke. But people did buy and sell such things. Her real-estate agent, Mary Jane, had assured her that someone would buy hers, too. A cardinal rule of real estate, Mary Jane had said, is that everything sells eventually.

Unfortunately, Mary Jane had grown disenchanted with Josephine, who was not cooperating with her. Josephine refused to put a FOR SALE sign on her front lawn, or to list her address in the paper so that people could drive by. The problem wasn't that she wouldn't do those things for Mary Jane; she *couldn't* do them, or explain why she couldn't, so she simply refused. She couldn't do them because her son, Ricky, didn't know she was selling the house. She was selling it behind his back, and as soon as she'd sold it, she was going to run away to Florida.

She drove around the big lot three times looking for a space, and finally parked all the way over by the duck pond, at the base of the hill, the fairy-tale castle looming above her, spooky and fundamentally beyond belief. Yesterday, when she was crying on the phone about nobody buying her house, Camilla told her the old Saint Joseph trick. Camilla thought everybody knew about it; she'd assumed Josephine had done it already. When you want to sell a piece of real estate, you bury a statue of Saint Joseph in the lawn and he brings you a buyer. She ordered Josephine to go immediately to the famous shrine forty minutes south of Boston on I-95, where they had all kinds of saint figurines, and which was a beautiful sight to see at Christmastime anyway. Camilla said it was unholy that Josephine, raised Catholic even if she never went to Mass anymore, had never been to the shrine in all her years of living in the area, and this made Josephine smile because Camilla had once told her—in the midst of Josephine's divorce —that the only unholy thing in life was bad matrimony.

■

Camilla knew that Josephine was running away. More than that, she approved completely. The idea was partly hers, in fact, and that was sad, because Camilla was the one person Josephine was really going to miss. The truth was, Josephine always liked Camilla more than she had liked Camilla's son, Sal, her ex-husband, who took after his father just the way Ricky took after Sal. Josephine had divorced Sal six years before, when Ricky was thirteen, and though most Italian mothers-in-law would have considered Josephine dead after that, the divorce brought Camilla and Josephine closer. The old lady knew her son was no good—she'd stopped crying over him long before Josephine did—and now, considering the way Ricky had turned out, Camilla had no use for her grandson, either.

The bad genes of men wove themselves through human generations like a corrosive thread, tainting the goodness of women. That was the thing you had to remember when you married a guy, Josephine thought. You were really marrying his father. And when you had a guy's son, you were having the guy.

Camilla, however, thought Florida was too far away, not to mention that Josephine didn't know anybody there. But that was one of the things Josephine liked about it: she wouldn't know anybody. The other thing was something she'd read in a magazine—that Florida was the leading edge of the United States, the first part of America to enter the twenty-first century. Florida was already *in* the twenty-first century, the magazine article had said, and that sounded pretty incredible to Josephine. And besides, she was tired of being cold eight months of the year.

She was cold right now. The temperature was below freezing as she stepped out of her car into the aurora borealis of the Christmas lights. The vehicles looked like ornaments on a gigantic tree as she walked past them into the headache-inducing wind. A great many pickup trucks seemed to be visiting the shrine today, most of them with rifle racks in their rear cab windows. The racks were empty, but you got the idea, and if you didn't get it, the bumper stickers helped you out. To judge from the bumpers, the Eastern Seaboard's spiritual nodes were Disney World, South of the Border, and this very shrine, and things did not look good for people who wanted to ban the handgun or burn the flag.

Were other countries like this, or was it just the U.S.A.? Josephine didn't know. She'd never been to another country. Well, Florida was practically one, according to that magazine, and she'd be there soon, in the holy land of Mickey and Minnie. She felt slightly blue. She would have liked to take Ricky to Disney World when he was a kid, but she never had. She'd never had the money.

Lately, she spent a lot of time looking back on Ricky's youth, trying to figure out just where he turned bad, what might have prevented it, which things she might have broken her back to change. It was one of those mental games she was always playing, the kind that make you crazy.

She stumbled into the Information Center with her eyes full of tears from the wind. An automobile was parked in the lobby—a brand-new Ford Taurus, stickers still in the windows, sitting on the linoleum floor. Josephine glanced around at the various doorways, but she didn't see any way they could have gotten it in. A young brother in a cassock sat at a table beside the car, with a stack of flyers and a gray metal box. He was raffling off the Ford to benefit the shrine.

"Excellent car," the brother said as Josephine picked up a flyer to read. "Automatic. Moon-roof. Cruise control."

"It's so strange that you're raffling a car," Josephine said. "I just almost had a terrible wreck in my own."

"Driver's-side air bag in this one," the brother said.

"I wasn't paying attention and I came around the bend, and I would've been killed except I saw all these lights and slammed on my brakes. That's what saved me, all your Christmas lights. This shrine just saved my life."

The brother shook his head in wonderment.

"Of course," Josephine went on, "I was coming here in the first place, so you could also say this shrine almost just got me killed."

"That makes us even," the brother said.

Josephine examined the flyer describing the car. "What I really need is a convertible," she said. "I'm moving to Florida soon."

"Convertibles are death traps," the brother said. He looked at her sincerely. "You in particular shouldn't have one."

The tickets were a dollar fifty apiece, and the drawing didn't take place for four more months. Josephine hoped to be long gone by then. "How come you're raffling off a car now," she asked, "when you're not holding the drawing until April?"

"So we can sell a lot of tickets," the brother said.

"Oh," Josephine said. She hadn't expected him to be so forth-right about it. He had a nice direct personality and a pleasant voice. He was pretty good-looking, too. "But you're lowering my chances of winning," she said.

"How much do you figure we're lowering them by?" the brother asked. He wasn't being sarcastic.

"Well, I figured you'd do the drawing in, you know, maybe a month."

"So we're cutting your chances by four. But if you bought four tickets, you'd be right back up there again."

"Oh, ho, what a salesman."

He pulled a stapled sheaf of tickets from his box. "We have booklets of five tickets for five dollars. You save two fifty, plus your chances go up to *better* than they'd have been if we held the raffle in a month." He smiled winningly. In civilian life this would definitely be flirting. "Did I mention the sound system?" he said. "AM, FM, auto-reverse cassette?"

Josephine was feeling lucky. If she actually won, she could always take a cheap one-way flight back from Florida to get it. Or a drive-away agency could have some college kid bring it down. Saint Joseph's hand would be strengthened, she thought, if she dem-onstrated a little faith and bought a book of tickets. She gave the brother the money and wrote her name and address on the coupon. "I'm looking for the gift shop," she said.

"Down below," he said, pointing at the floor.

Josephine laughed. "In the Other Place?"

The brother laughed, too. "You wouldn't joke about that if you ate in the canteen down there."

She looked for a set of stairs.

"You have to go back out and around," he said. "Stupid design."

She followed the sidewalk into an underpass, where the wind wasn't blowing. The cold stopped hammering its fist on her skull. She was about to walk down the concrete steps when she saw that the complex of brick buildings wasn't the shrine at all. The real shrine was an esplanade enclosed by the mounds of two more suburban hills, a park-like place full of shrubs and statuary and garden beds that must have been something in the spring. Josephine loved parks and public gardens. Even covered with snow, the landscaping made her happy—the winding stone walls, marble stairs like pearl inlay in the hills, rhododendrons as large as trees. She stepped out of the underpass into the mouth of this place. Most of the visitors were here, it seemed, strolling around among statues that turned out to be Jesus at the Stations of the Cross. In their heavy winter clothes the worshippers were hard to match up with the trucks outside. On top of one hill towered a marble crucifix at least twenty feet tall. A wide staircase led up to this gigantic Jesus, with a sign that said THE HOLY STEPS.

An elderly man in a blue suit and tan raincoat was climbing the Holy Steps on his knees. The stairs were strangely shallow—each one just a baby step—and it took Josephine a minute to understand that they'd been designed for this purpose; even the aged gentleman could do it while clasping his hands beneath his chin. At every step he stopped and crossed himself, and said another prayer. The Holy Steps numbered at least a hundred, and Josephine could now feel the cold through her fleece-lined boots.

■

The gift shop had the holy smell that made her feel ill, the smell Church buildings always had, no matter where she went. Perhaps some essential oil, the Essence of Holiness, was distributed worldwide by Religious Supply, purveyors to the trade. Josephine didn't know, but she should have, growing up the way she did in a Catholic orphanage. Not that she'd been an orphan. That would have been too simple. That would have been normal, almost. No, Josephine had had two living parents and she was *still* raised in an orphanage—a Catholic home for young women, actually, which housed orphans, bad girls, and plain unfortunates such as herself. From the age of nine, when her parents split up, to the age of fifteen, she lived there because her father was a bum who didn't give her mother any money, and her poor mother, just a girl herself, couldn't make enough on her own to raise Josephine.

Inside the shop's door an alcove decorated with bales of hay was labeled STABLES and held a dozen mangers of various sizes, each containing a Mary, a Joseph, and a baby Jesus, along with three Wise Men and a farm animal or two. The big mangers were half-life-size and beautifully done; they must have cost a fortune. Past the alcove, antiquity became the present, like switching a channel on TV. The store was big and modern, and full of pastel Post-It notes printed with chapter and verse, 3-D holograms of Jesus carrying the cross, religious desk-blotters, religious penholders, religious paperweights, religious fluffy troll-dolls in fluorescent colors, religious picture frames filled with sample photos of happy families who didn't exist.

Josephine grew more unsettled with every pious article she passed. She was starting to have an attack of her old religious asthma, when she looked up and saw a sign that said SAINTS. A whole wall was devoted to the miracle-workers, in alphabetical order, beginning with Anthony. She walked along until she got to Joseph, recognizable partly because he came right before the popular Jude, but also because he was holding the Baby Jesus, his son—or his stepson, or ward, or whatever their relationship was supposed to be, theologically. Josephine couldn't remember how it worked anymore. She glanced at the spot preceding Joseph, expecting to see Joan, but there was no Saint Joan. Only the men saints were there, no women, and no instructions on what to do with any of them, either. She'd expected lists of the powers each saint had, thinking that as long as she was here, she might get a few more to help with her other troubles.

In a corner of the store, racks of magazines bristled up the wall, heaps of sharp-looking periodicals with pictures of people playing guitars, going to flea markets, helping the poor in other countries. You could hardly tell they were religious magazines at all. They said nothing about sex being wrong, or the guilt and shame you were supposed to feel about everything. Josephine's entire child-hood seemed to have disappeared. But then, off at one edge of the rack, she spotted the pamphlets printed on cheap paper in loud, bleeding colors to match the things they were saying. This was the world she remembered. The pamphlets offered instructions on having the right kind of marriage, on raising your kids to be believers, on casting the Devil out of your home. One brochure was intended for a person thinking of becoming a monk—perhaps the very tract that had snared her friend upstairs.

She dug around a bit, and sure enough, she found a series on the powers of the saints. One saint was known as "The Heart Saint"; another was "The Cancer Saint." There was a saint you prayed to if you had arthritis, and a saint for mental illness. She expected but failed to find "Joseph, the Real Estate Saint." Physical maladies seemed to be the thing, so she flicked through every gaudy cover, hoping to see "The Dope Addict Saint" for Ricky, or even "The Cigarette Saint" for herself—she'd buy that one—but they didn't have those, either.

On her way back to the figurines, she passed through the chil-dren's section. Religion was a sunnier thing for kids today than it had been for Josephine. She could see where kids would like these books and games and jigsaw puzzles. An old-fashioned children's book about the saints called *An Half-Hour with God's Heroes* looked like something Josephine might herself have read back in Catholic school. She picked it up. It didn't contain the information she desired at this juncture in her fallen life—how to get a saint to bring people with money to your home. It was a storybook full of sweet little tales about the saints and the miracles they had per-formed, with ancient cartoon paintings to go along. It was great. Kind of great. She liked it. It was the kind of thing, she thought, that Camilla would like, too, and she decided to buy it as a present for her.

She put it under her arm and went back to the statues. If you wanted a dinky little Saint Joe for forty-nine cents, they had that, but such a thing was not going into Josephine's lawn. On the other hand, she wasn't springing for the $30 hand-painted ceramic number, either. The plastic Saint Joseph for $4.99 was a bland beeswax color, semi-translucent and perfectly hollow, but a good ten inches high and decently molded: you could make out the baby's features, whereas on the cheaper models the Saviour's face was kind of a smudge. She balanced it in her hand and discovered that she was having difficulty breathing. Religious asthma, for real this time. She practically ran to the checkout, where, under the suspicious eyes of the lady at the computerized cash register, Josephine clawed money from her wallet like a Saint Joseph junkie scoring a fix.

■

She ascended a different flight of concrete steps and found herself back at the Stations of the Cross, staring across a flagstone terrace at the Holy Steps. The old gentleman was almost to the top—all the way up on his knees. Dizzy, Josephine turned toward the parking lot, nearly knocking down a nun in a light-blue habit. The nun gave her the bad, scolding look of nuns everywhere, and Josephine was time-shifted back to the Catholic home, where a girl didn't simply live, she worked, and the nuns were her masters. Josephine had scrubbed the floors there a thousand times, and polished them once a month with Butcher's Wax from a can, buffing away the adhesive haze with a cloth-wrapped brick until her arm almost fell off. Yes, they would hit her hands with rulers if she didn't do it right; they really did that. She had worked outside for entire sweltering summer afternoons in her starched school uniform and dark knee socks, picking iridescent Japanese beetles off the roses and dropping them into coffee cans full of kerosene, where they died instantly, according to the nuns, though Josephine had seen them suffer intensely with her own two eyes.

The sidewalk led right to the open mouth of the big canvas tent that she'd seen when she arrived. She walked up to it and peeked inside. A veritable sea of votive candles was burning in there—

thousands of them, arranged in tiers, each flame in a green glass tube. You could light a candle here in the tent twenty-four hours a day. Josephine stepped inside, half expecting to choke, but a large hole in the tent top took the fumes away. Fifteen or twenty people were worshipping, one of them a bearded man in a shiny black parka and jogging pants, who was maintaining some kind of martial-arts stance before the candles, swinging his rosary like a lasso and mumbling to himself. His approach to God was strangely hostile, but he was getting the same reception as anybody else. And that hit Josephine like a rock: God didn't care about a person's approach. The human things people cared so deeply about on earth dropped through the screen when God scooped you up, panning for gold. Josephine wished they had taught this back in Catholic school. Her insight made her like God more than she could remember ever liking Him before. He was utterly indifferent to all the stuff she worried about. She felt free now to light a candle herself.

A sign said $3 DONATION. Three bucks to light a candle! You got a shot at a Ford Taurus for a dollar fifty. The new God she'd discovered wouldn't care whether she paid or not, but that was the difference between Him and His agents on earth. His agents wanted the cash. She glanced around; nobody was looking, but she felt guilty anyway. She slipped three singles from her wallet into the Plexiglas box, and stepped onto the wooden platform.

Dear God, she prayed, lighting a candle, *I wish I could say I believed in You a little more than I do. I used to, when I was a kid, and if You really exist, then I don't have to tell You. I don't believe in these candles, either, but I'm lighting this one for Ricky, my son. He's a junkie thief, as You presumably know. He's nineteen, but he won't get out of my life and go rob and torment someone else. Why did You let my son shoot dope and turn into a germ? He steals from me, his own mother, rips me off and lies to my face about it. Well, pretty soon he's going to wake up and find me gone. I'm here to get a Saint Joseph to sell my house, which is probably blasphemous or something, but You don't care about superficial things like that. I just got that point. So let*

*me ask You this: Why does anybody bother talking to You at all? You
know everything already. Why does anybody build a shrine like this?
Why am I burying a Saint Joseph? It's because actions speak louder
than words, isn't it? That's why it's three bucks for the candle, right?
I get it.*

She looked at Ricky's flame flickering in its green glass tube. It
was a small, inconsequential thing to put up against the wall of
crap her son lived behind. Once, before he stole her TV, she'd
checked out the heavy-metal videos he liked to watch when he
was stoned and under her roof—the Satan worshippers and leather
Nazis acting nasty with guitars they couldn't even play. This was
no turning of any generational wheel; it wasn't her own mother's
dismay over the Rolling Stones. This was her offspring growing
extra legs and wings and turning into a locust or something, and
Josephine had decided that the leaders of the country secretly
wanted youth this way, that it served some hidden government
purpose. How else could she explain the incredible collection
of losers she saw when she drove around town these days, every
guy Ricky's age looking just like Ricky, a tattooed doper who
smashed bottles on the kids' playground every night and lived
for nothing but whatever jolt he could get in the next fifteen
minutes?

She'd hung on till he was nineteen, and that was it. Blood was
thicker than water, but it wasn't thicker than a woman's whole
life.

So I'm taking action, she continued to God. *Maybe finding me
gone will make him change. I doubt it, but if You could help him do
that, that's all I ask. I'm not asking anything for myself. Well . . . I
am asking to sell my house. And I wouldn't mind winning that car to
have in Florida. Mine's just about shot. Oh, and Camilla. She's a great
lady. Take care of her for me. Thank You, God.*

She stepped down from the tiers of candles, away from the welter
of wiggling flames. Hers flickered with the others in its green glass
tube, but when she blinked her eyes, she lost track of which one
it was.

■

When she got home, an hour of daylight remained, possibly less. Today was her day off, and she was starting to wish she was going in. She hated the dark shroud that winter dropped over the afternoon. She was a chef at Cantami in Boston, one of the new Italian places where everybody went. The restaurant's kitchen had no windows and a million small distractions, and you didn't have to experience the untimely demise of the day.

She half expected to find Ricky in the house, or some evidence he'd been around—something missing or messed up somehow—but she didn't see anything. She'd thrown him out a year ago, when he turned eighteen. She would have liked to bounce him sooner, but he'd been remanded to her custody at sixteen, after sticking up a convenience store. Josephine had wanted him sent to reform school then, but the lawyer assured her that institutionalization only made kids like Ricky worse, and then they came home like mutant bacteria that nothing could kill. By this logic, Josephine was left alone with a full-fledged juvenile delinquent. A father's guiding hand would have been nice, but no court in the world would have let her ex-husband care for Ricky or any other kid, so it didn't really matter that Sal was halfway through six-to-eight for armed robbery—short time for that offense because he wasn't the one carrying the gun. Or so the judge had been persuaded to believe. Josephine didn't even know. She knew that Sal *had* a gun: she'd seen it a number of times—once pointed at her head. He claimed it wasn't loaded, but that was why she got her divorce.

When she threw Ricky out, he went to live with his girlfriend, and Josephine changed the locks on the house. But Ricky knew how to pick locks and came in whenever he pleased. Sometimes he wanted to spend the night. Sometimes he just wanted to steal something. Josephine couldn't keep him out, so she asked him not to come in when she wasn't around. He came the next day and stole her toaster oven. He called that "borrowing." By now Ricky had borrowed almost every fenceable thing Josephine owned—her TV and VCR, her stereo, her clock radio, two toaster ovens, a nice floor lamp—along with whole cartons of cigarettes, and cash if she was stupid enough to leave any around. The television set had become his symbolic object, even though Josephine liked to eat toast as much as she liked to watch TV. Every time he came around, he promised to bring the television back. If it weren't so pathetic, it might have been endearing, this insistence that he had the TV and would return it next time, when Josephine knew perfectly well he'd shot it into his crotch the same day he stole it. That was where Ricky and his friends stuck the dope, in the hairy parts of their groins, so they wouldn't have marks the cops could find easily.

She made a mug of strong black coffee, and got her garden spade from the basement. She put on her parka and cap and gloves, and stuck Saint Joseph in one of her cargo pockets. Thus outfitted for the wars, she glanced out the kitchen window into her tiny back yard. Something was terribly wrong out there. Everything beyond her property line was gone. The world had broken off like a cardboard picture and fallen away. Her snow-filled birdbath was still there in the foreground, along with her revolving clothesline like some weird antenna on its aluminum mast. After that, it was empty gray sky. A spasm of terror sealed Josephine's windpipe. Even in her panic, unable to breathe, she blamed herself: God was punishing her after all for burying Joseph, slicing the world right off at her door.

When she shook her eyes into focus, everything was normal again. Yes, she'd been raised by the nuns—when in doubt, assume holy wrath. The cold, cloudy sky was almost the same shimmering gray as her neighbor's weathered fence, and the two things—gray sky, gray cedar boards—had feathered together in a visual trick, making her yard look like the edge of the earth. She almost laughed, but she couldn't quite do it. A vision of doomsday shakes a person up, even when it's an optical illusion. She got the Old Grand-Dad from the cupboard and glugged some into her coffee, had a slurp, and headed out into what had just been, for a second, the end of the world.

Saint Joe belonged dead center in the lawn, she decided, sipping her fortified coffee. She kicked away some powdery snow and set her mug down. The ground felt hard. She dropped the point of her spade; the lawn was like rock. With a purposeful whack, she got maybe a sixteenth of an inch in. She wanted to cry. Then she reflected that the ground would be most frozen near the surface, and softer the deeper she went. Three or four inches down it might not be frozen at all. She had to be the most naturally optimistic person she'd ever met.

She thought about the shrine as she dug. She hadn't said a prayer in years, and now she remembered why. Praying was absurd. If God existed, He knew your every thought. He could only laugh when you tried to single out certain ones for His special attention. If God existed, every single thing you thought would be a prayer. Everything you *did* would be a prayer. Your *whole life* would be a prayer, Josephine thought, and when she thought that, burying Saint Joseph suddenly made more sense. It was superstitious, but at least that implied action—throwing salt over your shoulder, carrying a rabbit's foot, wearing specific socks when you played gin rummy. Superstitious people were the most religious of all, Josephine decided, because they lived their beliefs. Their weird obsessions were their ongoing prayer. That made gamblers like her ex-husband the priests and rabbis of the group. Their whole lives were offerings to luck—and what was luck if not fate, and what was fate if not God? Sal was a hood, but he was a spiritual hood —Josephine saw this about him for the very first time. And there he was now in his monastery cell, like the young brother she'd met today. The young brother selling raffle tickets.

She hooted at the sky and sipped her drink. It was a cold drink now, but that was what she needed, whereas before she'd needed something hot. Everything taking care of itself. The statue's resting place looked pretty good. All she really had to do was get him deep enough so the dogs didn't dig him up before the sale. After her exertions over his tomb, the hollow Saint Joseph seemed to weigh nothing in her hand. He seemed to float in space before her eyes. She set him down on his back in the hole, but found that she couldn't shovel the dirt on top of him, not right on his face like that. She turned him face-down, but that seemed worse. When she picked him up again, half-frozen dirt had sifted into his open base. You could see it through the translucent, cream-colored skin: Saint Joseph turning brown as he filled up with soil.

She washed him in the kitchen sink and put him in a Ziploc freezer bag, and when she got back outside, she told herself she'd done her best, plopped Joseph in his hole without looking, and scraped soil over him till he disappeared. She tamped down the remaining earth and threw a few spadefuls of snow on the spot. Then she looked around to see if anyone had been watching. She felt furtive and guilty, not uplifted by the magical presence of a sacred personage on her side. She needed to perform some better ritual, something to improve the efficacy of this whole bad act. She closed her eyes to conjure up an image of her soul at peace, and one came to her—her soul in a hot bubble bath with some more Old Grand-Dad.

■

She poached herself in the tub and thought about food. Her struggle with the earth had left her ravenous and helped her appreciate the hunger that Sal used to have back when they first got married. He was working as a stonemason then, and came home at night ferocious for the pastas and cheeses and spicy meats his mama had stuffed him with his whole life till then. Josephine, a girl from a tuna-casserole family, prepared meals that Sal didn't even consider food. And so, nineteen years ago, Camilla had come over to teach Italian cooking to her son's twenty-year-old bride.

The phone rang out in the kitchen. Josephine slid her ears into the water to make it go away. She had old Camilla to thank for a lot of things—her career as a chef, her changing real-estate luck, even her dinner tonight, which she'd brought home from Cantami yesterday because she knew she wouldn't want to cook today. Lying back in the tub like a dragoness, bourbon fumes escaping her nostrils, she relished the food awaiting her—linguini with calamari sauce, one of her favorite things in the world. Camilla had taught her to make it. In honor of Camilla, Josephine was going to find someplace great to cook in Florida, some incredibly classy restaurant where she'd knock their eyes out and get articles written about herself in the paper. She'd send those articles to Camilla, and Camilla would come to visit her. They'd wade together in the blue Atlantic Ocean.

She appeared in her kitchen in her terry-cloth robe, feeling immensely better. The phone machine wasn't blinking—her caller hadn't left a message. That meant Camilla had called; she wouldn't talk to "jukeboxes," her word for telephone-answering machines. Dinner resided in two takeout containers in the fridge: from one she plopped cold linguini onto a plate; from the other she poured the nice-looking red sauce with its rings and tentacles of squid. She covered it all with plastic wrap and put it on the microwave carousel. She'd been against zappers at first, but they were surprisingly all right for pasta dishes. Her carpenter had built the microwave into a cabinet on the wall for her, or it wouldn't have been here at all.

She opened a bottle of Chianti and poured herself a glass, flipped on the back-yard floodlight and stood at the sink window with her wine, fantasizing about the real-estate calls that might come in as early as tomorrow. It was night now and frigidly cold, even to the eye; snowdrifts stood frozen in strange attitudes, like waves about to break. She thanked the Lord for alcohol. Sharp gusts of wind blew powdery snow into the air, where it sifted like silver-blue glitter through the plastic rigging of her revolving clothesline. Saint Joseph, earthly father of the Christmas manger, was out there under the ground, irradiating her property with saintliness.

She got the cordless phone and pushed Camilla's speed button. The microwave started beeping the instant the number rang. The bells in Josephine's life always went off all at once. She popped the oven door and lifted a corner of the plastic wrap, averting her face from the steam.

"Hi, Ma," she said when Camilla answered. "It'sa me."

"It'sa you, bad girl," Camilla said.

"I'ma no bad girl," said Josephine. They always played this game. She clamped the phone between ear and shoulder so she could grab her wine, and walked herself and her comforts into the dining room. "Hey, Ma, you calla me?"

"I no calla you."

The food was too hot to eat, but she shoved in a forkful anyway. "Oh. O.K.," Josephine mumbled around the pasta, huffing puffs of steam to save her mouth. "Guess what?"

"No eat when you talk!" Camilla said.

"Sorry. I'm starving."

"What you eat over there?"

Josephine was burning her tongue with a hot calamari tentacle, and it took her a few seconds to get the answer out.

"You get fresh squid?" Camilla asked.

"Nice and fresh, Ma. From the restaurant."

"Why you so hungry? You no hava lunch?"

"I'm hungry from burying Saint Joseph. The ground is like a rock."

"You get nice saint?"

"Got a nice big one. About a foot long. Real nice."

"Hold Baby Jesus?"

"Of course, Ma. That's how you know it's Joseph. 'Cause he has Jesus."

"You bury like I tella you?"

"What do you mean, like you tella me? I buried him. He's in the ground. I put him in a plastic bag so he wouldn't get dirty."

"I tella you, head going down."

"No, Ma. You did not tella me that. What? Straight down?"

"Straight down!"

"Ma, I buried him good, in a nice plastic bag in the back yard."

"Back yard! No back yard! Front yard!"

"You did not tell me front yard!"

"I tella you!"

"Ma, I live on a busy street. People will see me."

"How you gonna sella you house?"

Josephine tossed her fork onto her plate and stood up from the table. "Are you really telling me this isn't gonna work?"

"I tella you, Josephine!"

"You did not tella me, Ma!"

"I tella you!"

■

She burst out the back door of the house in her jeans and boots and goose-down parka, cursing Chianti vapors at the arctic darkness beyond the range of her floodlight. She had her spade in one hand, her wineglass in the other. The wind had blown the snow into drifts across the yard, and now she couldn't find the spot where she'd buried the saint. She stamped around, kicking at the snow. Chianti sloshed out of the glass, staining her sleeve. She drank some more, and then ran the shovel around like a locomotive's cowcatcher till she found the soft spot she'd made before. She forced herself to go gingerly from there, so as not to disembowel the saint with her spade.

It was too much to ask that she be left alone. Mr. Crocus, her neighbor on the side with only a naked privet hedge, came out into his own postage stamp of a back yard to walk his hateful yippy dog, Felicia. Josephine very much doubted that Felicia had to go. She almost never saw Mr. Crocus walk the dog in winter; she was sure he let the little rodent relieve itself in the basement until spring and saved its business in mayonnaise jars. No, her nosy neighbor had seen her outside with a shovel, cursing and stomping, and he had to know what she was doing. Josephine pretended not to see him, and went on with the exhumation.

"Josephine!" he called out over the hedge. "What are you digging there?"

She looked up and feigned surprise. "Oh, Mr. Crocus!" she said. "What am I digging? A begonia. An exotic begonia tuber I bought mail order. I decided it belonged in the front yard after all, and I couldn't sleep till I moved it." With unmistakable finality, she added, "Good night, Mr. Crocus."

"You don't plant begonias this time of year," he said.

"These you do," she replied, scraping the soil. "They're perennials."

Saint Joe's plastic shroud glistened in the dirt. Josephine grabbed it and extirpated him like a root. This brought Felicia past the point of self-containment. She howled ghoulishly and tried to tear through the bare hedge while Mr. Crocus yelled and slapped her with her leash's leather handle.

"But you have it in a plastic bag," he protested.

"That's how you do this kind of root. You trick it into thinking it's winter."

"But it is winter."

"Yes, Mr. Crocus. *Here.* But not where the root comes from."

She put the saint in her cargo pocket, fetched her glass from the snow, and raised it in a toast. "To your health, Mr. Crocus! To Felicia!" She tossed off a swig and wiggled her fingers goodbye.

"Can I see this root, Josephine?" he called out. "I'd like to see this root."

"Gotta get it in the ground," she called back, hurrying up the narrow driveway on the opposite side of the house. Her fury at her neighbor made the digging easier this time—or maybe the front yard got more sun and didn't freeze so hard. She was working beyond the small well of light from her front-porch fixture, and couldn't see into the hole, but when it felt deep enough, she pulled Saint Joseph from her parka pocket and stuck him in, head down—no, she was still several inches shy. She could have bought the forty-nine-cent Joseph and buried him with a teaspoon, but she had to be grandiose. Did the spirits care about the size of your saint? She tossed him on the snow, and chopped like a madwoman at the base of the hole. Even in fleece-lined gloves, her hands were going numb.

Felicia began barking on the second floor next door. Josephine looked up to see the dog's master peeping through the window curtains. *Croak off, Mister Crocus!* she barked at him in her mind. Given her exhaustion, the cold, and the Chianti, she couldn't be sure she hadn't yelled it out loud. She must have, because suddenly her neighbor's window went dark. Or actually, no, the whole side of his white house lit up. Josephine thought she must have burst a vessel in her brain, or for some other reason was hallucinating. Then she saw that her arms were lit up, too, and throwing shadows across the blue-white lawn; the lawn itself was lit up, the shovel, Saint Joseph in his Ziploc bag on the snow. She twisted around to look. Her mental curse at Mr. Crocus had blocked the sound of a truck pulling into her drive and stopping halfway, as though about to turn around. She was kneeling before a hole in her lawn at eight o'clock on a frigid night, caught like an animal in someone's lights. She thought of the rifle racks she'd seen at the shrine.

She waited for the truck to back out and go away. Instead, its lights snapped off, though its rear end was still technically out in the street. It wasn't a truck. It was the smashed-up van of Ricky's jackass of a friend Alfie, whom she could see, in the glare of the streetlight, sitting behind the wheel. Her son was in the passenger seat. They stared at her through the windshield in the relative dark. Then they pushed open the creaking doors and stumbled out of the van.

Had it been summer, you could have seen their tattoos. As it was, they wore scuffed black leather and deformed ski caps. The spectacle of Josephine digging a hole in the lawn seemed to focus their wobbling attention, straighten them out momentarily, though they were clearly on goofballs of some kind. They moved in slo-mo, like androids whose joint grease was thickened by the cold. Josephine plunged Saint Joseph in the ground head-first and pulled dirt over him with her gloves. Then she stood and shoveled in the rest, and tramped it down with her boots. The representatives of drugged youth arrived as she finished. Ricky just stood looking at the dirty place in the snow. Alfie was the first to speak.

"Hi, Missus Vitale," he said, looking her up and down without even pretending he wasn't. "Whatcha doin'?"

"I'm not *Missus Vitale*. There's no such person. You can call me Miz Sessions. *Miz* Sessions."

"Excuse me, *Miz Sessions*," the sarcastic bastard said.

"Whatcha doin', Mom?" Ricky said.

She answered, "You're not supposed to come here when I'm not around."

This point seemed to dumbfound Josephine's son. He licked his lips and blinked his eyes. "But you are around."

"I know I'm around. You're supposed to call first."

"I did call."

"Oh, that was you. Well, you didn't get any answer, right? That means I'm not around." She gestured at the van. "You got my TV?"

Ricky looked at the van himself. "I forgot it. What are you buryin'?"

"None of your business."

"That's not very nice," Alfie said. "My mom doesn't talk to me that way."

"You don't even know where your mom is, schmuck," Ricky said. "Shut up." He turned to Josephine with a smile. "You buryin' the money and jewels?"

"Yeah, right, Ricky."

Josephine felt someone looking and glanced up at the window next door. When she did, Ricky grabbed the shovel from her hand. With one swipe of its blade he unearthed the plastic freezer bag. He pulled on its edge and plucked Saint Joseph from the ground.

"Hey, it's a religious thing," Alfie said.

"Give him a medal," said Josephine.

Ricky held the saint up in the yellow light from the front porch. He peered into its hollow bottom and shook it, but nothing came out. He poked at the hole in the ground with the spade.

"There's nothing else," said Josephine. "Just Saint Joseph."

"Is that who this is?"

"Can't you see he's holding the Baby Jesus?"

"Oh, yeah. So what are you buryin' him for?"

"It's an old good-luck tradition. You bury a Saint Joseph for Christmas. I'm doing Christmas traditions this year."

"You bury him and he brings you good luck?"

"That's right."

"Huh," Alfie said.

"You gettin' religious?" Ricky asked.

"I've always been religious," Josephine said. "But now I'm born again."

"*You* are? Born again?"

"That's right. So give me my saint and take off, O.K.?"

"I need to talk to you about something."

"I don't have anything, Ricky. It's gone. You took it all."

"He might, like, have some news to tell you," Alfie said.

"Will you stay the hell out of my life?" Josephine said to Alfie. She turned to her son. "You wanna talk, you can talk. Inside. Alone."

"Go wait in the van," Ricky said to his friend.

"Hey, it's, like, really fuckin' cold out here," Alfie said.

"Don't you know you're not supposed to talk that way in front of me?" said Josephine. "Go turn on the heat in your stupid van."

"The heat doesn't work."

"Then freeze."

Josephine picked up her wineglass, pulled Saint Joseph from Ricky's hand, and climbed the front-porch steps. Ricky followed her.

"Hey, I might not be here when you come out, Rick," Alfie said.

"Then he'll stay here tonight," said Josephine.

"I have to go somewhere with him," Ricky said.

"Then go."

"I gotta talk to you, Mom."

"Then talk."

Ricky turned on the steps to face Alfie. "Just wait for me, O.K., idiot?"

■

Josephine wished she hadn't left her Chianti bottle on the kitchen counter, but she had, and now Ricky made a point of smirking at it while she took off her parka. In his simplemindedness, her having a drink leveled the moral playing field between them. If she now tried to pretend she hadn't been drinking, the field would tilt in his favor. So she uncorked the bottle and poured herself another glass, even though she didn't want one. She threw Saint Joseph on the counter and lit a cigarette, too. Never apologize, never explain. It worked for Ricky. It seemed to be working for her. He had nothing to say. He took off his cap but not his leather jacket. His hair was cut in the goofy homeboy mode, the temples shaved away.

"I guess I don't get offered a drink," he said.

"You're gonna mix booze and those goofballs you're on?" Josephine said. "You're not bad enough as it is? You want to be a vegetable now?"

"I ain't on any goofballs," Ricky said.

"Who do you think's gonna take care of you when you're a giant slug? Me? Don't count on it, pal."

"I didn't even want a drink," Ricky said. He opened the fridge. "Is there anything from the restaurant around? I'm pretty hungry."

"I ate what there was. Today's my day off. That's why I'm here, right? You didn't expect me to be here. You came 'cause you thought I wasn't around."

"I told you. I came to talk to you."

"You can have peanut butter and jelly and a glass of milk."

"That's O.K. with me. I'll take that."

"Take it. You know where it is."

She took the wine bottle to the dining-room table while he rattled around in the kitchen. She stubbed out her cigarette and lit another one. She was going to quit smoking when she got to Florida. People would see her jogging by the ocean in fluorescent shorts. In time, her lungs would turn pink, as though she'd never lived this dirty life. Time would go backward. She'd be young again. She'd pass Ricky on her way back, looking like Methuselah under his wicked dope.

He came out with a white-bread sandwich and a glass of milk. He'd had countless identical meals at this very table as a boy, and it was mockery—the props remaining exactly the same though the plot had changed so utterly. There should be a different kind of bread to make sandwiches from when your heart was broken, Josephine thought. Milk should come in different colors, so you could tell at a glance which part of your life you were in. "What's on your mind?" she said.

Ricky was flipping through *An Half-Hour with God's Heroes* with one hand, eating his sandwich with the other, looking at the book and then at his mother, and shaking his head. He closed it and pushed it away. "Well," he said, and clacked the table with his long, dirty nails. "I guess I'm gonna be a father."

Josephine had been taking a drag on her cigarette, and she choked on the smoke. "*What!* Don't be ridiculous. You're not becoming any father."

"It's not ridiculous. She just told me today."

Josephine stood up so fast her chair fell down. She pointed at Ricky with her cigarette. "Then she's not very pregnant. She can get an abortion right now."

"She says she's not. She says she's having it."

Josephine righted her chair. A finger of wine remained in her glass, which she took to the kitchen and threw down the drain. "I'm having a cup of tea," she said. "You want one?"

"No."

"You want anything else?"

"I gotta go in a minute."

She put water on to boil. "Where do you have to go?"

"To Charlene's."

"What are you going to tell her?"

"Nothing, Mom. I told her everything already."

"Like what?"

"Like she shouldn't have the kid."

"That's right! It's a sin for her to have this kid! A sin!" She heard what she was saying, and stopped. She hadn't realized she believed in sin anymore. Ricky sat there stupefied, staring at her. Not only was she born again, she had the whole thing backward. She barreled on. "You're a drug addict! She works in a lousy diner! This kid is gonna have no life! Zero!"

"I'm not a drug addict," Ricky said.

"You're stoned right now!"

"I'm not a drug addict."

"When did you stop?"

"A while ago."

"You're lying. You know who you sound like? Your father. You lie exactly like your father."

"If you hate my father so much, how come you married him? You weren't knocked up with me. You didn't have to marry him."

He always did this when they got to this point. Maybe she should have been grateful he still followed the old script. Maybe that meant he had human feelings left, and wasn't just a lab animal sucking a nozzle. Maybe he was sorry his life had gone this way. "I've told you why. I fell in love with him. I didn't know who he really was."

"He probably didn't, either," Ricky said.

This stunned Josephine. It was the most thoughtful thing she'd ever heard Ricky say. "Are you gonna live up to your responsibilities and support this kid?" she said.

"Yup."

"How?"

"I'm gonna work."

"You've never worked in your life! And what about Charlene?"

"She's gonna work, too."

"You're both gonna work. So who's gonna take care of the baby?

Me? Is that what you think? Is that why you're in such a hurry to tell me?"

"Well, a lot of mothers would do their share," Ricky said.

"Their share! Are you kidding me?" She was screaming above the screeching teakettle. She went out to the kitchen to turn it off.

Ricky hiked up in his chair to look through the gauzy curtains on the living room's picture window. "I gotta go. He's freezing out there."

Josephine came into the dining room and suddenly she started to laugh. "I could pour boiling water on him for you," she said. "Want to?" she added conspiratorially, widening her eyes. "Let's pour boiling water on him!"

Ricky snorted at the idea. Then he stood up and led her through the dining room and living room and out to the front door.

"Did you really stop?" Josephine asked. "Tell me the truth."

"I stopped."

"Come back here tomorrow morning and tell me that. Come for breakfast."

"O.K., fine. I will."

He stepped into the crackling air, and she closed the door. Through the small windowpane she watched him get into Alfie's van and drive away, and then she walked down the front hall to the kitchen. She was about to make her tea when she noticed her purse on the counter with its flap unlatched. Inside, the snap was undone on her red leather wallet. She walked her fingertips through its worn compartments. He'd taken thirty of her forty bucks, and her extra pack of cigarettes, too. He wasn't going to Charlene's. He was going to gangland to buy some dope and nod out somewhere. Once, back when Josephine was legally charged with his life, she'd gone to the bad part of Boston to find her son. Half the stores were boarded up and the big theater's marquee was blank. She found Ricky and his friends in a dive called Vaughn's Rib Room, where a rack of baby backs was only $6.99, and that included the slaw, the beans, the slice of white bread, and the realistic sound of pistol fire out in the darkness nearby—no extra charge for the gunplay unless you got hit through the window while minding your business and gnawing on a bone, in which case your luck was so bad that it was now or later for you anyway, and it might as well be now.

CAN YOU DANCE

TO IT?

■

We three kings of Collegetown crossed Main Street in the dazzling light and flung open the black door of Rafferty's Bar. It was that brief moment in clear autumn afternoons when the sun ignited our beautiful lake, suffusing downtown with gleams and flashes like a five-minute occupation by the forces of good. Rafferty's door swung shut and cut us off from all that. We blinked in the cool darkness, surrounded by the spectral forms of pinball machines and the Ms. Pac-Man on which I'd recently damaged my right arm in a tournament with some of my students. This was back in my days of teaching at the college, before that part of my life came to an end. The doctor had my arm in one of those modern slings, all Teflon and Velcro as befit the high-tech nature of my wound.

Rafferty's was a vast old place. A voice called to us from deep inside it, where the names of beer shimmered in the void like approaching spacecraft. "Hey, the gang's all here," the voice said. "And it's not even Friday."

It was Russell, the man we were after. We couldn't see him yet, but he could see us—white-haired widower Sam, middle-aged divorcé Max, and youngest, never-married me, like three Russian dolls that fit inside each other. We were only one-third of the gang he had in mind—the Alienated Professors Club, which met every Friday at this hour in Rafferty's Bar. Judith herself, seven months pregnant with Russell's child, was a founding member. But, true, it wasn't Friday, and we weren't in Rafferty's for our weekly kvetchfest.

"That's right," Max called back. "It's Tuesday."

"Then this must be Bora Bora," Russell replied.

"Only for the lucky people on the cruise," said Sam.

"Luck!" Russell laughed into the darkness. "My mistress!"

Judith had told us to expect a jolly fellow, and here he was, his body tending bar but his soul already counting its chips in Atlantic City. Russell didn't know that federal agents had just been on campus looking for Judith, but he perceived his blunder with the word "mistress," the carelessness of giving up a card for no reason. His laughter stopped abruptly. In the dark, beneath an old Ray Charles tune on the jukebox, I sensed him cursing himself.

"Let me see if I have this straight," said Max, using Jack Webb's voice from *Dragnet*. Max was chair of the Philosophy Department and thus my boss. He'd begun doing the *Dragnet* voice years before as a way of keeping himself amused in class, and now it was a professional deformation, like the carved-up hands of a sheet-metal worker. He could no longer discuss Nietzsche or Hegel or Heidegger except in Jack Webb's voice. "First he says the gang is 'all here' when the gang is conspicuously *not* all here. Then he substitutes a metaphysical mistress for a physical one—both statements serving to erase, as it were, a particular individual."

"Screw you, Max," Russell said. "That's my third statement."

Our irises finally opened to reveal a few old regulars at tables, a few more at the far end of the bar, Russell himself pouring the drinks. It was what he was supposed to be doing, what Rafferty paid him to do, but we didn't expect to find him actually doing it.

"One-armed bandit!" he called to me. "I'll be seeing a lot of you soon!"

"So we hear," I said.

Judith had given us this news twenty minutes before, when we pulled her from a supplies closet in the Humanities building, wrapped her in a quilt, and smuggled her to Sam's warehouse loft in the trunk of Max's Toyota. Our pal Russell had finally bought his ticket for the Greyhound—one-way to Atlantic City, leaving tomorrow. For months he'd been studying the science of card counting, pumping his memory up, practicing by fleecing his professor friends in all-night blackjack marathons. Now he figured he could take the dealers of southern Jersey, and from there Reno, then Vegas, then early retirement in Honolulu. And never mind anything he might be leaving behind.

We sat down at the bar. "We'll have whatever you've been having," I said, noting the freshly washed shot glasses he'd arrayed bottoms-up on the rubber nubs of a green drainage mat. He was stumbling some, but still lining up the glassware in his meticulous way. I was surprised to see him this gone at four in the afternoon, until I remembered that it probably wasn't four in the afternoon for Russell. It was probably midnight now; it might even be tomorrow. Russell had switched over to casino time, where the boundaries of a day can expand and contract and slide around.

"No, I have something special for you guys," he said. "Something special and rare." And from down around his knees he produced a tall, clear bottle and plunked it on the bar. The label depicted a woman in a red miniskirt on a green-and-white field, caught mid-step in some ecstatic dance, the word "Ouzo" printed across her waist. It reminded me of "The Peppermint Twist" by Joey Dee and the Starliters, and I began to hum that tune.

"The last remaining evidence of the Greek space program," Russell said, as he started to break the seal.

Max grabbed it out of his hands and passed it to Sam, who put it in his canvas satchel along with the Chinese text on silk painting and the big book on Oskar Kokoschka he'd been showing me earlier in the day. Sam, the senior painter in the Art Department, had taken upon himself my visual education. Years before, Max had received similar tutelage.

"So, you've been talking to Judith," Russell said.

"More than talking," said Max. "We've been playing hide-the-pregnant-lady."

"We thought you might like to play, too," Sam said.

"Aw, I thought we were gonna have fun."

"Girls aren't fun?" Sam asked.

"They are at first," Russell said.

Judith was the Philosophy Department's aesthetician, our specialist in truth and beauty. Like me, she was coming up for tenure in a couple of months. Unlike me, she had a chance. In my six years at the college I'd done a number of questionable things, but my dissertation wasn't one of them. Judith was not only a bona fide Ph.D., she was a pal, and everyone wanted to see her stick around. She wore the hippest shoes and stretch pants on campus, and she organized our monthly Motown dance parties, some of the only wholesome fun we ever had anymore. It was at one of Judith's dances that I'd first met Russell—the same night she met him, in fact, back when he first hit town to work in the vineyards of a farmer he knew down the lake.

"*You* teach at this college?" Russell had said that night as he shook my hand. He'd been playing cards for a few weeks with Sam and Max and some other profs, and I'd heard all about him—the big Oklahoman who was taking the faculty's money in any game they cared to name. "*You're* a philosophy professor?" Russell said, staring at me.

"I don't look the part, huh?"

"I guess the haircut fooled me, the little tail thing there in back. Or maybe it was the purple corduroy bedroom slippers."

"Not the string tie?" I asked, fingering the state of Texas it had for a clasp.

"Yeah, that, too," he said. "I'm from those parts, you know."

"I've heard."

"Damn, seeing you makes me think I could have been a professor, too."

"Oh, you would have been good," I said.

He seemed genuinely morose about it. "The things that pass you by in life 'cause you just don't know."

"You just nailed a major philosophical problem right there."

"*Damn*," Russell said. "And I'll tell you another thing. I can sing about as good as Robert Goulet."

"That's something I'd save for just the right time," I said, and then, across Judith's living room jammed with dancers, I saw it happen—the instant she and Russell saw each other. Their attraction annihilated space and time. Instantly, Judith was at Russell's side. "Is this the gentleman from Oklahoma?" she said.

"Why, yes, ma'am, it is," Russell replied, his voice gone slippery, his nostrils flaring, his cowboy boot pawing the ground. Apparently, his singing voice was the least of it.

"I need to borrow him," Judith said to me, and danced Russell away.

It was two years later now, and we'd grown fond of Russell in the time he'd been orbiting Judith, roaring into town like a comet and flaming in our midst for two or three months at a time. Across Rafferty's mahogany bar, Max said, "There's something you don't know, mister."

"Don't worry," Russell answered. "I know it all. Inside out. Double."

"No," said Max. "You don't. Events have taken a sinister turn."

■

Judith was an Argentine whose visa had expired more than a year before. Nobody knew why they kept turning her down, but her repeated applications for renewal had all been denied. We suspected the malignant influence of our provost. It was his job to plead Judith's case to the authorities, see to it that she be allowed to stay, yet just last week he'd called Max, not to report on his progress with the Feds, but to express the trustee position on tenuring unwed mothers. The provost liked to "ride herd" on the faculty. Still, we'd assumed the campus was consecrated corral.

No cop had set foot on the grounds since 1972, when a mole exposed the student protesters' plan to blow up the cafeteria.

But this afternoon two federal agents had strolled right into the Humanities building with a warrant for our pregnant friend. Some students (who would later graduate with highest honors) saw them in the lobby, smelled a rat, and tipped us off. We hid Judith behind the mimeo machine in the supplies closet, locked the door, and took up lounging positions in our office doorways around the Humanities reception area.

The tired-looking men in bad suits came up the stairs. They flashed their IDs and asked us where Judith was.

"Judith," Max said in Jack Webb's voice. He looked around at the rest of us. "Anybody got any information on Judith's whereabouts?" "Whereabouts" was one of Max's favorite words and he relished any opportunity to use it.

"She might be in New York," I volunteered. "She likes to disco there."

"The woman in question is an illegal alien," one of the agents said.

Six or seven profs were standing in their doorways by now. We all acted stunned and amazed.

Max turned ceremoniously to our receptionist, the trusty Maria. "If anyone would know of Judith's whereabouts, it would be this lady right here."

"Haven't seen her," Maria said.

"Wish we could do more to help," Max told the agents.

They saw how things stood and they went away. But they vowed to come back, and we believed they would. They were too dull to have been sent for show. No, Judith's manila folder had found its way down to the worker ants of the system, the bureaucratic plodders whose bland tenacity was a force of nature. Given enough time and brown shoe leather, they would create the Grand Canyon.

There was only one thing left to do: get Judith married to a citizen of the United States. The father of her baby seemed the elegant, economical stroke. True, he was the worst husband material imaginable, but Judith persisted in liking him. She couldn't explain what it was about Russell, she said; he was just her type. Thus, we'd come to Rafferty's Bar like the Three Sisters of Fate to give Mr. Wrong his last chance to do the right thing. If he refused, we had an alternate plan: Max would marry Judith himself. Max and Judith already had what Max, a Marxist, called "history," and this plan also satisfied his highly developed sense of duty to his staff, something we all cherished him for. It seemed rather too highly developed in this case, however, since I had volunteered to marry Judith first.

Our news about the Feds had flung Russell into a funk of gambler's superstition. He'd been less than a day away from making his escape, and now this. You could see what he was thinking— that he'd gotten jinxed somehow.

Sam handed over the key to the freight elevator up to his loft. "She's expecting you."

Like a sleepwalker, Russell tried to hand the key back. "Sorry, fellas, I have to work," he said.

"We're covering for you," said Sam, leading him out from behind the bar and stepping in to take his place.

The sight of his own face in the big mirror seemed to wake Russell up. "I just want you guys to know something," he said. "That baby was her idea. I was always against babies. This could have happened to you!"

He saw that we were the wrong audience for the distress signals of the cornered male. "I'm saying she tricked me into it!" he exclaimed, taking another tack, the appeal to reason and justice.

"Stole your sperms," I said.

"That's right!" he replied.

Max joined me in examining the classic tin ceiling of Rafferty's place—stamped with an intricate filigreed relief and freshly painted a dill-pickle green—until Russell huffed off to the black front door. When he reached it, he spun around to face us again. "Everything's a trick," he said bitterly, and stepped backward into a lozenge of apricot-colored light.

"Indeed it is," said Sam, who spent most of his life in pictorial space and who was now stacking a pyramid of shot glasses to do the one where you cascade the whisky by overpouring the uppermost glass. He flourished the bottle like a magic wand. "Bourbon is a witch," he said. "I am a witch doctor."

■

We had tended bar for a half hour when Rafferty showed up. He was a big pink-faced man who sold real estate and sang baritone with the local opera. The bar was a sideline.

"You look good back there," he said to Sam. "I think you missed your calling. Johnnie on the rocks."

Sam poured him a big one. Rafferty was already up to speed on Russell.

"The fantasies of grown men are the worst," he said, sipping his Scotch. "Everybody knows you can't card-count in casinos anymore. They shuffle six decks together in the boot. It doesn't matter how good your memory is. The house wins."

"And then there's the small matter of the baby, Raff," I said.

"Yeah, and then he goes and knocks up this girl. The guy's a loser."

We told Rafferty about Immigration. He jumped right off his bar stool in one motion. I couldn't believe he could do that. Real-estate salesman or not, he was still an old Leftie. "No! Not federal agents on a college campus!"

"G-men," Max said. "Two of 'em."

"Big as life," I said.

Max leaned into Rafferty's face. "Brown shoes," he said significantly.

"Oh, that's no good," Rafferty said, sitting back down. "That's bad."

"Rafferty," said Sam, "the girl has to get married, tomorrow, and the bum she's with doesn't even have a full-time job."

"All right, all right," Rafferty said. "I'll use him six nights. By himself except on weekends. He's a pain in the ass, but I think he keeps the damage down. The kids respect him."

We all embraced the big man. "All right, all right," he said.

"Let us buy you dinner at Stella's," Max said.

"I can't eat at Stella's anymore," said Rafferty. "You guys eat there?"

"Once in a while," we said, backing away toward the door.

"Who's tending bar here?"

"Cover us for dinner, O.K.?" said Sam, as the door opened and the sunset hit our eyes, and we seemed, for a moment, to dematerialize into the pure manifestations of Being we had apparently devoted our lives to believing we were.

Our little town had one of everything—one Chinese place, one steak place, one Bar-B-Q, one avocado-and-sprout—except for sub shops and bars, of which it had about fifty apiece. Stella's was the Italian place. This dinner was probably my five-hundredth there. Sam and Max, both long ago tenured and left for dead, must have been well into four figures at Stella's by then. It was an old shoe of a restaurant with homey food served in a decor so red you seemed to be dining inside a living heart. Personally, I could have gone for a steak, but steak was out on the bypass at the Chanticleer Grill, and from a window table at Stella's downtown we could keep an eye on Sam's second-floor loft, kitty-corner across the street.

"I hate the idea of spying on people," said Max, once we had our antipasto and our first carafe of local red wine. His doctorate was in ethics and he was always saying things like that. We'd been staring across the street like people at a drive-in movie, watching the large industrial windows above the furniture store. Sam had the whole second floor of the building—one huge open space except for his bathroom in back, all of it painted hospital white. He did his pictures in front, at the wall of windows filled by a perfect view of the lake.

"Is it spying if you can't see anything?" Sam asked.

"This is not seeing anything?" said Max. He turned to me. "How many times have you given the Plato's Cave lecture?"

"And now I'm seeing it. Just the way Plato described it."

What we could see, from our seats at street level, was the top half of a wall and a large swatch of Sam's ceiling. It was dusk now, and Russell and Judith had all the lamps blazing in the loft. As they moved around, gigantic shadow-forms of a man and a woman hurtled across the open space like Mr. and Mrs. Frankenstein. They were either dancing or duking it out; nothing else could account for the titanic story we saw enacted on the wall. Every now and then the people themselves strayed close enough to the windows to pop into view, just the tops of their heads lit from below, and it was shocking to see them appear that way, so 3-D and so small, like seed kernels released by the great, dark creatures to propagate shadow-beings throughout the world.

We were almost finished eating when Russell suddenly burst from Sam's street door and hurried off down the sidewalk. Max went to call Judith from the old wooden phone booth in back. Her giant shadow answered the phone. Max gesticulated in the rear of Stella's restaurant, and then, across the street, Judith's shadow gesticulated up in Sam's loft.

"So what happened?" we asked when Max got back.

"They danced for a while and then they had a fight."

■

On account of Sam, I was looking forward to getting old. He had many winters on his hoary head, and their snow had leveled out life's hills and valleys for him. All things of the world delighted Sam equally now, even the spectacle of his town's demise. He'd come there forty years before, when it was still considered the most beautiful spot in the state and our two-lane road was the big highway. People from everywhere stopped to see the summer houses and eat lunch by the lake. Then somebody decided to build the Thruway seven long miles north of town, and now only the college and the army base stood between us and nothingness.

Our search for Russell took us past many old landmarks, and Sam remembered some of them for Max and me—the boarded-up ballroom on Exchange where throngs once danced to the Dorsey band, the big theater on Market where Sinatra once sang. Our own Rafferty sang there now. We stopped in the sad Greyhound station that was once a whorehouse, and verified that Russell had not boarded any buses for anywhere. We checked all the joints we'd ever seen him in, right down to the tiny one near the tracks whose sign merely said "Bar." We checked all the addresses where Russell had ever crashed. Even in a town so small, it took a while. Nobody had seen him anywhere. Max was looking more and more like a married man with a kid on the way when—at ten o'clock, to be absolutely sure—we finished up with a swing down by the water.

We found the usual hot cars in the lot at the head of the lake, local kids drinking beer and listening to brain damage on their tape machines. They hooted at Max's little Toyota. Farther around the big asphalt crescent of the lot, where the streetlights stopped and the sandy beach became a long plain of shiny stones, we saw Russell and a woman sitting on the bumper of a snow-white Jeep. Max pulled up and parked nearby. Russell saw who it was and wearily pushed off from the woman's car. He walked out on the stones, all the way out to where the water began, lit a cigarette and smoked with his back to us, looking across the lake at the string of mercury lamps lighting the bypass running south out of town.

The woman was holding a joint and looking at us with alarm.

"Hi there, Leslie," I called out to her.

She looked me up and down for a second and then she smiled. "Hey, it's you," she said. "You remembered my name."

"Oh, Leslie," I said. "Of course I remembered." I turned to Max and Sam. "Leslie works at the hospital. She does physical therapy there."

"That's the best kind," Sam said.

"Yeah, yeah," Leslie said.

Among friends now, she had a toke on her pot.

"Leslie working on your arm for you?" Max asked me.

"No, this I haven't seen," she said. "Haven't seen any of this guy for a while now."

This was true, but for a few months the previous year I couldn't walk into a bar in town without encountering Leslie. Her MO was to come on ridiculously strong and then disappear with somebody else. I danced with her a few times and bought her drinks. The one time she decided to take me home, she phoned out for Buffalo hot wings when we got back to her place, even though it was two in the morning by then. When they arrived she spent a long time at the door with the delivery guy, who'd drawn a happy face on the Styrofoam takeout container and written "Hi, Leslie!" above it. We ate the wings with their Roquefort sauce and Leslie told me things about herself that she probably didn't remember telling me now. She told me her philosophy of life, which was that life was a game. She told me that she liked professors better than guys from the Ag station, but that guys from the army base were best of all. She told me I was a good listener, and then she passed out.

Here in the parking lot, she offered her joint to the three of us.

"Sorry, ma'am, we're on duty," Max said.

"Professors go on duty?" Leslie asked. "Down at the lake? At night?"

"Hermeneutics Division," I explained.

"Oh," she said. "Sounds serious."

"It is, ma'am," Max said. "We have to question this suspect here."

"Good luck. He's one sad case."

"We know," Sam said. "Let's just book him."

"Is it about the girl or the money?" asked Leslie.

"How about if you tell us?" said Max.

"Well, he took all this money from some suckers at cards, and figured he'd stake himself to a big roll in Atlantic City. He asked me to go with him. Promised me the time of my life. When I turned him down, he got all morose and said it didn't matter, 'cause he just found out he had to get married."

"He said that?" Max asked.

"Yeah. It's a shotgun deal. He's taking it pretty hard."

We stood there for a minute watching Russell sitting out there on a large black stone. I'd walked this stretch of lake shore many times with Sam in the evening. He liked a cigar after dinner, so we'd buy some stogies at the magazine store on Exchange and stroll the water's edge puffing away and talking about art. Sam was painting big abstract landscapes in those days—masses of green and brown and blue plucked from the world around here—and he would tell me the right way to look at the lake, how to empty myself of all thoughts of lakeness, and just see the thing.

Which was what I was doing now when I noticed that everybody was looking at me. Without realizing it, I'd been humming the Joey Dee and the Starliters tune. More than humming it, actually, I was giving it the full combo rendition—bass line at the bottom of my throat, drums and cymbals with my tongue and teeth, melody carried somewhere up in my nose.

"He always does that," Max told Leslie.

"Didn't know you were a musician," Leslie said.

"Oh, I did some backup vocals in the old days. Played a little tambourine. Nothing too heavy. That was 'The Peppermint Twist.' Remember that one, Leslie?" I said, though the song had probably come out before she was born.

"Nope," Leslie said. "I don't. It's an oldie, huh? I don't much go in for oldies. Can you dance to it?"

"That was the whole idea, Leslie. It was a dance. The Peppermint Twist. The song came on, and you did this special dance that went with the song."

"Oh, one of those," Leslie said.

"Leslie's not interested in those," Max said. "Leslie does her own dances."

"Correct," Leslie said. Then she jutted her chin at my arm in its sling. "So what happened?"

"Ms. Pac-Man."

"Ouch. We're seeing more and more of that." She tilted her head toward the north side of town, where the hospital was. "Well, stop in, maybe I can do something."

"I might do that, thanks."

"Can I stop in, too?" Max asked.

"What's your problem?"

"General dislocation."

"It has to be specific before I get involved."

"That a girl," Sam said, nodding his head at the moonlit lake. He was watching a tall, rugged Oklahoman approach us on the glistening stones.

I retrieved the ouzo from Sam's satchel in the car, opened it, and gave it to Russell when he arrived. "Congratulations, Pop," I said.

He took a slug. "It's really as long as they say, isn't it?" he said, passing the bottle back.

"What's that, Russell?"

"The arm of the law."

"Oh, that. Yes, indeed it is."

"You can run," Sam said, having a swig, "but you cannot hide."

"You can't even run," said Max.

I looked at Max's face in the lavish moonlight—the original stuff from the sky along with the reflected version from the surface of the lake. You can read minds in light like that. Max was thinking, *I almost belonged to someone again.* I knew the way he felt. I'd had somebody once myself, right here in this very town, but she left for a better deal in a better place. We'd all had them at one time or another, companions who were suddenly gone when the tide went out, leaving us like porpoises famous for their brains who, finding themselves beached, nonetheless continue to smile inscrutably and sing to one another.

"There's a big Motown dance party this weekend to celebrate Russell's marriage," I told Leslie. "Maybe you'd like to come."

"Me? Oh. Would I be, like, your date?"

"Sure."

"Oh, well. Gee. Thanks. O.K."

"She probably never shows much enthusiasm," Sam said. "This probably means the world to her."

"It does," Leslie said. "You gonna be able to dance with that wing?"

I tried a few steps there in the parking lot and the arm hurt pretty bad. "You're right. I should probably start some therapy on this immediately."

"You probably should," Leslie said.

She got into her virginal Jeep and rolled the driver's window down. "So long, fellas," she said. Then her passenger door swung open and she waved me in.

"What about our card game?" Russell said. "You owe me money."

"He should be home writing his dissertation," Max told Leslie. "He's deliberately trying not to get tenure here."

Sam handed Leslie the ouzo bottle. "Good muscle relaxant," he said.

We waved goodbye to my friends and launched into the night. When we reached cruising altitude, somewhere out over the lake, Leslie patted my injured arm. "You're gonna have to stop playing that stupid game," she said.

"I know it," I replied. "And it's kind of a shame. Because there's these little blue guys that come after you? The bad blue men? And I just learned how to keep them from gobbling me up."

PILTDOWN MAN,
LATER PROVED TO BE
A HOAX

■

Down at the asylum, the best-behaved patients were out walking around loose, roaming the grounds in their bathrobes and pajamas or sitting on benches staring at the road. Some wore regular clothes, but you could tell they were patients whenever a car went by. Patients had a special way of watching a car. They followed its path as though it magnetized their faces, their heads swiveling together in sync; then they gazed down the empty road long after the car was gone, as though, like a movie in reverse, it might come reeling back. Only a tiny old man was ignoring the cars altogether. He was off by himself on the lawn beneath the massive gray buildings, making his way among the flower beds in his tattered blue robe. At each bed he knelt to speak to the plants, putting his lips close to specific flowers, gesturing to make himself understood. Blossom after blossom failed to respond. I could see the pain it was causing him, the umbrage he was taking. Finally he began to cry. Then he wrenched a clump of daffodils from the ground and lashed them into slivers against a nearby rock.

I was across the road behind a tree. I'd just hiked down from the mountaintop where my family lived—down the old deer-hunters' path and across a field—and I was hiding behind one of the big maples lining the hospital road. Every minute or so I stepped out and stood beside its trunk and waved to the patients on the lawn, and they waved back to me. Then I hid behind the tree for a minute before coming out to do it again. It was a game I'd been playing with the patients since the beginning of spring. First they would see a cornfield and trees, then a dark-haired twelve-year-old boy, then only trees and a cornfield again. They loved things like that. This time a few patients hid behind trees on their side of the road, too, but they lost track of the game and forgot to come out.

I was already late getting over to my friend Clayton's house. When I crossed the road, patients flocked to me like ducklings. Their gauntness did not prepare you for the way they could move, if moving entered their minds. They were terribly gaunt. Even the stout ones seemed gaunt somehow, around the mouth and eyes. I knew they had food to eat because I ate it myself; Clayton's mother worked in the hospital kitchens and gave us whatever the patients were having. Maybe they just did the wrong things with it. Many of the men had dried egg-yolk patches in the stubble on their cheeks.

I revealed a few secrets to them. "The fish refuse to have their pictures taken," I said. "The bumblebees are meeting to decide what to do." The patients nodded enthusiastically—a stiff, whole-torso nodding accomplished from the waist. "There's a city in the sky," I added, looking up at the sliding clouds. "They're having a party today."

They were eager to tell me things in return. "The doctors play violins all night and never let us sleep," one patient said. Another said, "They have factories on the moon where they make all the money." "They're selling our sunsets to the Chinese nation," I was informed by a third.

I knew these things—they'd told me already—but I put on a good show of surprise and indignation. Then I said goodbye and proceeded across the lawn. The man in the blue robe was still kneeling by the rock, gaping at his scraps of yellow flower on the grass. "I'll be back soon with rubies and diamonds," I called to him over my shoulder. He looked up at me, and for a second he forgot his troubles. The patients hiding behind the trees were still pretending I wasn't there. Out of courtesy, I pretended the same thing about them.

■

The asylum occupied a gigantic parcel of state-owned land bisected by a brook that bubbled amid the Gothic gray buildings where people went to live when they lost their minds. The place was much larger than any nearby town, and it suggested boundless bureaucratic mystery as you drove past it on the road—as though a medieval principality had sprung up from dung in the cow country forty miles west of Manhattan. In my whole first summer on the mountain I never saw the asylum except that way, as a passenger in my parents' cars. They had forbidden me to go down there to play.

My father owned fifty acres of land on the mountain overlooking the asylum—not the whole mountain, as Clayton always said to embarrass me. Compared to real mountains like the Rockies it was just a hill, but for New Jersey it was a mountain. We'd moved there the summer before, between my sixth and seventh grades, to escape the colored people my father said were taking over our native city of Newark. My father had been driving an oil truck in Newark when I was born, but he'd worked his way up till he had his own heating-fuel company in the city. He sold it to start another one in the sticks of Jersey and build us a house on the land he'd bought, where he envisioned a whole mountaintop development of superior homes. So far, ours was the only one. In his flight to the country my father was ahead of his time; no one else was ready to buy lots for houses that far away from everything except a lunatic asylum. That was why the asylum was there, my mother said, because it was the middle of nowhere. She, too, had wanted to get out of Newark, but she thought the state hospital was a fatal flaw in my father's plan. She'd heard bad stories about the asylum, including the one about the escaped patient who had appeared the previous year on the streets of a neighboring town —barefoot and crazy and brandishing a razor blade.

Our new house was surrounded by acres of wooded land, yet when the leaves fell off the trees that first autumn, I could see, on the horizon, small but unmistakable, the Empire State Building and the Statue of Liberty. I could see the hospital, too, down in the foreground, where Clayton lived in the workers' barracks. School had begun by then, and Clayton was my only classmate from our remote corner of the township. Working for the asylum made Clayton's parents employees of the state, and the state took care of its people—or so his mother, Mrs. Parker, always said. She liked the state for the way it helped her raise her family. The Parkers had five children, Clayton and four younger girls. "I don't know how we could ever do for them *out there*," Mrs. Parker had told me, meaning out in the world where my family lived.

We didn't have this concept of the benevolent state in our house on the mountain. My father worked for himself and did not like the state. He said the state was hurting those hospital workers by giving them too much and taking their incentive away, and this was the only connection I ever heard my father make between himself and the hospital people, because the state was hurting him as well, with taxes and regulations that seemed designed to keep a man from having ambition and doing business.

I believed him about his taxes, but I didn't get the part about the workers having too much. As far as I could see, they didn't have anything and never would. Their barracks lay huddled in a grassy basin at the edge of the hospital grounds—scores of chalky, lime-green lozenges like an army encampment, each the size of two railroad cars, with a small brick porch at either end. When I first went down to play with Clayton in the fall, I didn't understand how two whole families, not just one, could live in each of those barracks buildings. The rooms were small and dark; there was a tiny stove and a sink, but not really a kitchen. Once, when we were filthy from jumping into the cinder pit, I asked Clayton how many times a week he took a bath, and he said he'd never taken one in his life. He laughed when I didn't get the joke: the barracks had no bathtubs, only showers.

■

I ran down the grassy slope and across the parking lot. Clayton answered when I knocked on the flimsy barracks door, his big-toothed smile floating in the dim entrance of his shabby house. His parents worked on Saturdays and his sisters were out playing somewhere. It was getting toward lunch, but it seemed he'd just gotten up. He came out into the sunny parking lot blinking his eyes.

"Weren't you expecting me?" I said.

"Sure," said Clayton, looking at the sky. "I was expecting you."

We talked about what to do. The choices were not infinite, and we'd end up doing them all anyway—playing in the tunnels, getting lunch from Clayton's mother, buying stuff at the hospital store, jumping in the cinder pit—so the only question was in what order. I was trying to think of a way to avoid the pit altogether today. Clayton had vowed to push me off the highest part of the cliff the next time we went there.

"Let's go down in the tunnels," I said.

"Too nice out," said Clayton.

"Let's go look at the cows. We never do that anymore."

"I don't want to see any cows. Let's go to the pit."

Our game at the cinder pit was to pretend we were para-troopers—sprinting from the road's edge to the cliff and then leaping out into empty space. Clayton jumped into the pit's deepest place, where the drop was more than twenty feet. I stuck to the shallow end, where it was less than ten. Clayton lived for danger, which was one of the main differences between him and me. The other main difference was that he was black. For a long time I assumed that all black people liked danger more than white people did, because I didn't have anybody to compare Clayton to. He was the only black student in our entire school.

"I'm not going off the high end, Clayton."

"Oh, Gabe," he said, knowing I disliked that nickname. He punched me in the arm. "I was only kidding about that."

We crossed a lawn into the center of the asylum and took the wide tree-lined boulevard past white gazebos and a band shell where the patients heard music in the summertime. The springtime grass was tender and pale green. The forsythia had long since lost their yellow flowers, but azaleas still burned like gas jets at the base of every stone-faced building—as though Mr. Parker, an asylum groundskeeper, had gone around adjusting them like the flames of his own little stove at home. The hospital's reservoir sparkled in the distance, a polished blue platter in an evergreen grove. Puffs of steam rose from metal grates in the grass, the exhaust from the tunnels that connected the whole hospital underground. I caught the sour institutional smell of the subterranean kitchens where Clayton's mother cooked.

From one of the towering gray buildings, a voice called to us. When we looked up, we saw a woman on the fifth or sixth floor, a paper-white face behind the bars of her window. Framed by stone blocks, she resembled a plant trying to grow beneath the dark weight of a rock. Only a few hospital structures had bars on their windows; these were the buildings for the criminally insane. Clayton said that the people behind those bars had done especially nasty things, like killing their entire families.

"I know who you are," the woman called out, slipping her arm through the bars and pointing at us. Her hair hung in oily strings.

We walked to the base of her building. "We know who you are, too," I said, pointing back at her.

This pleased her immensely. She clapped her hands and left her window. When she came back, she had a plate of spaghetti in her hands. She held it up for us to see.

"That looks good," Clayton said. "You're supposed to eat that." He rubbed his belly for emphasis.

She spilled the spaghetti out through the bars. It slid down the building, a shimmering trail of sauce and noodles on the stone façade.

"There goes your lunch," I called to her in a scolding voice.

"There goes my lunch," she called back with enormous joy.

We left her like that and walked on toward the pit.

"What do you think it's like?" I asked Clayton. "Being crazy like her."

"I think it's like being high!" he said.

"What do you know about being high?"

"I've seen lots of high people. What do you think it's like?"

"I think it's like being on another planet. Mars, say!"

"What's so good about that? They don't have air up there!"

"You bring your own air, Clayton. Didn't you ever read Tom Swift?"

"No. Who's that?"

"A kid in some books."

Clayton just shook his head.

"You think we'll ever get like that woman?" I asked him.

"You will, for sure," he said. "It runs in your family."

"You don't go crazy from having it run in your family."

"Don't you know anything? Going crazy is a hereditary thing. Everybody knows that. Count on it."

A few years before this, my father's father had become senile. He started traveling across the city of Newark to see people who were no longer alive, stopped strangers on the street and claimed to be their friend. He thought his reflection in the mirror was another person, and sometimes he didn't recognize his wife. He was only fifty-seven years old when they took him away, and that was the thing my folks marveled over with their friends, the way a person's mind could evaporate at any time. My grandfather lived in a home where they kept him on drugs all day. My parents had taken me to visit him and I'd seen the miserable situation he was in. I'd bragged to Clayton about how bizarre it was—the way he had his meals in a high chair like a baby and didn't even know my name.

"Well, what about *your* family?" I said now. "How about your old man? Talk about crazy!"

"Yeah, but he's not *crazy* crazy," Clayton said.

∎

The school we attended was a bad place twelve miles away, populated by greasers and hoods and sniffers of glue. I should have lasted five minutes there, but I arrived in the same van that brought Clayton to school and I was shielded by his protective coloration. The nastiest thugs left Clayton alone, though they despised black people in theory. It was rumored that I, too, lived at the lunatic asylum. Clayton and I allowed this mistake to go uncorrected. He became my closest friend. My parents were appalled by this turn of events, but what could they say?

My friendship with Clayton consisted of countless little riffs we played over and over, but the special seal and symbol of our brotherhood was a prehistoric being known as Piltdown Man. Early in the year, our teacher, Mr. Marsh, had done a lesson on him in history class. They'd unearthed Piltdown Man's skull in England somewhere. It had the cranium of a human and the jaw of an ape, and this made Piltdown Man the original human being, the missing link, the hairy angel who'd vaulted evolution's monkey-chasm to become the thing we were today. Single-handedly, Piltdown Man had crossed the dark threshold into species-hood.

Mr. Marsh told us all this in his usual boring way, but then something inspired the man. It hit him that he should become Piltdown Man to show us, and this he did brilliantly—stooping over to half his height so that his arms slid out of his jacket sleeves, swinging his arms ape-fashion, grunting and bellowing as he lurched back and forth the length of the blackboard. He was a tall, goofy man with a crew cut and a bad complexion, and he was perfect as the man-beast responsible for all humanity. Clayton and I regarded each other with bugged-out eyes, our heads nodding up and down. *Yes, yes!* our startled faces said. *This is the real stuff! Check this out!*

Nobody said anything out loud. Nobody laughed. The whole class was transfixed by Piltdown Man. Because the insane were never far from my mind, I wondered if Mr. Marsh was ready for the funny farm—as people always called it who didn't know exactly where the farm was located and what it was like. Then students around me started cackling. Clayton had joined Mr. Marsh at the dawn of human time. He was up from his desk, hunched over and grunting in the back of the room, doing a stunning black version of Piltdown Man.

The two of them carried on this way for a minute to our general delight, groaning and gesturing to each other across the room. It was Mr. Marsh's most successful interaction with Clayton. Then the big white ape-man cast his eyes around our world of people and people's things. "Piltdown Man!" he boomed, straightening up to become Homo erectus again. "Later proved to be a hoax."

We sat there with idiotic grins on our faces.

"Hoax?" Clayton finally said, still dangling his arms. "What hoax you talking about?"

"Piltdown Man," said Mr. Marsh. "Discovered, nineteen-eleven. Proved to be a hoax, nineteen-fifty-three. Those bones turned out to be fake."

"What!" Clayton cried out.

"That's right," Mr. Marsh said with enormous satisfaction. Astonishing Clayton, laying Clayton flat out with disbelief, was the greatest pedagogical achievement he could hope to have in our class.

"With people believing in him all that time?" Clayton said, returning to his desk. "Nineteen-eleven to nineteen-fifty-three?"

"Yup," said Mr. Marsh.

"How could anybody do that?" I said. "Make fake bones like that?"

"Well, they were very clever," Mr. Marsh answered with a smile. "Kind of like you guys."

"Bull*shit!*" Clayton said.

The girls gasped and the boys snorted like little pigs. Mr. Marsh's happiness disappeared. "I don't want to hear that again, Clayton," he said, for probably the three-hundredth time. Like all the teachers at our school, Mr. Marsh had to take great care not to appear to be picking on Clayton.

"You told us Piltdown Man was real," Clayton stated.

"I did not," Mr. Marsh replied.

I said, "You showed us how he walked and everything!"

Mr. Marsh turned to face me. "Gabriel," he said kindly, "I was showing the class what people *thought* Piltdown Man was like. When they believed in him."

"Well, how are we supposed to figure that out!" Clayton cried. "You're supposed to be teaching us stuff, and instead you're getting us all confused!"

Mr. Marsh leaned on the blackboard's eraser tray and rubbed his eyes.

"Did they get in trouble?" one of the girls asked. "The people who did the hoax?"

"They never found out who did it," said Mr. Marsh.

"They never got caught?" the girl exclaimed.

"They got away with it?" cried one of her friends.

"Yes," he said, looking at Clayton and me. "They got away with it." He stared over our heads. "The perpetrators of that hoax took the secret to their graves," he said, as if to himself.

His remark chilled the room. The idea of being in one's grave withered the triumph of not getting caught, and the class settled down. Mr. Marsh opened his English book and started diagramming sentences on the board. But Clayton did not agree that history was over. He raised the wooden top of his desk and put his head inside. The metal book-cavity was empty and made an echo chamber for his voice. *"Piltdown Man!"* he bellowed.

Mr. Marsh spun around. "Clayton, that's enough," he declared.

My own desk had books and papers inside, ruining my echo. *"Later proved to be a hoax!"* I cried, but it came out muffled and indistinct.

We were sent to the principal's office. I was brave until they separated me from Clayton. Clayton was brave the whole time. He'd been to the principal's office many times before. The principal told me that if we ever again called Mr. Marsh "Piltdown Man" we would be expelled. "We weren't calling *him* Piltdown Man,"

I said. "We were saying it about ourselves." And only in saying this did I understand it was true. The principal, being the principal, didn't get the point.

We stopped making our joke in class. But like dogs we kept returning to the rotten thing we'd found—roaming the halls and playgrounds in the Piltdown crouch, grunting and hollering his name followed always by the heart-wrenching "Later proved to be a hoax!" Piltdown Man became our universal sign of everything the world contained. The authors of our textbooks were Piltdown Men, our classmates were Piltdown persons, all schools and governments and works of men were frauds. But the purest form of the Piltdown hoax on earth was the lone black boy among the whites, the indisputably impossible creature.

■

The cinder pit was just off the public road that looped the hospital grounds. A guardrail kept cars from driving where the shoulder of the road thickened to become the cliff. The pit resembled a quarry. Bulldozers moved the glistening blackness and loaded it into trucks for the asylum's icy roads in winter. The cinders themselves were a loose, oddly lightweight substance, like crushed pumice stone, but dirty. Walking across the pit, you sank past your ankles and the coarse, sooty grit filled your shoes. It was a filthy place to play. The cinders turned my skin jet-black, which my mother bemoaned when I fouled her tub and washing machine, but which gave Clayton as much pleasure as seeing me blush in school. Cinder soot didn't make his skin any darker, and he couldn't turn red in the face. Nothing showed up on Clayton.

The pit was a prehistoric place where Piltdown Man would have felt at home. I always thought of him when we went there, that cave dweller no one believed in anymore. I stood on the cliff and imagined Piltdown Man on the desolate black plain below, wandering the primeval landscape in his crouch, human but not really, hunting and foraging, his eye out for a mate, never imagining that someday people would call him a hoax.

We took a few jumps off the cliff, me from the shallow end, Clayton from the thrilling peak, plunging knee-deep into the granular stuff and then scrambling back up the side to do it again. When I wasn't looking, Clayton grabbed me in a headlock and dragged me to the highest place. He said he would count to three, but he jumped on two. I went over head-first, fell short into the scooped-out face of the pit, and somersaulted twenty feet down. When Clayton saw I wasn't dead, he laughed. I was still struggling out of the cinders when a voice spoke to us.

"That was a brave one, that time," the voice said. "That one was good."

We looked up and saw him emerge from the trees, a tall black man in hospital clothes. He'd been hiding in the woods beyond the pit, watching us drop into the soft, receiving lap of pulverized darkness.

"Let me have a look at these young fellows," he said on his way toward us. "Oh, these are two fine young Negroes. Two fine-looking Negro boys."

"He's not a Negro," Clayton said.

"Of course he is," the man said. "Look at that rich, dark skin."

"That's dirt," Clayton said. "He's white. I'm black."

"Oh," the man said, sidestepping away as if afraid of me. "Can we trust him?" he asked Clayton.

"Maybe," Clayton said.

"Sure, you can trust me," I said.

"How do I know?" said the man.

I didn't answer. Instead, I hunched my shoulders and dangled my hands at the ground, and started walking around like Piltdown Man. My knuckles brushed the cinders as I slogged across the pit. I heard grunting and looked up to find Clayton doing it with me. We lumbered around like space baboons on a shimmering black moon. The man's mouth gaped open as he watched.

"What's that!" he cried.

"What's what?" I said.

"What you're doing!"

"We're not doing anything."

"You're doing something!"

"We're just being normal," Clayton said. "You trying to make us feel bad? We can't help the way we are."

For a second the man got serious and spooky, then he gave us a sly face and started walking like Piltdown Man, too. He made us look like amateurs. Compared to him, we didn't even know how to do it. Even gawky Mr. Marsh couldn't come close.

"Nice!" said Clayton. "Very nice!"

"You're the missing link!" I said.

The man jumped back. "Who said I was missing?"

"Nobody said you were missing, man," Clayton said. "Be cool."

"Why did he say I was missing?"

"He was talking about something else. Nobody's missing."

"Nobody knows you've escaped," I said.

The man stared at me. Then he started to laugh.

"How long you been in this joint?" Clayton asked him.

He thought about this with some amusement. "I forget," he finally said. "What are you boys' names?"

We told him our names. He shook our hands in an elaborate way, enveloping them with his left hand while shaking with his right. "My name is Luther," he told us.

"You shake hands like a king," I said. "I'll bet you're a king." I'd met a number of kings and queens while playing at the asylum with Clayton. Luther was the only one who really looked the part—the noble bearing and the outsized face. You needed a big face to be a royal personage, or you looked silly on a throne.

"I'm a prince," Luther said.

"Where's your princedom?" I said.

"Africa. You boys have any cigarettes?"

"We don't smoke. Aren't you kind of old to be a prince?"

That cracked Luther up. His laughing mouth was full of gold. "I was kidnapped to keep me from becoming King," he said. "That's why I'm still a prince." He paused. "I could die a prince and never be King. Unless I return to my people and reclaim my throne."

"What work crew they have you on?" Clayton asked.

The hospital had barns full of cows and pigs, large fields for growing the white cow-corn they ate, fenced-in tracts of other vegetables. Farm work was part of the rehabilitation practiced there. Driving past the asylum in good weather, you saw crews of patients tending to the animals and plants.

Luther looked down at himself. "They took me to a patch of dirt and gave me a hoe," he said. "Me, a prince."

"So as soon as you had your chance," I said, "you went over the wall."

"Did I?" Luther replied. "I don't remember that. What wall?"

"It's an expression. You don't actually need a wall to do it."

"And now you have to get back to your people," Clayton said.

"Yes. But first I need food and money. And cigarettes."

"Where are your people, exactly?" I asked.

"I told you," Luther said. "Africa."

"Yeah, but what part?"

He didn't answer.

"Nigeria?" I suggested. Mr. Marsh had been trying to teach us something about Nigeria recently, though I couldn't remember what.

"Yes!" Luther said. "How did you know?"

"You look like people in pictures from there. Nice in Nigeria this time of year?"

"It is so beautiful," Luther said. "The sky is bright red every night and all the people are singing. I must get back to my home. Soon, I must start out soon."

"Nigeria is ten thousand miles from here," Clayton said. "You're not gonna make it three miles to town. You're wearing chain-gang clothes, Luther."

"That's why I was hoping you boys could help me," he said.

■

The Administration building stood majestically at the head of the asylum's tree-lined central boulevard, with four columns of polished purple marble and a wide white staircase up to its elegant doors. It looked particularly grand from the grassy ridge we were standing on. Two Jersey state troopers had their cruisers parked in the circular drive around the fountain. They were out talking with hospital security cops and some men in suits.

"Look at this, Clayton," I said, squeezing his arm. "They're on to Luther."

"How do you know that?"

"What else could it be? We can't go back there now. Luther's on his own."

"Gabriel, you are such a baby. Those cops could be here for anything. They make the rounds. I live here, remember? Cops are here all the time."

"Not state troopers."

"It's a *state* hospital, man."

My father had told me that Jersey state troopers were the meanest people on earth, meaner than Marines. "I'm not messing around with them, Clayton."

"You are such an infant," he said.

We walked up the boulevard toward Administration. At the base of an adjoining building, wide metal utility doors to the tunnels were standing open. Two black men in white uniforms were unloading a truck, stacking boxes of food on bright chrome carts for the kitchens. When we got close enough, I saw they were Jimmy and Earl, two of Clayton's neighbors in the workers' barracks.

"What's going on?" Clayton asked when we reached them.

Earl, the older man, answered him. "Something," he said.

"Like what?"

"Don't know. Something not good."

"You can tell the way folks are acting," Jimmy said.

"How are they acting?" I asked.

"Scared," Jimmy said.

Clayton pushed me along. "I'm hungry," he said.

He led me into the mouth of the tunnels, down the concrete

ramp into the broad dim corridor beneath the ground. Naked bulbs
burned in small cages on the ceiling. Their murky yellow light
looked the way the tunnels smelled—a sour smell of medicines
and the fermentation of old age. Orderlies pushed patients strapped
to tables along the concrete floors. People in wheelchairs rolled
themselves from one building to another, nurses bustling past them
in white leather shoes.

You could walk around the asylum grounds all day and never
imagine the tunnel world that existed beneath you. When I played
down there with Clayton, we ran around pretending to be in a
dungeon or escaping from evil pursuers. We spied on the strangest
people we could find, took stairways we'd never noticed before,
surfaced inside buildings far from where we'd first gone in. Sooner
or later we showed up in the basement kitchens to get food from
Mrs. Parker. She was a nice lady with a formal, dignified way of
speaking and carrying herself. She always seemed glad that Clayton
was friends with me. Today she was at a big stainless-steel table,
making baloney-and-cheese sandwiches on mushy white bread.
Clayton and I stood silently beseeching her while she hummed a
tune and layered meat and cheese on many slices of bread. I tried
to think of a way to let her know what we were doing.

"We're starving, Mom," Clayton said. "Can we have two sandwiches each today?"

"How are you ever going to lose any weight, Clayton?" Mrs.
Parker said. "You eat all the time and you don't get any exercise.
You don't go out for a single sport."

"I'm going out for football next year," Clayton said.

Mrs. Parker raised her face to laugh. The shelf of her bosom
heaved up and down. "Do you think I believe that nonsense?"
She looked at me. "Gabriel, are you ill? You don't look well today."

"I'm not very hungry all of a sudden, Mrs. Parker."

Clayton glared at me. "He just told me he was starved!"

"Does Clayton eat the food I give you?" Mrs. Parker asked.

"No, ma'am. I eat it. I'm usually hungry."

"Maybe you let yourself get *too* hungry this time," she said.

"That can happen. Eat your lunch and see if you don't feel better."
She completed our sandwiches with mustard and lettuce leaves,
and turned them over to us in waxed paper bags.

I looked back at her longingly as Clayton dragged me away. We
left the kitchens and ran through the tunnels till we were under
the building where the chambermaids had their headquarters.
Clayton knew all the women who cleaned at the asylum; they
lived in the workers' barracks, too. Two maids, Margaret and
Shirley, were on the sofa in the lunchroom when we ran in.

"We're putting on a play in school!" Clayton told them. "Can
we get some of those old clothes you have? For costumes for it?"

"You never acted in any play, Clayton," Margaret said, her
dark, white-stockinged legs crossed on the sofa, cigarette smoke
coming out of her nose. "Besides, we don't have no clothes to fit
you."

"No, it's older kids acting in it," he said.

"What kind of play?" she asked me.

"It's kind of about the roaring twenties," I said.

"I like that," said Shirley. "What characters you looking for?"

"Men," I said.

"I know that! What *kind* of mens?"

"A tycoon and a politician," said Clayton.

Margaret and Shirley seemed dazzled by the idea of characters
like that. We followed them to big canvas hampers full of patients'
unclaimed clothes. They pawed through the bins until a musty
miasma filled the small back room we were in. When they were
finished we had two whole outfits, a winter one and a summer
one—jackets, pants, shirts and socks, two old-fashioned pairs of
shoes. There was even a hat, a brown fedora hat. The women put
it all into a paper shopping bag.

"Hey, when is this play?" Margaret called as we ran away down
the stairs.

"Don't know yet!" Clayton called back. "We'll get you tickets!"

"You better, Clayton Parker!" she cried.

We went back underground and resurfaced at the hospital store.

The goods in this store were subsidized by the mysterious entity of the state. You could get cakes and candy for a penny, soda for a nickel, whole packs of cigarettes for a dime. I always bought treats there for Clayton and myself. This time he wanted to do the buying, and asked for money before we went in. He got soda and corn chips and candy bars, and brought them to the counter. "Two packs of Luckies for my pop," he said to the clerk.

At the phone booth outside, he dropped in one of my dimes and dialed my number. Clayton knew that my mother made a regular Saturday trip to town, and with this knowledge he had conceived a plan. I tried to tell him it was crazy, that it wouldn't work, but he wouldn't listen, and so I got on the phone with my mother and asked her to stop and pick us up on her way.

■

Luther poked his head out from behind a tree as we crunched into his hiding place in the woods. When he was sure we were alone he scrambled out. "Look what my mates have brought me!" he said when he saw the shopping bag slapping Clayton's leg. "Good work, my young princes!" He sat on the fallen trunk of a tree and wolfed a baloney sandwich while Clayton told him the plan.

Fear was closing off my throat so that I could hardly breathe. I kept looking at my watch. "She'll be here in less than half an hour," I said.

"What about money?" Luther said.

"He has money," Clayton said.

I had fifteen dollars left in my wallet, saved from my allowance over the winter. I said I had ten, and that much I turned over to Luther.

"Good boy," he said.

"I want something in return for that money."

He dragged heavily on a cigarette. "What?"

"I want to know if you're crazy. If you're really insane."

He blew smoke at the asylum. "They think I am."

"What do *you* think?"

"I think they're right."

"Was your father crazy?"

"Yup."

"How about his father?"

"Same."

"See?" Clayton said.

"That's what you wanted to know?" said Luther.

"Not really," I said.

I stood by the side of the road above the cinder pit and watched for my mother. Her blue station wagon appeared in the distance. I thought of the many times I'd ridden that stretch of road in that very car. This was how the patients saw me coming, I thought, and for a strange moment I felt like a patient myself. My mother pulled onto the shoulder beside me. "You've been in that pit again," she said, but kindly, because she loved me no matter what I did.

A pathetically false smile possessed my face. "Mom, could Clayton's uncle catch a ride to town, too?"

"Clayton's uncle?" she said. "Doesn't he have a car of his own?"

I wasn't prepared for this question. If a man wants a ride to town, doesn't that imply he has no car? I stood there stupidly, certain she knew I was up to something, until she looked behind me and smiled.

"Hello, Clayton," she said.

"Hi, Mrs. V.," he said. "My uncle has a car, but it's not here. He lives in Philadelphia. He's been visiting us. We would've called a cab to the train, but Gabriel said you were coming this way anyway."

"It's fine, Clayton," my mother said. "Where is he?"

Clayton affected great embarrassment, flapping his arms and covering his eyes. "Let me check on him," he said, and ran down the overgrown slope beside the cinder cliff.

"I guess he stepped into the woods," I said.

"What for?" my mother asked.

I looked up at the sky. "I guess to go to the bathroom, Mom."

She lowered her eyes at the dashboard. "Oh, I see," she said.

In a few minutes, Clayton and Luther clambered up the embankment. Luther was wearing the heavy brown tweed suit. It was the hottest day of the spring so far, probably eighty degrees. I couldn't imagine why Luther had chosen the winter clothes. Then I remembered: he was crazy. He carried the half-empty paper shopping bag and held himself elegantly erect.

"Mrs. V.," said Clayton, "this is my Uncle Luther."

"Pleased to meet you, Luther," my mother said.

"Ma'am," said Luther, taking off the brown fedora and bowing from the waist beside her driver's window.

Something I hadn't realized about Luther in the open air became intensely clear when we were all in the car. He smelled bad. He smelled, in fact, like an asylum patient, and there was no mistaking or ignoring it. My mother looked over at me in the passenger seat. I never saw her smile more insincerely. She rolled her driver's window down. "Let me know if that's too much air for you, Luther," she said, pulling out onto the road.

"I like air," Luther said.

"And no wonder," my mother said. "You're overdressed for this weather."

I poked her thigh as if to say, *Jesus, Mom, they're poor. Those are probably the only nice clothes he has.* I saw her catch my meaning.

"Did you enjoy your visit?" she said.

"Yes'm," Luther said. "Didn't expect to stay quite as long as I did."

"Family visits can just go on and on, can't they?" My mother laughed.

"Yes'm, they sure can."

We drove past the well-kept older homes on the shady road between the asylum and town. I wondered what Clayton and Luther thought when they saw places like that. The town was a village, really, and just as it began there were two big stone churches, Lutheran and Episcopalian, one on either side of the road. They were churches from an earlier time, cathedrals compared to the modern Catholic one my family attended, a depressing brick rectangle next to a filling station.

Luther ogled the Episcopalian church, pressing his forehead against the car window and gaping at the ivy-covered stone and the mythic figures portrayed in stained glass. I braced myself to hear him claim to be Jesus or one of those colorful saints, but he didn't say anything.

The train station was at the beginning of town, before the stores began. The maroon-and-silver train was sitting there. My mother pulled in and the three of us got out. "Thanks for the ride, Mrs. V.," Clayton called to my mother in the car. "See you, Gabe," he said to me, and winked.

"What do you mean?" I asked. "Where are you going?"

"To Philadelphia with my Uncle Luther."

"What are you talking about, Clayton?" I whispered.

"You knew I was going," he said loudly, so my mother could hear. "I told you that."

"No, you did not tell me that."

Luther doffed his hat for my mother again and backed away. I started to follow after them.

"Gabriel, come on," my mother said. "You can say goodbye to Clayton here. How long are you going for, Clayton?"

"Two or three days," he said.

"You can survive without Clayton for a couple of days," my mother said to me, and I got back into the car.

For a half hour I trailed behind her through the stores. I didn't want candy or comic books or any of the things I'd always wanted in town before. When we drove out, the train was gone. I controlled myself all the way back to the asylum, certain I would see Clayton walking home by himself on the side of the road. But I didn't. On the ride up our mountain, I broke down and told my mother everything. She didn't believe it. She called Mrs. Parker, who didn't believe it, either. I was sent up to my room while she called my father at work. I looked out my window, but I couldn't see the asylum buildings below us or New York City on the horizon;

the trees were already green enough to screen that all out. When my father got home, his low voice resonated through the house exactly as I imagined the voice of a Jersey state trooper—a terrifying sound bereft of animation or joy.

He called me downstairs and I told him what we'd done. He didn't hit me—my mother didn't allow hitting in our house—but he didn't have to hit; when I was finished, he turned his back on me and walked away. I returned to my room upstairs, where I deciphered enough muffled words to gather that he was calling the police, and that Luther and Clayton would have a reception when they arrived in Philadelphia.

■

The next day was Sunday and my father told me to dress up and get in the car. I'd made my Confirmation the previous fall, and now that I was a man it was supposed to be my decision whether to continue worshipping or not. I had decided against it, and hadn't been in the church since Confirmation day. I would have to begin my confession with this information and then go on to my secular sins. I rode down the mountain nearly faint with dread. But instead of taking me to town, my father pulled into the asylum grounds, drove to the workers' barracks, and parked. I didn't know he even knew where the workers' barracks were. I thought the asylum part of my life was separate from him. He was bringing me to apologize to Clayton's mother and father.

"But the whole thing was Clayton's idea," I said.

"Get in there," he said.

Mrs. Parker answered the door when I knocked. She was wearing a fancy dress and stockings and shoes. She motioned for me to step inside. Mr. Parker stood in their little living room in a suit and tie; he looked at me, but his face was utterly blank. The four girls sat on the sofa in dresses, with bows in their hair. I didn't understand what was going on. Then I realized that they'd been to church themselves, or were about to go. I'd never seen Mr. and Mrs. Parker dressed as anything but a cook and a groundskeeper, and seeing them now in their Sunday clothes staggered me. I started to cry. When I stopped, Mrs. Parker told me that she and Mr. Parker had had to plead for their very jobs after what Clayton and I had done.

"I'm really sorry, Mr. and Missus Parker. I apologize," I said, sniffling and backing away, but Mrs. Parker took hold of my arm. Clayton had asked to see me, she said. "He knew I was coming?" I asked.

"Your father called us," she said, and she led me to Clayton's bedroom door.

He lay on the bed in his tiny, dim room, the only one of us not wearing Sunday clothes. His lips were cut and his cheeks were swollen, and his blackened eyes were puffy slits.

"Well, look who's here," Clayton said. His rubbery words were hard to understand. "Nice, huh?" he added, indicating his face.

I couldn't think of anything to say. "I'm sorry, Clayton," I whispered finally. "I got scared something would happen to you."

"So you made sure something did."

"No, I didn't. I didn't make sure of anything. I was worried, that's all."

"You're always worried about something," he said. "You are such a mama's boy." He sat halfway up on his bed. "What were you worried about this time, Gabe? That I was gonna ride the train for a few hours and then go home? Big deal. You never rode a train before?"

In fact, I had never been on a train. "My parents always had cars," I said.

Clayton flopped back down on his bed and laughed.

"What's so funny about that?"

He laughed until I thought he was crying. "I don't know," he said between spasms. "It's just so funny. Your parents always had cars."

"I can't do anything about the way my family lives," I said.

He didn't answer me. I took a step or two farther into his room.

"Hey, Clayton, listen," I said. "When this all blows over, we can go to the pit and you can push me off the high part. You can push me off as many times as you want."

"I don't think so, Gabe," he answered without looking at me. "I don't think we'll be going there anymore," he said, and we never did.

THIS IS A NATURAL
PRODUCT OF THE
EARTH

■

The Transamerica pyramid was even more fantastical in life than in the pictures of it Raymond had seen, a dagger thrust from the center of the earth in the name of life insurance, and as he crossed the Bay Bridge, the entire city delighted him, sliding over his windshield in the sun. San Francisco's exotic face spoke to Raymond, saying he'd done the right thing when he moved to California two weeks ago. Maybe, when he and Christine had some money, they could move up here from San Jose. He followed Mary's instructions into Berkeley, parked the car, and walked up onto Telegraph Avenue. They were supposed to meet in front of Cody's famous bookshop—it was easier than her trying to explain on the phone how to get up to her house in the Berkeley hills—and when he arrived, late, she was waiting for him. But he didn't realize it. He stood on the corner for five minutes, looking back and forth between the rollerskaters in the street and the books in Cody's window. Finally, a woman at a magazine stand walked over and kissed his cheek.

"I thought this might happen." She laughed.

He was too stunned to laugh himself. In Boston six years before, Mary's hair had been short and straight, bluntly cut into a helmet by herself at home. Now it was down to her shoulders and permed into cascades of bouncy ringlets. Her disdain for fashion had been complete, but today she was wearing a red silk dress and red leather pumps, makeup on her eyes, and a grapey color on her lips. She looked great—sexy, if you could still say that—but she didn't look like Mary.

"He finally shows up in California," she said. "But what's this strange taboo against visiting people? You had to wait until you *moved* out here?"

Raymond's never having been off the East Coast was one of their standing jokes. In every letter, and the yearly phone calls on their birthdays, Mary insisted that he come out and see the marvelous West. He could stay with her as long as he liked, she always said, and the girlfriend was welcome, too. Every year Raymond said he would, and every year he didn't.

And now he actually lived here—with Christine, his girlfriend, who was attending the Stanford Business School. He had a new job with a Silicon Valley importer of high-end computers from Japan, turning painful documentation ("Activate vector object and transform to specified output") into plainspoken user's guides ("Click on the thick line and then choose an item from the 'Output' menu"). For the past four or five years—most of the time since he'd last seen Mary—he'd done similar technical writing for outfits on Route 128 around Boston. He never could have predicted this career for himself, but he was surprisingly satisfied doing it. Most people in the industry were decent folks, and he liked to play with hardware. On some level it engaged his soul.

"You could have come out here years ago and been a West Coast saxophone player," Mary said. "This is a great place to be a musician."

Raymond only laughed—he'd heard this so many times. Trying to be a jazz musician was what he'd been doing when he and Mary knew each other in Boston. He worked in a photocopy shop on Boylston Street and practiced at night, jammed with music students, played an occasional gig. But he was twenty-seven with a master's in English, and Boston was crawling with eighteen-year-olds who'd never done anything but play saxophone. Nothing mattered to those kids except the horn, and in the end Raymond saw that he'd never be obsessed enough to live that life.

He'd met Mary because she and her daughter, Melissa, moved into his building on Marlborough Street. When he asked her what she did, she said she was a revolutionary. She'd been married to an older man, a sixties political organizer; the politics outlasted the husband. Later, he found out she worked in a hospital as an LPN. Her plan was to get the RN degree she'd abandoned when Melissa was born, and become a barefoot doctor somewhere in the Third World. When she left Boston five years ago, she and Raymond had been lovers for a year. She left because California was warm and friendly and conducive to human life, and nursing school was almost free for state residents. He had wanted to go with her, but she was taking Melissa and no one else.

Now they were finally together in the Café Mediterraneum, Mary's favorite place, having the gigantic caffè latte served there in pint pub glasses. At eleven in the morning, the place was still full of people talking and reading and having coffee and pastry. Some were clearly Berkeley students; others looked like the lords and ladies of the Valley whose Porsches and BMWs idled next to Raymond's old Datsun at every light in San Jose. At a corner table sat a wildly bearded, heavyset man in a dingy T-shirt, reading a dog-eared copy of *Das Kapital* and looking like Marx himself.

Mary sipped her latte and shook her head. "Well, *you* look exactly the same," she said. "It's spooky, like I just saw you yesterday." She smiled. "But you're not the same. The body snatchers got my friend. This has really become your life now, huh? Writing computer poop for corporations? You were an artist, Raymond. You've completely sold out."

He smiled back. Mary's California transformation was entirely in the cosmetics and couture. She was the same old Mary. He'd never been an artist, and as she must have remembered, he could needle right back. He touched the sleeve of her red silk dress. "When you sell out, it's usually for money. I see you've managed to get along without any. This is just something from the Good-will."

She looked down at the front of herself and tossed her springy hair. "Actually, the Goodwill in Berkeley is very good. I've been there. Not for this particular dress, which just happens to be my very best dress that I wore especially for you. But I started this, right?"

"You started it. I do what I do for a living and it's fine." He sipped his coffee and glanced at a man by the window who was, in turn, glancing at Raymond and Mary from behind a yellow paperback of *Realism in Our Time*.

"O.K., you gave up the saxophone. But you didn't give up trying to follow girls to California. And now one of them has taken you up on it. I should have grabbed you when I had the chance, huh?"

"No, you were smart. I was a bad bet. Probably still am."

"You don't mention her in your letters. I ask all these questions and you don't answer. This makes me suspicious. You can't possibly think you're supposed to spare my feelings or something. I mean, I left you, right? So what's the story? Are you in love here, Raymond, or just involved?"

"How do you tell the difference?"

"Oh, come on. You were in love with me, for instance."

"Was I?"

"Yeah, you were."

"O.K., that'll be my reference. Am I in love? It must get harder to tell, the older you are. Christine's great. I like her a lot. It's lower-key than it was with you. She doesn't harangue me about overthrowing the government."

"She just harangues you about doing the dishes."

"Nope."

"Business school, huh?"

"Yes, business school, and I know what you're thinking. I see the image you've got, and she's not like that at all. The whole world is business, kiddo. It's just what people do all the time. There's no such thing as life without business. Going to business school doesn't automatically make you Lucifer's servant, the way we used to think it did."

"You're sure about that?"

"I think I'd know if Christine was Lucifer's servant."

"Her head would spin around or something."

"Right. Or she'd like spicy food."

Mary's pub glass thumped on the table. "She doesn't like spicy food?"

"No, not particularly."

"Oh, my God! Raymond, Raymond. How can you possibly live with someone who doesn't like spicy food?"

"Easy. Hot sauce on the side."

∎

They walked along the streets, Mary showing Raymond the things she loved about Berkeley. It was her favorite place in the world, she said, except maybe for New York, but they didn't need any more revolutionary nurses in New York. Plus, it snowed there. And you could see the whole world in Berkeley, anyway. Not to mention eat it. She was taking him to a Mongolian place for lunch.

On the way, Raymond saw a music store and took Mary in to buy her a gift—John Coltrane's *Crescent*, one of her old favorites that she didn't have for her new CD machine. In Boston, Coltrane had been Raymond's great inspiration, and it was possible that he and Mary had become lovers because she loved Coltrane, too. He wasn't sure anymore, but he used to learn Coltrane solos note for note and play them for her, he remembered that. These days, he hardly listened to jazz anymore at all. He listened to loud electric pop that entered his blood like sugar and kept him revved up all the time.

Mary, however, still listened to Coltrane, who sounded new every time she heard him, as though he were alive and playing that moment. She made cassette tapes of Coltrane for Charles, her husband, and he listened to them in prison on a little head-phone machine. Sometimes the music got him through the bad days. But every day's a bad day in prison, one after another out to the vanishing point, and if a person's going to stay sane in a situation like that, he needs real evidence of what's waiting for him at the end. And so Mary had decided not to wait until Charles got out to marry him.

She'd met him three years before, after his attempted escape. He smashed his leg jumping from the prison wall, and they brought him to the locked police ward in San Francisco General, where Mary worked as a nurse. The surgeons had to put a lot of screws in his leg in two operations that kept him in the hospital a month. By the time he went back to jail he and Mary were friends. She visited him every week. She brought him cigarettes and books to read—fiction and poetry and political thought. When Charles was finally paroled, he moved in with Mary to start a new life.

Raymond heard the first installment of the Charles story in a letter from Mary, and he'd been full of admiration for the never-ending adventure of her life. He'd also been appalled. The man was a lifelong needle user and Mary, the battle-zone nurse, wasn't even mentioning AIDS. In her next letter she read Raymond's mind and volunteered that Charles was HIV negative, and if he weren't she'd know how to deal with that. Her letters were happy for a while, and then they weren't. A year ago she wrote that when a junkie gets out of jail, all the old friends come around, wanting him to get high again. Charles had promised to stay straight, but it was like promising to hold back a train. The only free life he knew was out on the street. He was shooting dope again, breaking and entering, the whole nightmare. While Mary was at work one night, the cops showed up with a warrant and turned the place upside down—her place, all her own things—and took Charles away again. He was forty and he'd been in Sing Sing, off and on, for almost half his days on earth. They put him in Folsom this time. That's where Mary'd been married four months ago—Folsom.

"I talk to him twice a week on the phone," she told Raymond now, over a Mongolian hot-pot into which one dunked noodles and onions and strips of meat. "But I haven't seen him since our wedding. The prison's having a lock-down, which means no visitors, no privileges, no leaving the cell. Usually you have a lockdown if there's been trouble, if they're worried about a riot or something. There hasn't been any trouble. They're just doing it to lean on people. It's a long drive, and I could only go once a week, no matter what. Every week I call on my one day off, and every week they say still locked down."

She laughed. "After six months in prison, if you're married to somebody, you're supposed to get conjugal visits. In our case they're going to count from the wedding, not from the time he went in, just so we know what they think of white girls who marry black junkies in their jail. That makes four more months before I can finally lie down next to my husband. Assuming I ever see him again at all. Incredible, right? But what do they care? They're free, it's not their life."

Raymond spooned more peanut-chili paste into his bowl and thought, as he had thought many times before, that he could never have foreseen Mary's present life. Then he recalled that he had failed to foresee his own. He knew that if Martians landed tomorrow they'd say, "Hey, look, they put all the black and brown ones in jail," but Mary was describing a life so bizarre it was hard to believe it really existed. He couldn't imagine being in prison, or being married to someone who was. "Do you want me to help you bust him out?" he said. "We could do it tonight, unless there's a moon."

"That's the spirit," Mary said. "It's all a bad joke anyway. And then we can hide out at your place in San Jose, right? Christine won't mind." She lifted some noodles from the steaming broth. "He was supposed to come up for parole this January. They always said if his behavior was good they'd forget the attempted escape. Now, for no reason, they're not going to forget. Just like that, an extra year out of his life." She pointed her chopsticks at Raymond. "This is why white men *need* black men to be junkie slaves. You realize that, right? So they can have somebody to do this to. I'm only telling you this as an illustration of the way the world works. For your education. It's not a plea for pity. They can't break me down. I can wait. And Charles can wait, too. God knows he's had plenty of practice."

"And then, after this particular practice session, Charles gets out—again—and comes back home to you, again—"

"Totally different, Raymond. Totally. We're married now. He never had anything as good as a wife to lose before. He's learned his lesson."

They finished lunch and walked up Telegraph till they were back where they started. They visited Shakespeare & Co., and when they came out Mary took Raymond by the arm and turned him onto a side street up the hill. After a couple of blocks, at the beginning of a residential neighborhood, she stopped beside a large vacant lot. It was about an acre of land with a patch of dirt for every patch of crabgrass. A few old garbage barrels were scattered around, a few winos lying on the benches.

"I'm only giving you one guess," Mary said, "because it's so easy."

"One guess," Raymond said.

"About what this is."

"It's a vacant lot."

"Come on. No ideas? Nothing at all?"

"No."

"This," Mary said, "is People's Park."

Raymond stared at it for a minute. "Not *the* People's Park."

"Oh, yes," she said. "The very one. Remember? You were young, your generation was going to change the world forever. An amazing peaceful revolution was just automatically going to happen because you wanted it to."

"Right," he said. "I remember. But I can't believe this is it. *People's Park.* I heard so much about this."

Mary laughed. "If you put your ear to the ground you can still hear The Grateful Dead." Some dandelions were growing at the edge of the sidewalk. She bent down to pick one. "Flower Power," she said, putting the dandelion in Raymond's jacket lapel. "I *know* you remember Flower Power."

■

They got Raymond's car and drove to the Co-op supermarket where Mary was a stockholding member. At the Co-op, the shoppers were the owners.

"Why don't they have these in Boston?" Raymond said. "This is great. Boston's not hip enough for a Co-op supermarket?"

"They'll have them someday," Mary said. "California's the future of everything."

He wheeled the shopping cart through the aisles while she picked out the things she wanted. She was conceiving a fantastic home-made Mexican dinner, with all the things she'd always made for him in Boston—nachos with guacamole, chiles rellenos, chicken enchiladas with sour cream, rice and beans. The shopping cart made Raymond feel glad, all the good food piled in it. In the beer section, he added two six-packs of Dos Equis, the amber kind.

"*Two* six-packs?" Mary said.

"In case you make the food really hot."

"A wishful-thinking sensualist. You're gonna fit in just fine out here."

In grains and legumes, she picked out the rice while Raymond hefted the various brands of pinto beans. They all seemed about the same, but one brand distinguished itself with a message printed on its plastic bag.

Raymond read it aloud. "*Please note. This is a natural product of the earth. Even with diligent processing using the most modern equipment available, we suggest you examine the contents carefully, sort out any foreign substances (small stones, particles of soil, metal, etc.), rinse with drinkable water before cooking to assure maximum wholesomeness.*" He tossed the bag into the shopping cart. "No apologies for lowly origins. I admire that in a bean."

"I like the part about the pieces of metal," Mary said. "Metal, for God's sake. Where did the metal come from?"

"From the Iron Age," Raymond said. "Iron man would mix metal with his beans. They needed that back then, because they had an iron-poor diet. But now, with the better nutrition the hip people have here in Berkeley, most folks don't need metal in their beans anymore, so they tell you right on the package you can take it out if you want to. I like this company. Let's get two." He tossed another one into the cart. "How can you go wrong? Forty-nine cents."

"That's why Mexicans eat rice and beans, my friend. Because they're poor people. They live in the dirt. But do the Mexicans need our pity? They do not. Meanwhile, rich white man is living off the top of the food chain, eating all these cows, torturing poor geese so he can have pâté de fois gras. Pretty soon, all the cows and geese are dead. Rich white man doesn't know what to do. He has to take over somebody else's country so he can get something to eat. But he's soft and weak, he's had it too easy. Poor brown man eats a big helping of rice and beans, beats back the pasty white conqueror, assumes his rightful place in the world."

"That's how it's gonna happen, huh?"

"It *is* happening, Raymond. And you'd better watch out, Silicon Valley capitalist."

"I'm just a guy who shows people how to use their computers."

"Oh, I see. Power to the people," said a twinkling Mary.

"That's right," Raymond said.

■

He drove the car into the Berkeley hills while Mary gave him directions. The roads became steep and narrow, twisting around on themselves and snaking through dark groves of tall, straight-trunked eucalyptus trees with strips of bark peeling down their sides like loosened bandages. He could smell the strong, minty fumes in the air. Spectacular redwood-and-glass houses jutted straight out of cliffsides high above the road.

Mary had her passenger seat tilted back like a lounge chair, reclining in it with one foot on the dashboard and her arm stuck straight out the window. She smiled at Raymond from behind her shades. "Nice up here, huh?" she said, amused by his wide eyes.

"These people are fearless," he said, pointing to a sleek, glassy mansion hanging in the air above them. If it fell that moment, it would drop a hundred feet straight down on top of their car.

"Not fearless," Mary said. "Learning disabled. People in the California hills are proof that money makes you dumb. Every three years or so, the big storms come and wash some of these places right down into the valley. I'm telling you, whole houses have sailed across this road in mud slides. And every time it happens, the rich folks grab the insurance and do it all over again. They don't get it."

"But that's not about being rich in California," Raymond said. "Poor farmers in Kansas rebuild after tornadoes and floods."

Mary wasn't listening. "My landlady's house will someday plunge into the abyss," she said, "where it belongs. But that's not the best thing about it. The best thing I saved for last. Are you ready for this? Timothy Leary used to live there."

"*Doctor* Timothy Leary?"

"He used to own my house. Isn't that great?"

"That's unbelievable. Timothy Leary. In his wild acid-party days?"

"The whole zapped-out gang, right here in Berzerkeley."

Mary's road ran along the edge of a cliff. Through breaks in the dark trees, Raymond could see the deep shiny blue of the Bay and the whiter matte-blue of the sky. "Right here," Mary said, and he pulled to the side of the road. When they got out of the car, her house looked like a small brown A-frame with redwood steps through ground ivy and flowers down to the plain front door. But when they walked in, Raymond saw that only the topmost level of the house was visible from the road. Below the balcony they were standing on, two huge floors of it hung out in the air like the lower jaw of a mouth dropped open in amazement. The opposite side of the place was almost entirely glass, and in it Raymond could see both bridges—the Bay and the Golden Gate—and all the blue Bay water between them, and the beginnings of San Francisco and Marin on either side.

He had to laugh. "Those poor, deprived acid freaks."

Mary laughed, too. "Yeah, they had it tough, didn't they? Stuck in this little shack trying to forge ahead with human consciousness. The view must have been distracting."

They carried the groceries down one flight to the kitchen. Raymond opened beers for Mary and himself. Out in the big living room, a woman stood up from the pillow-piled sofa, a silhouette against the bright window-wall. He thought it must be the landlady, until Melissa stepped out of the shadows—a tall, willowy version of Melissa.

"It can't be," Raymond said.

"Of course it is," Mary said. "Who else would be inside watching TV on such a gorgeous day?"

"Hi, Raymond," Melissa said, giving him a hug. "I know, I'm a big girl now."

"I guess so," he said, hugging her back. "Have a beer with us? It's happy hour."

"I'm too young to drink."

He brought his Dos Equis out to the living room and took a sip. Then he gestured with his head toward the kitchen and made a questioning face at Melissa. Mary was banging things around in there and ignoring them.

"We're fighting," Melissa whispered.

"Scarcely noticeable," Raymond said.

They sat down on the sofa. "So," Melissa said, "I had this image of you as my mother's East Coast beatnik sax-player friend. It's hard to picture you doing computers in California. Do you have a Porsche or a BMW?"

Raymond hooted at the high ceiling. "Everybody's young in California, but nobody's innocent. Those aren't technical writers driving those cars you see, Melissa. We drive old beat-up Datsuns. I'm the invisible man, the unknown soldier."

"I didn't think you were famous or anything."

"Well, good. No disappointments. And how about yourself, young lady? Porsche or BMW?"

"I'm not getting anything. I don't like it here. I'm going to live with my father in New York."

"What's-her-name said you were thinking about doing that."

"Not thinking."

"It'll be lonely for her without you."

"Yeah, I know."

"Do you like your new stepfather?"

"Give me a break, Raymond. He's a junkie. He's in jail."

"I know. Did you go to the wedding?"

"She made me."

He stood up and walked over to the sliding glass doors leading out to the redwood deck. "You're really going to leave that view out there? Some people would kill for a vista like that. Talk about scenic."

"I'm not much of a scenic person," Melissa said.

"Well, let me ask you this, Melissa. Are you much of a Mexican-food person? We've got an amazing Mexican dinner coming up."

"I'm going to a slumber party."

"They still have those? Incredible. But slumber parties don't include dinner, do they?"

"This one does."

"I see. So, first you have your hamburgers and watch a little TV, your favorite hunky star, whoever that is. Then you all put on your jammies and talk about boys."

Melissa smiled. "Yeah, pretty much."

"Your daughter's not having dinner with us," Raymond called into the kitchen. "She has other people she'd rather be with. People her own age. How about that?"

"Grownups are boring," Mary called back. "We're old. We don't understand anything."

"That's right," Melissa said.

■

Coltrane's *Crescent* was playing in the living room. In the kitchen Mary prepared food while Raymond washed the dirty dishes stacked in the sink and all over the countertops. The dishes were left by Joan, the landlady—casseroles and saucepans half-full of moldy food, and numerous plates and glasses. But no silverware.

"I keep saying I'm not cleaning it up again," Mary said. "I keep pushing it out of the way. If it gets so bad that I can't cook, I take Melissa to a restaurant or order takeout from somewhere. Finally I can't deal with it anymore and I clean it all up."

"There's no silverware," Raymond said.

"There is, but Joan doesn't use it. Silverware frightens her. She eats everything with her fingers."

Raymond glanced back into the large open atrium of the house.

"She's not here," Mary said, "though she'll probably waft in at some point. She's in terrible shape. On first glance she looks all right, your basic Berkeley hills woman in her forties—liberal, trendy, narcissistic. She looks like she belongs in a house like this. Then you realize she's completely tranquillized. She gets doctors to give her whatever pills she wants. She wears expensive clothes but she can't get it together to take them to the cleaners; she just wears them filthy. She can't remember things, like turning off the stove. In the middle of a conversation she suddenly stops making sense."

Mary put her enchiladas in to bake, and then she and Raymond took the nachos and beer onto the deck overlooking the Bay. It was a buoyant early evening, the sky orangy-pink with sunset, electric lights beginning to twinkle down in the cities. A low-lying bank of fog was rolling in across the water like a white coverlet being pulled up to the chin of a sleeper.

"Joan, poor Joan," Mary said. "She got married and her rich husband moved her into this wonderful place in the wonderful Berkeley hills, and then after a couple of years he found somebody he liked better. I know, a totally new thing in the history of human life. But Joan wasn't ready for it. Is anybody? Maybe some people are. I'm sure Joan was shaky to begin with, but being disposed of by this guy did damage. She got a lot of his dough plus this house in exchange for letting him go. She has a son who's about Melissa's age now. He was only a baby at that point."

Raymond listened to the music coming through the sliding screen door. The redwood deck seemed to float in space on Coltrane's sublime improvisations. For some reason Mary was telling him a sad story after he'd finally come all this way to see her, when all he wanted to do was savor the magic of his new life in this amazing place.

She drummed along on the redwood railing with her palm. "So Joan stayed here by herself with this kid, and just drifted into her own little world. She never had the vaguest idea how to manage her life. One day last year she went to the bank and they told her almost nothing was left. She advertised to share the house, to keep going. I loved the land up here so much I figured I could deal with anybody. But she's too weird, even for me. I have to get out of here when Melissa leaves in the fall. This was mostly for her sake, anyway. I wanted my kid to experience something nice like this, something that wasn't a rotten city apartment. But nothing I do is right for Melissa. All she wants is to live with her daddy, her wonderful, wonderful daddy."

"Daughters feel that way about their dads. Especially when Dad's not around."

"I know, but this is *my* daughter. I raised her, pal, *raised* her by myself with my own two hands. He did nothing, *nothing*, and all she can think about is being with him. She says she hasn't stayed with him in a long time, and she'll be back after a year. She'll never be back."

"You don't know that."

"Yes, I do. I know it. He's getting married, by the way."

"To that same woman he was with?"

"Yeah, to that same woman. The one Melissa likes. The one who is not a black man in prison."

Raymond tapped the bottom of his beer bottle on the redwood

deck and looked out at the lights coming on like fairy dust across Berkeley and San Francisco, remembering the first night he'd ever spent with Mary in Boston. He'd woken up well before dawn to find that Melissa, eight or nine years old, had crawled in under the covers and was sleeping between them. He couldn't stay in the bed with Melissa there. He got up and sat in the living room, smoking cigarettes and looking at magazines, and finally he went back to sleep on the sofa, where Mary found him in the morning. She explained that Melissa sometimes slept with her when they were alone, and once or twice she'd done it when a man was there. It wasn't all that peculiar, Mary thought. After a few more visits it started to seem normal, and in the end, when they moved away, he almost felt that Mary was taking his daughter from him—though he knew it was sentimental, and that Melissa didn't feel that way about him.

"She's fifteen now?"

"Fourteen," Mary said. "Making me forty-three. An old lady." She sipped her beer and smiled at him. "I console myself with the thought that I can still lure a younger man to my romantic cliff dwelling."

He was five years younger than she was. "Remember that old math problem about ages?" Raymond said. "You start out being twenty-five times older than your children. Then six times, then four, then two. If you and me and Melissa live long enough, we'll all be the same age someday."

Mary laughed. "Brother, you better go back and do that problem again."

He got up to get some more beer, walking slowly toward the kitchen through the darkening house, stopping to look up at the exposed beams of the high cathedral ceiling, the embroidered woolen floor pillows and wall hangings that looked Peruvian, the polished wooden floors picking up the colorful glow of the sky. He was still having a hard time believing he was in the house where Timothy Leary had lived at the birth of the New Age. He tried to imagine those legendary goings-on in this very place. It made him laugh. A dozen years ago when he'd often thought about Leary, or five years ago in Boston with Mary, or this morning, he would never have been able to predict being here now.

And then, in a stranger's extravagant house at sunset, the brute unknowableness of life almost overwhelmed him. You couldn't know what would happen to you in five minutes, never mind tomorrow. You couldn't know anything. He thought about Christine, who could easily slip out of his life into the vastness of California, the mud slide that might wash this house down the mountain, the earthquakes he'd been trying not to think about since moving to San Jose.

Crescent had finished playing some time ago. Raymond put it on again. He hadn't heard this music in several years. He watched the advancing digital numbers on the CD machine and breathed deeply in and out. He wanted to enjoy himself, not be frightened or sad. When the old familiar music began to play, the simple fact of it made him happy again.

He brought two more beers out to the deck. Mary reached up for his arm and pulled until he sat down between her legs on the reclining chair. She smiled at him in a specific way, and he recognized the smile, recalled it from years ago. He shook his head. "You can have some shoulder, that's all."

She laughed, and then she took him up on it and cried. He held her and patted her back, but saw himself doing this as if from far away. He felt sorry that she was sad, but he himself was not unhappy. He told her everything would be O.K., though in fact he had serious doubts. After a while, through the sliding screen door, they smelled the dinner burning. Mary cursed and laughed at the same time and ran to the kitchen. Raymond found her standing beside a smoking oven, poking a fork into a dish on the counter.

"I forgot to turn it from broil to bake," she said. "It's only burned on top, though. It looks O.K. under that. How stupid can you get?"

"I like burned food," Raymond said. "Really, I do. That carbon tang."

Mary smiled brightly. "Well, you came to the right place."

■

She was reclining against one arm of the long sofa, her legs up on the cushions, talking about something, but Raymond, sprawled the same way at the other end of the sofa, had lost the thread of what she was saying. He had two plates of Mexican dinner and any number of Mexican beers inside him. KJAZ was playing on the FM receiver, and he kept losing himself in the music, or in looking past Mary's head at the glass doors to the redwood deck. He had wanted to have dinner out there, but the air had suddenly turned too damp and chilly for eating outside. The fog was completely upon them now, and the great vista that had been there before was gone. The redwood deck floated in a pearly void. Even the trees on the slope below the house were invisible.

Raymond sipped from his beer bottle and looked at Mary. She was talking about Charles, he realized, making a complicated point about herself and her husband. He waited until she finished speaking, but the gist of it did not materialize for him. He patted her ankle and smiled. "Everything's going to be all right," he said. She nodded her head and seemed reassured by that.

Then the front door of the house opened on the level above them. A woman and a boy stepped onto the balcony and stood there, as if waiting to be asked to come all the way in.

"Joan, what's wrong?" Mary called up. "Did you have trouble in the fog?"

"It's foggy out there," said Joan.

"We had a neat wreck," the boy said. It had been dark for hours, but he was wearing surfer sunglasses connected to a satin cord around his neck.

"No," Joan said. "I just couldn't see."

Raymond followed Mary to the top of the stairs. Joan held out her car keys for him to take. He put on his jacket and groped along the wooden walkway until he could see that Joan had run her car off the road and into a tree at the top of her steep front lawn. The left front fender was dented and the headlight was broken, but that was all. If she hadn't hit the tree, she would have come all the way down the slope and through the foggy balcony windows above the living room. He climbed up to the car and started it, and backed it up onto the level part of the road. When he looked down, he couldn't even see the house.

"Everything's O.K.," he told Joan when he returned her keys. She seemed to know that already, or to have something else on her mind. She and her son were still standing aimlessly in the balcony-foyer with their jackets on. "All you have to do is get somebody to bend your fender back. It scrapes the tire a little bit."

"You could do that for me," Joan said.

"No, I'm sorry, I can't. I'd need a crowbar or something, and I can hardly see out there."

"You could do it in the morning," Joan said.

"I won't be here in the morning. I have to leave tonight, soon. You can find somebody else to do it."

"You can't drive tonight," Joan said. "You don't want to go out there now."

"Joan, don't start scaring people," Mary broke in. "Jimmy," she said, "is it clear downtown?"

"Downtown is cool," Jimmy said from behind his shades. He scuffed his checkerboard sneakers on the balcony and plucked at the rubberized printing of his black heavy-metal T-shirt.

"The fog's just up here," Mary said. "Happens all the time. Suddenly you drop out of it and it's crystal clear."

Joan was staring at a place about a foot below Raymond's face. When he looked down he saw the wilted dandelion in his jacket lapel. "We were at People's Park today," he explained to Joan. "We were reminiscing about it. Remember Flower Power?"

Joan looked at him uncomprehendingly. Finally she said, "There was a big earthquake in L.A. tonight."

"There was?" Mary said. "Then why didn't we hear about it? We've had the radio on, they would have talked about that."

"It was a big one," Joan said. "They said it could travel up here."

"Joan," Mary said. "Earthquakes don't *travel*. They happen where they happen. If there was an earthquake in L.A., that's where it was—L.A."

Joan rubbed her car keys between her hands and breathed deeply. "It's doing something to the weather up here already," she said. "Like what a volcano does. Can't you smell it? Something's wrong with the weather."

"Joan, I think you're really tired," Mary said. "I think driving in the fog upset you. You need to get some rest. Jimmy, doesn't your mother seem really tired to you?"

"How would I know?" Jimmy said.

"Well, would you at least try to convince her that everything's all right?"

"How am I supposed to do that?"

"Joan, everything's all right," Mary said. "Go to bed now, O.K.? Go to bed." She pulled Raymond's arm until he followed her downstairs. They collected the dinner dishes from the dining room and stacked them in the kitchen. "Did she freak you out?" Mary asked.

Raymond took his sunglasses from his jacket pocket and put them on. "Yeah, but everything's cool now," he said. They giggled.

"California kids are unbelievable," Mary said. "They're much worse than we ever were." She counted the empty beer bottles. "You O.K. to drive?"

"Sure, I'm fine." He looked at his watch. "It's later than I thought, though. I better get going. She'll be worried."

"You could call her and tell her you have to stay," Mary said. She put her arms around him. "If you told her the fog was really bad, that would be the truth. Or your car might not start. This kind of moisture makes a lot of cars not start. It's really common around here." She pulled the limp dandelion from his lapel and tossed it on the counter. "But I'll bet your car is real reliable."

"Surprisingly so, for such an old one."

"Just a thought."

"No harm."

She put on her slippers and walked him outside to the staircase leading up to the road. His car was barely perceptible up there.

"Can you find your way out of the hills?" she asked.

"How would I know?" Raymond said, bouncing his shoulders and snapping his fingers.

"I can't let you drive." Mary laughed. "Get back in my house."

He looked out at the fog. It wasn't any better. It might have gotten worse. He tried to think his way back to the highway, but he couldn't. He decided that driving downhill on any street would eventually get him there. He wouldn't be able to remember any instructions Mary gave him anyway.

"There's something wrong with the weather," he said, and he started to chuckle again. But he wasn't thinking about the people in this house. He was thinking about music, about how much he used to love to play the saxophone. Tomorrow, he thought, he would start looking for some people to jam with in San Jose.

"It's so sad," Mary said. "We shouldn't be laughing at them. She sort of scared me tonight. Do you really think there was a quake in L.A.?"

"Let me check," Raymond said. He got down on his hands and knees and put the side of his head against the redwood boardwalk. He stayed like that for a full half-minute or more. He was trying to listen to the earth, to see if today was the day it would shake the humans off its back like a beast they'd provoked. He couldn't hear anything at all.

He stood up, laughing, and kissed Mary goodbye. "We're safe for one more night," he said. "I can't guarantee anything after that."

EVERY GOOD BOY

DESERVES FAVOR

■

If you wanted the book on Karl, the official version of his creative life, it went something like this: As a very young man he'd achieved minor fame by writing a suite of chamber works that bounded harmoniously away from the atonal bog where serious music was shrieking and splashing like a sinking dinosaur. Karl's sunny compositions had the new sound of a time beyond great world wars—the innocent, optimistic 1950s. They won a major prize, got recorded by a first-rate quartet, and for music from the hand of a boy they were surprisingly influential: most experts still listed Karl among the originators of the epochal return to consonance. But Karl himself, it was said, seduced by false muses and beatnik foolishness, had abandoned his original inspirations to devote the rest of his career to inferior experiments in chance and randomness worthy of no greater fame than he already possessed.

The critics who made these judgments had no talent or imagination, and no respect, and they had utterly missed the significance of Karl's later work. They didn't even know what *chance* and *randomness* meant. Nevertheless, their opinions had shaped his destiny. He was fifty-eight years old, and those precocious chamber pieces were still his only regularly performed compositions. When he wrote them, only a few players in the world could do them right; conservatory students played them passably well today—students who were often surprised to learn that Karl was still alive.

One of his own former students was in his studio as Karl's car crunched down the long, graveled driveway through the woods; lights were burning in the barn's second story, and Jennifer's beat-up Japanese sedan was parked in the cul-de-sac. Karl had been on campus the entire day, teaching in the flourishing summer arts program invented by his wife, and he hadn't seen Jennifer since their fight the night before—their third or fourth fight in a week. Jennifer was now Karl's assistant at school, though she hadn't bothered showing up today. She copied parts for him at his studio, too, and in her free time she did her own work up there. He pulled his Land Rover into the spot between her car and his wife's Volvo wagon. It amazed him that he'd been famous when he was not much older than this young woman in his workspace right now. He had been the youngest professor ever to hold an endowed chair at the college, back when the trustees were convinced they had the next Charles Ives on their hands.

Lights were burning in the house as well. He saw the shadows that Gloria cast on the walls as she moved around, preparing dinner. When he stepped out of his vehicle, he caught the rich scent of a roast coming through the kitchen's screened windows. He smelled freshly mown grass, too, and looked through the barn doorway to see it on the rubber tires of the tractor. On its ground level, the barn still housed heavy equipment for the farmer who worked some of Karl's land and mowed the meadows. The vast former hayloft was Karl's music studio. He climbed the stairway up to it. "And what's this my nose detects?" he called out in his fairy-tale woodsman's voice, flaring his nostrils and sniffing loudly as he entered the cavernous place. "Methinks my nose smells blood."

"Boil and bubble," Jennifer said, her back to him at the distant kitchen counter. "Toil and trouble."

Karl's studio was bigger and better-appointed than the homes of most professors at the college, though he'd kept it, except for the bathroom, one large, unbroken space. He stood in front, where picture windows looked into the woods from the walls framing his grand piano poised on glossy floorboards beneath the skylight-studded ceiling. In the year since he'd begun his masterpiece, Karl had worked in the barn much of every night, sleeping on the sofa-bed for a few hours before dawn. He needed very little sleep these days.

"More blood, my darling?" he said, switching to the voice of a soap-opera husband. "But, sweetheart, you've made so much blood already."

"*I need more blood,*" Jennifer replied, doing the vampire voice.

He strode across the gleaming floor to join her at the stove. Three large pots of blood were simmering there, Jennifer stirring them with a wooden spoon. Karl tried to bite her neck like Dracula, but she wouldn't let him. He used to bite her neck all the time. In the blood's bubbling turbulence, he saw the chaos that wasn't chaotic, the randomness that wasn't chance. But he saw that in almost everything. Jennifer liked her blood fairly thick, with plenty of clots. She seemed especially pleased with this batch. She had discovered recently that if she reserved some cornstarch until the blood was good and hot, it produced numerous misshapen lumps that looked grotesque sliding down her arms and face.

Jennifer was a performance artist. The blood was a prop in her act. There were many props in Jennifer's act, but blood was the unifying device. She concealed plastic sacs of the homemade blood in various articles she had with her onstage—a child's fluffy teddy bear, her pearl-encrusted evening bag, the bodice of her white bridal gown. For an hour she paraded about to her own synthesizer score, acting out dysfunctional family relationships and decrying bankrupt, oppressive governments, while the Barbie-doll world hemorrhaged around her. Everything she touched turned to blood. For her finale, she decorated a wedding cake with a bleeding pastry bag.

In Karl's opinion, her act was an embarrassing, juvenile cliché.

It was also a fraud. Jennifer did not genuinely have the elemental fixation upon blood that she portrayed herself as having. An obsession with blood was a serious thing. No, it was merely that bodily fluids were good for one's career in the performance game —itself the most depraved development Karl had witnessed in his many years in the arts. He had assumed she'd grow out of it, but she was doing quite the reverse, and now people in New York City were participating in her delusion.

"Why don't you stay for dinner?" Karl said. "Gloria's making a roast. Rare, the way you like it."

Jennifer deigned to chuckle over this, and then turned off the burners on the stove. Her blood was finished boiling. "I was going to clean up in here."

"You can do it later." He pinched her waist. "I'll help."

She created her blood in his studio because her own apartment had a useless kitchenette, whereas Karl, in his prosperity, had a full set of professional pots and pans, not to mention a six-burner Viking restaurant range, and that was just the barn.

"Karl, I don't really feel like having dinner with you and Gloria."

"You've had dinner with me and Gloria before."

"I'm trying to concentrate. I don't feel like feeling stress."

This batch of blood was for Jennifer's biggest engagement to date—opening for some famous fake in a New York performance space this weekend. She'd written new material for this occasion, and she was nervous about it. Karl blamed their fighting on this.

"I didn't get to see you at all today. I'd like you to stay."

She sighed. "Fine, if you insist. Let me change."

■

He came down the barn stairs into the late New Hampshire day and smelled again his wife's cookery emanating from the house. *A man enjoys a nice roast in the evening,* he thought, to cheer himself up, and at that instant his heart thing happened again—starting like a bird trying to fly in his chest and then escalating into a punching bag that made him sit on the steps, holding the railing and panting to ride it out. This happened to him two or three times a week, yet his doctors maintained that nothing was seriously wrong with him. Their diagnosis was garden-variety arrhythmia —an irregular heartbeat—and they weren't inclined to do much about it. At Karl's insistence, they'd rigged wires all over his chest for twenty-four hours at a time, the surveillance of his quavering ham hock pouring into a recorder clipped to a canvas belt. Later, they plotted his data on long paper scrolls. The black bursts on the green graph paper looked like the Reaper's palm prints to Karl, the Reaper advancing on hands and knees like a cannibal, yet one doctor after another said it was a well-known, non-fatal phenomenon. They told him to cut out coffee and booze, and stop worrying.

But Karl was more up on these things than the doctors were. For years he'd been studying the phenomenon of chaos, of which heartbeat arrhythmia was a perfect example. Chaos was not nothing. It was not the absence of purpose and structure. Chaos might even *be* structure—what human beings called structure—or maybe it was structure seen from the other side. It was reality's essential ingredient. Everything had chaos in it. But chaos could amplify and feed back, propagating until it destroyed any system it was in. Scientists had lately discovered these things about chaos, but Karl had intuited the truth decades ago. Had he been a scientist, he'd have the Nobel Prize by now. In his music, he'd explored chaos when it was ridiculed and reviled. Now chaos was respectable, but Karl wasn't. Most of the fundamental properties of reality that Karl believed in—mind over matter, to take an obvious example—would eventually be discovered, too, and presented to the world on television shows, but Karl wouldn't be around to see them.

The devils stopped playing their bongos in his rib cage; they were finished laughing at him for the moment. He looked up the steps, half expecting to find Jennifer staring down at him, but the landing was empty. He rose and walked gingerly across the graveled drive as though in his stocking feet. No one except Jennifer knew this, but the masterpiece he was composing was about his erratic heart. That was the genius of it, its beauty and raw, flawed life. That was even its title, *Heart Chaos 1*. It literally began with the anti-rhythms of his own mortal pump going berserk, captured one day when he held a tape recorder to his chest despite his mortal terror. Later, he transcribed it verbatim into his overture. When it was done, *Heart Chaos 1* was going to express perfectly what chaos really was—the music of the world.

His attack left him shaky and weak and craving a slice of roast. He entered the kitchen and joined Gloria at the range, where she was stirring a broad sauté pan of creamy sauce with vegetables in it. A large pot of water boiled on a back burner.

"This isn't a roast," he said.

"Who said it was?" Gloria replied.

"It smelled exactly like a roast. I smelled it."

She turned to face him. "Karl, this smells like a roast to you?"

He bent over the sauce and inhaled. "No, it doesn't. Not anymore." The aroma dispelled most of his disappointment. He loved creamy sauces for pasta, though they were too rich and he had no business eating them. He'd brought home bad cholesterol numbers a year before. He had no business eating roasts, either, but a person tired of broiled eggplant slices with lemon juice. "Trying to kill me again," he said.

"Out to get you," said Gloria, stirring green peas into the simmering cream.

She was twelve years younger than Karl, his first student-affair from his first year at the college. It was thanks largely to her that the small, pretty campus of brownstone buildings was still a college at all, and not some ashram or corporate retreat. The place had been in serious trouble when Gloria left Admissions six years ago to take over the Development Office. Now the college had the beginnings of a well-invested endowment, the hiring freeze was lifted, applications were up. In meetings with the trustees, the provost tried to take credit for the school's salvation, but everybody knew Gloria was the brains behind it.

"Jennifer would like to stay for dinner," Karl said.

"Fine. There's plenty to go around."

A bottle of white wine was already standing open on the kitchen island. He poured himself some and refreshed Gloria's glass. "Fair warning, though. She's in a stinker of a mood. I think she's terrified she doesn't have her new lines memorized or something, that her big act isn't going to go over in New York. She's been quite unpleasant lately."

"Well, we'll have to stay off that subject, then."

"Or we could get on that subject. We could quiz her. Give her a test, try to trip her up."

"Karl."

He looked out the window to see Jennifer crossing the cul-de-sac between the barn and the house. She'd changed out of her blood-spattered clothes into clean jeans and a T-shirt that said AMERICA HAS A REALITY PROBLEM.

She pushed open the kitchen's screen door and stuck her head inside. "Hi. It's me."

"Hello, Jennifer," Gloria said.

"We're not having a roast after all," Karl said, sipping his wine beneath the massive oval rack of hanging pots. "We're having fettuccine Alfredo."

"Primavera," Gloria said.

"Excuse me, primavera."

"Great," Jennifer said.

"Karl was positive he smelled a roast," Gloria told Jennifer.

"It was uncanny," Karl said.

"Maybe you were smelling a roast in your brain," Jennifer said. "A roast from your past that once made you happy."

Gloria laughed. "That's very funny," she said.

Karl didn't think it was all that funny. It was exactly the kind of thing Jennifer was always saying, the prototypical Jennifer statement. She would float around New York City saying things like this, and soon some people would be having a lot of fun with her.

"You could put that in your skit," Karl said. She disliked having her act called a skit. She didn't care for "act" either.

"Maybe I will," Jennifer said. "A roast in the brain. I like it."

Karl caught Gloria glaring at him over her shoulder. "Wine?" he asked Jennifer. "Or would it fog your mind?"

Jennifer laughed. "Nothing could fog my mind more than it is already."

The girl was the most amazing fount of truth sometimes. Karl poured a glass and handed it to her.

Gloria slid coiled noodles into the boiling kettle and stirred them around, then turned to bestow a gracious smile upon Jennifer. "What's your mind so fogged about?" she asked.

Whenever Karl watched Gloria socialize, he understood how she could put on her handsome tailored lady's suits, fly around the country with her computer, and come home with her briefcase full of money for the college. Karl couldn't get a Rotary Club to give him twenty cents. Gloria had "people skills" in spades. She made people feel good about themselves. Somebody had to do it.

"I'm fogged from working on my show," Jennifer said. "I've been rewriting my script and rewriting my music and trying to memorize everything and stay calm about it."

"Plus doing your work for Karl."

"Yeah, that, too."

"Plus making lots of blood," Karl added.

"Right, let's not forget the blood," Jennifer laughed.

"Are you excited about performing in New York?" asked Gloria.

"Of course! I'm psyched. I'm nervous, too."

"It's really important to work there, I guess? As opposed to other cities?"

"Oh, totally," Jennifer said. "I mean, people do performance in, like, Seattle and *Minneapolis* and stuff, but it's not the same thing. People in New York recognize two or three area codes, and if you don't have one, they don't even call you. To tell you the truth, even living up here is becoming an impediment to me."

"I'm not surprised," Gloria said. "We're sort of in the middle of nowhere here. Aren't we?"

"Living here is an impediment?" Karl said. "Since when?"

"Maybe Jennifer is just realizing it," Gloria said.

"That's it exactly," Jennifer said. "It's just dawning on me. All the work for this show has made me realize how much harder it is not to be there."

"Makes perfect sense," Gloria said.

"Are you saying you're thinking about moving to New York?" said Karl.

"I've thought about it, yeah."

He stepped out from behind the kitchen island. Gloria had her eye on him. "When?"

"If I did it, I'd probably do it pretty soon."

"Jennifer, school starts in two months. You're supposed to teach sections of the intro course. You wanted an Instructor appointment. I got you one."

The blood had rushed to Jennifer's face. She stood looking mortified, her wineglass trembling and her free hand stuck in a back pocket of her jeans.

"Karl," Gloria said, "they can easily find a replacement for Survey of Western Music."

"That's not the point, Gloria."

"Then what's the point?"

He looked at Jennifer and squeezed an exasperated laugh out of himself. "I guess the point is, when were you planning to tell the department?"

"I wanted to get this performance behind me and then figure it out."

Gloria put her hand on Jennifer's shoulder. "I know more about this college than he does. Take your opportunities. Somebody else will cover the course." Suddenly, the noodles foamed and boiled over on the stove. "You two are making me forget what I'm doing! Go sit down! Both of you!"

When they were all at the table with portions of dinner before them, Gloria poured more wine and proposed a toast. "To Jennifer's success in New York. I'm sure you'll be great."

"Thank you," Jennifer said.

Karl was fuming in his chair. "Here's wishing you minor fame," he said, and smiled witheringly before sipping his wine.

"Thanks, but I think I already have that," Jennifer said.

Karl heard this like a schizophrenic hearing voices. He looked to see if Gloria had heard it, too, but he couldn't tell. "You don't say," he said.

"Yeah, I think you could say I'm kind of minor famous." She turned to Gloria. "Some pretty important critics in New York are talking about my work."

"Karl's been telling me," Gloria said. "Congratulations."

Jennifer shrugged her shoulders. "I mean, you know it's not real," she added. "You don't let yourself believe in it. You don't think about it when you're working. But as long as you don't, it's not a bad thing. It helps."

"That sounds like a very wise attitude," Gloria said, smiling and touching Jennifer's arm. "For someone so wonderfully young."

Karl sat like a man turned to stone. "Indeed," he said. He had told Jennifer those very things, in those words exactly.

■

He didn't pretend to be jolly at dinner, though Jennifer and Gloria did, and when dinner was over, Jennifer announced that she was going out to the barn to clean up her blood, and then she was going home to get ready for her trip to New York. Karl remained at the table with the second bottle of wine, while Gloria cleaned the kitchen. For some time, he'd felt that he was living in a bad knock-off of the world, or that the world itself had taken a bad fall on the head and suffered from amnesia now. Nobody remembered anything. Everything Karl saw in the arts was a watery reflection of something he'd seen firsthand decades before, but nobody was saying that. Nobody seemed to recall that all the currently fashionable gestures had been made before, and made better, by better people in a better time. But the most galling thing was that Karl felt, without being able to prove it, that Jennifer had stolen her whole blood business from him.

Gloria finished in the kitchen and came into the dining room. "How about that America with that reality problem," she said and laughed, but Karl didn't laugh back. "Oh, Karl, cheer up, will you?"

Karl poured the last of the wine into his glass. Cheering up, promoting good cheer, was actually Gloria's profession, for what was fund-raising if not leading the crowd in a cheer? Institutional endowment people were really brilliant con artists, but he didn't see how she could stand the life. Once in a while, he attended some college event with her, and watched in horror as hundreds of people cheered each other. "I'm disappointed to see how little I taught someone who seemed to be a gifted student. It's a common syndrome we professors suffer from. Jennifer turns out to believe that if she doesn't get opportunities for exhibitionism in New York, her creative life isn't worth living."

"Well, for what she wants to do, that's true, isn't it?"

"And what's that? What she wants to do?"

"Her theater stuff. Whatever it is."

"She's not doing theater stuff, Gloria. She's perpetrating a hoax on the public. It's the same thing in music and painting—kids getting lionized for discovering their belly buttons."

"You were lionized as a kid," she said.

"For discovering my belly button?" he cried out.

"For having something new to say."

"These kids do not have something new to say. But that's not even the point. The point is, she'll be eaten alive down there. Devoured like prey."

"Lots of kids go to New York to do art and don't get devoured like prey."

"Jennifer will be devoured. She puts out a certain vibration. She invites it." And then, as though one thing followed from the other, he said, "I don't like helping people and then being treated with disrespect."

"She's young, Karl."

"I wasn't like that when *I* was young. Were you like that?"

"I don't know. You tell me. You knew me then."

"No, you were not like that. You were infinitely better than that. Kids today are off the map. This whole fucking civilization is out the window." He stood up from the table. "I'm asking her to leave right now. I'll clean up her mess myself. I have work to do tonight."

He kicked across the driveway, splashing gravel against the cars. In his twenty-five years at the college, plenty of pretty girls had thrown themselves at him, and he'd slept with a number of them. True, girls threw themselves at other professors, too, and some of those professors practiced restraint. But none of those professors had lived through the experience of minor fame.

He stomped up the studio stairs, stood beside his grand piano, and called across the high-ceilinged space, "You expected me to leave her for you, didn't you? That's what this is all about."

Jennifer swung around at the sink. "Are you kidding me? I think *she* should leave *you*."

"You think it was fair to dump this news on me in front of my wife?"

"Karl, don't talk to me like the big father, O.K.?"

He barked a bitter laugh. This was the major theme of their recent fighting—Karl's being the big, controlling father. When she studied with him at the college, his being the big father was the thing she'd loved; he happened to know that, even if she wouldn't admit it now. "All right, Jennifer, fine. But I hope you're planning to be careful what you say. There are people who would assume I took advantage of you."

She snorted. "Who do you think seduced who, anyway?"

He was going schizo again, hearing things. "What?"

"I said, who do you think started this? I seduced you, not the other way around."

He must have drunk more wine than he realized. He was going in slow motion and Jennifer was in normal time. He stood there saying nothing.

"I decided to have an affair with you, and I initiated it," Jennifer went on. "Think back."

"And now you've initiated another one with some boy in New York."

"That would be none of your business if I did."

He looked around the studio for her red milk jugs. "Jennifer, I don't see your blood."

"It's in the car."

"Then why don't you go join it?"

When she passed him on her way to the stairs, he said, "You know, something occurred to me tonight. You never did your blood thing until I told you about my heart symphony."

"You're paranoid, Karl. You're sick. I have my own ideas."

"Do you? I think I've had a pretty big influence on you."

"Influence? I *hate* your music."

■

On one of his bookshelves he had a few excellent cigars in a humidor, cigars he'd been saving for the right visitor or some special excuse to celebrate. He loved cigars, but he wasn't allowed to smoke them anymore. He snipped one and lit it, and squirted a volume of blue smoke into the air—a textbook example of chaos, swirling smoke, along with the weather and the flight of butterflies.

He was a first-rate composer, the real goddamn lifelong thing, and he was going to put his feelings into his music and have a good night of work, no matter what. He was not throwing away his discipline because he'd crossed paths with a self-deceived suburban girl. He was coming out of this just fine. But first he had to clean the studio kitchen; he couldn't write with Jennifer's bloody mess staring back at him from across the room. He clamped his cigar in his teeth and started washing one of the pans covered with congealed stage gore. It was even more realistic dry than wet, and when it did get wet it dissolved and got all over his hands, and upset him. He started to succumb to nasty Charles Manson imagery and graphic imaginings of the bloody metronome throbbing away behind his breastbone. He threw the saucepan back in the sink and pulled a folding Japanese screen in front of the whole affair.

He paced the floor, hazing the big studio with blue smoke. It came over him, in that sickeningly palpable way you can't endure for more than a second or two, that he was going to die. *What an abomination*, he thought, almost out loud. *That a man like me should return to dust.*

He stood at the piano and looked at his messy score. It didn't tell him anything. Nothing transcendental was clamoring to get out of him at the moment. He sat on the bench, opened a manila folder, and unfurled a length of green paper portraying his monitored heart. He'd gotten some sections of these graphs from the clinic, and he'd been consulting them while composing *Heart Chaos 1*. They'd proven surprisingly inspirational—the physical shapes on the paper suggesting sound and structure to him, telling him what to write. He found a burst of heart-static he liked, and played something on the keys to go with it, but what came out was the most pointlessly ugly music he'd ever heard in his life.

He got up and walked to one of his big picture windows. Beyond his reflection, small lights were flashing like the eyes of nightspirits. It was July, and fireflies were floating around by the hundreds, tails lighting and then fading to black, here and there, you never knew where, all of it looking perfectly random to human beings not privy to the secrets of firefly love. A three-quarters moon washed its ghost light over the mowed meadow beneath the window, and when Karl raised his eyes to look more deeply into the pasture, his heart gave a massive, terrifying pulse. Someone was out there in the meadow, lurking around his secluded house in the middle of the night. He opened his door quietly and stepped out onto the landing. The intruder was hiding something in the underbrush, or looking for something hidden there. After a few seconds, he saw that it was his wife, hovering at the billowing tangle of brambles that lined the edge of the meadow. "Gloria!" he called out to her.

She spun around in the moonlight. "You scared me!" she cried.

"I scared *you!*" he answered, and clomped down his staircase, thinking, *I who might never come back from a scare like that.* He walked toward Gloria through the lightning bugs, ducking their lethargic, flashing bodies. "What are you doing?" he said from afar.

"Picking raspberries," she replied, speaking into the bushes.

"For what?"

"Because they're feeding the birds out here, or just falling on the ground and rotting."

Deep thickets of raspberries bordered the meadow in back of the house. In years past, Karl and Gloria had made pies from the fruit of these bushes, but they hadn't done it this year or last, or maybe not for a few years. Fresh raspberry pie seemed almost a dream-thing to Karl now, a creation tasted on vacation in some exotic place and not available in ordinary life at home.

He reached his wife beneath the moon. "Are you planning to make a pie?" he asked.

"I don't know what I'm planning to do," she said. She had a large plastic tub from the kitchen, big enough to hold berries for two pies at least. She had a snifter of brandy, too, glinting on the freshly mown grass, completely out of character for Gloria. Karl was the late-night-brandy type, not her.

"Can I have a sip of your drink?" he asked, and when she didn't answer, he picked it up from the ground and had one.

She took it back from him and had a sip herself. "You smell like a cigar," she said.

He looked down at his left hand. The cigar was hanging between his fingers. He'd forgotten it was there. "I was in the mood for one."

"Having a party?"

"No more than you, it seems."

"We're both having a party," Gloria said. "But not the same party."

"You're not really the party type."

"I'm not a fun person?"

"I meant the type for that kind of party."

"What kind?"

"Never mind. I'm losing track of this conversation." He took a puff on the cigar, but it was no longer lit. It seemed that some utterance needed to be made, some accounting of himself to his wife. "Listen," he said. "I've been wanting to talk to you. I'm sorry I've had to work so hard lately."

"But you've always worked hard," Gloria said. "Is there something unusual about your working hard now?"

"I feel especially under pressure. I feel I have a lot of work to do in a limited time."

"We all have limited time, Karl, including you. But not because there's anything wrong with your heart." She put down her brandy snifter and continued to pluck the biggest berries out of the tangled, moonlit leaves. "But you *have* been especially passionate about your work this year—sleeping out in the barn all those nights and everything. You've been especially intense about whatever you're doing out there."

"What I'm doing out there is creating a masterpiece," Karl said.

"Aren't you always?"

"I don't know what you're saying, Gloria."

"You told me once that in order to be able to create anything at all, you had to feel you were creating a masterpiece. You said that was the only possible attitude toward work. Didn't you tell me that?"

He had, in fact, told her that, and it was true, but he made a mental note to stop telling people things. "Except that this time I'm really doing that."

"Really? Does it worry you to be so sure? You told me that artists are never sure it's a masterpiece, but that's a good thing, because being sure is bad. The point is not to be sure and to do it anyway, on faith."

Life chose this instant to reveal to Karl that the "1" in *Heart Chaos 1* would be one of his little jokes, because there would be no *Heart Chaos 2*. After *Heart Chaos 1*, he would write no more music. He would fall silent. He just couldn't take it anymore. He was feeling surprisingly good and righteous about this decision when, out of the blue, he remembered the radical black student from the 1960s who, in some curriculum dispute, had become briefly famous for calling Bach, Beethoven, and Brahms "old dead punks." Karl hadn't thought about this in years, and the memory of it cheered him out of all proportion to its real significance. He actually broke into a grin. "I guess I've told you just about everything, haven't I?"

Gloria laughed the way people laugh sometimes when the doctor touches a place that hurts. "No, not quite everything," she said, and held out her plastic tub for the few berries he'd picked.

When he opened his hand above her container, she pulled it away and his berries fell on the ground. He stared at their dark bodies on the matted grass mowings.

"Young Jennifer stopped in to see me as she was leaving," Gloria said.

Karl stopped breathing and waited for his heart to self-destruct, but the perverse vital organ beat on like a clock. "Oh? And what did she have to say?"

"The part I can't get over," Gloria continued, "is that you disliked her so much. You thought she was silly. You ridiculed her all the time."

"I did not ridicule her all the time."

"Yes, you did, in all sorts of little ways."

The situation was getting completely out of hand, and he was not going to allow that to happen. No person living on earth understood self-discipline and control better than Karl did. He stood up straight and composed himself. "Did Jennifer tell you how much she hated my work?"

"No."

"Well, she told me. She didn't spare me one speck of nasty truth tonight. But back when she wanted me to do things for her, my work was the greatest. You want the topper? She shamelessly stole her whole blood idea from the symphony I'm working on."

"You're writing a symphony about blood?" Gloria said, with a look of disbelief.

"It's not about blood as such."

"Then how could Jennifer steal it?"

Karl thought back to the experience of waking up this morning, and wondered where he'd missed the sign. There had to have been one. A day like this would not arrive unannounced. "I don't deny that I made a mistake with Jennifer."

"Really," said his wife, wafting the brandy snifter beneath her nose.

"I should never have kept her here after she graduated. I thought she was ready for responsibility, but it only prolonged her adolescence. I thought she was a mature person, but you were right, Gloria: she's young. She didn't even show up on campus to do her duties today. She left me to do the things she gets paid to do, but let me ask you this: Who does the things I get paid to do? Jennifer has a serious problem. It's going to hold her back in life."

"Is it a reality problem, do you think?"

"Yes, it is. She thinks she's the center of the world."

Gloria sipped her brandy, and when Karl reached for the snifter to have some, too, she pulled it away to keep to herself. "The center of the world," she said. "That's a crowded place."

MAKE ME WORK

■

The pink vanity mirror in Anthony's hand was like the one that enchanted princesses always have, the long-handled oval glass they consult to learn their fortunes. He was supposed to be using it to examine the back of his head; instead, he was tilting it this way and that to get the big picture from the wall mirror behind him. Nuong, the owner of Shear Satisfaction, appeared in this panorama in her blue smock and black leggings, a plummy color on her lips, her own hair a flawless black helmet. Anthony was enthroned in her chair, encased in a floral-printed cone from which his head emerged in ruthless relief. The rest of him seemed not to be there. To his right and left, other people sat beneath similar capes, and their nether parts also seemed to have disappeared. That was the point. The head was what concerned the denizens of this place, only the head, and the reflected scene told you so instantly, the way fairy tales told you things. In Anthony's mind the mirror spoke with Nuong's Vietnamese voice. *Leave heart at home*, it said. *Matters of head handled here.*

"Flying!" said Nuong herself, lifting Anthony's long hair and tossing it into the air. "Poof!" she exclaimed at the penumbra of fluff that floated back to his shoulders.

"Flyaway," Anthony said, helping her. "I have flyaway hair."

"Flying away!" Nuong affirmed, making her hands into birds flapping skyward. "Wispy! No good! Must cut!"

It was a time when formidable men wore ponytails—pigtails at the very least—but today, after ministering to Anthony's hair for more than two years, Nuong was saying that his fine-textured tresses had become too thin to be worn in any kind of tail any longer.

She brought her pretty face close to his. "Fact of reality, Anything," she said in commiseration (that was how she pronounced his name), and then, holding her index fingers apart to show the length, she said, "I cut this much, O.K.?"

"That much, Nuong! But that's all there is!"

"Not healthy!" Nuong said. "Must go!" she declared, and scissors magically appeared in her hand, their silver lips smacking at the definitive outward sign of Anthony's remaining youth and hipness. He was an interesting, creative guy, a sound-man for TV and films, but after Nuong was done, how would soulful single women know that? How would those rare creatures tell him from the good corporate citizens gripping Cambridge and Boston like a chest infection?

"Don't do it!" he cried out.

Nuong jumped back in surprise. Up and down the sweeping mural of the big mirror, disembodied heads swiveled to look at him.

"Let me think about it for a minute, O.K.?"

"Think?"

"Yes, think, Nuong. Maybe, you know . . . say goodbye."

"Oh! Goodbye! Sorry!" She laughed, and went off to check on a lady whose hair resembled, in its slick coat of red gel, the vital organs of a large animal.

He was facing the street, but watching it in the mirror behind him—reflected twice until it was right-side-out again. A college kid was skating across the four lanes of Mass. Ave. on fluorescent-blue Rollerblades, wearing electric-camouflage harem pants and a red T-shirt barking MAKE ME WORK in big green letters. He was bullfighting the cars, dancing with them to whatever he had on his CD player, its wires going into his head. In the present epoch kids like this were Republicans—hard to believe, until you talked to them. This one would make a fascinating corpse when he finally screwed up, but until then he was having a wonderful time. What kind of corpse would Anthony make, he wondered. He was thirty-nine years old, and lately envied the lives of surf bums and fraternity boys. If he were struck down today by a runaway truck, would his dying thought be, "Why didn't I party more?"

The kid leaped onto the sidewalk and coasted to the door of Shear Satisfaction. He was coming in for a haircut, or for something—"haircut" not really covering the situation on his head, which was dead-white and shoulder-length on the left, shoe-polish-black and buzzed to an inch or so on the right, with purple highlights like fake gorilla fur. The hieroglyphs carved into the black side were growing back. Maybe that's why he was here, to have his hieroglyphs repaired. Anthony lowered his mirror to check the kid out as he motored by. The kid checked Anthony out, too, with obvious contempt.

I was at Woodstock, dude! Anthony said to the kid with his mind. *That's right! Me! The old guy having his tail chopped off! I was there in the mud when it really happened, young cock! Not like this jive you punks are into!*

He raised his mirror to look at the street again. A black Alfa-Romeo had parked in front of the shop. When the driver got out, a spear of ice entered Anthony's heart. It was, unbelievably, a man named Robert, who'd been Anthony's best friend nearly a decade ago, until Anthony started sleeping with Robert's girlfriend, Sarah.

∎

Anthony slid down in his chair and hid his face behind the mirror. He had to brace his arm against the chair to keep it from shaking. His day had finally come. After stealing Sarah from Robert, he'd avoided his former friend, and not long after that, Robert had left town. In all these years Anthony had never seen him again.

Nuong reappeared beside his chair. "Say goodbye yet?"

He couldn't remember what she was talking about. In Anthony's six years with Sarah, Robert had rarely crossed his mind; the knife he'd put in his best friend's back had somehow entered his own brain as well, severing all memories of the man. But Sarah had left more than two years ago, and now Robert often popped into consciousness like a martyred saint, cloaked in the shimmering raiment of betrayal.

"We cut, yes?" said Nuong, tugging on Anthony's failing hair.

"Let me think a little more, Nuong. Please."

"Think more, Anything? You think so much! Maybe go home and think, O.K.?" she said, reaching to unfasten his cape.

"No, Nuong! Just another minute!" Anthony whispered as Robert, in the mirror behind him, made straight for his chair. He had a gorgeous head of wavy brown hair—hadn't lost a strand in all these years. What was it like for Nuong to work with hair like that? Anthony wondered. Wouldn't such hair be the Venetian light of her craft, her Stradivarius, the ultimate engagement of her special gifts? He saw that he'd never been more than hackwork for her.

"Oh, hi!" Nuong said to Robert.

Robert ran a hand through his flourishing locks. "Big meeting this afternoon, Nuong. Do I look O.K.?"

"Need trim," Nuong said.

"How soon till you're done with this one?" said Robert, and glanced into the big mirror where Anthony's reflected face floated cameolike in an oval frame. Their eyebeams met like a physics diagram. Somewhere, someplace, Anthony had seen the smile that bloomed across Robert's features.

"Can it be?" Robert said. "Is it possible?" He put a finger on Anthony's mirror and pushed it aside, as though setting back the hand of a clock. "Nuong! Do you know who this is?"

"It's Anything," she said. "You know Robert?" she asked Anthony.

Yes, Anthony said, but no sound came out. Instead, the smile came to him: Orson Welles in *The Third Man*, toying with Joseph Cotten on the Ferris wheel.

Nuong tried Robert. "You know Anything?"

"Oh, yes," Robert said. "Yes, indeed. I know Anything very well." He crouched down and clapped his hand on Anthony's knee through the barber's cape. "Anything! It's so great to *see* you! How have you *been*, old pal?"

"*Been all right*," Anthony said, sounding like a flying insect in a paper bag. His voice box had filled up with used motor oil. *"And yourself?"*

"*Oh, very well*," Robert said, imitating the sound Anthony was making. He straightened up. "Anything is a dear old friend of mine, Nuong."

"Oh! I never know!"

Robert circumnavigated the barbering chair. "You've kept your long hair all this time, Anything," he said. "There used to be so much more of it, though. You're thinning out quite dramatically on top, old friend. I'm sorry to say it doesn't look very good worn at this length." He turned to Anthony's stylist. "What do you think, Nuong?"

"I tell him same thing!" she said.

"Is Anything a Shear Satisfaction regular?" Robert asked her. "A steady customer of our humble enterprise?"

"Good customer," she answered, nodding her head.

The sludge drained from Anthony's vocal cords. "Our humble enterprise," he repeated, looking back and forth between them.

Nuong smiled shyly and took Robert's arm. "My husband," she said.

■

A barber's cape is strangely like a force field from science fiction —someone in charge must lift it from your body before you can move. Anthony sat without arms or the power to leave his chair, his head laid bare like a monkey offering its brains for supper.

Robert spoke to Nuong in a foreign language.

"You speak Vietnamese now?" Anthony said.

"I married a woman from Vietnam. I wouldn't bother to learn her tongue?"

"What were you saying?"

"I was offering Nuong the male perspective on your situation."

Perspective, Anthony thought, as Nuong gathered his hair in her hands. He'd recently done the sound for a nature film, yet another documentary about eagles and hawks. The public appetite for predation was apparently insatiable. Like all such films, it was told from the predator's point of view. But what about the point of view of the prey? he wondered now. What about the rabbits and rodents into whose lives those raptors plummeted like hydrogen bombs? Wasn't their story interesting? Wasn't it noble? So why did no one ever tell it? He heard a metallic whisper behind him, like a closing door. When Robert stepped into view, he had a ponytail in his hand.

Anthony marveled over how recognizable it was, even apart from his head. Seeing his ponytail was like an out-of-body experience. It was he, but it was over there. "Put it back!" he told Robert.

Robert chuckled through his teeth. "Wonderful," he said.

"What?"

"I said I'm afraid that won't be possible." He started playing a rhythm against his palm with Anthony's hair, the way a drummer brushes a snare. It seemed complex and Latin—a samba or cha-cha.

Anthony raised his mirror to see the back of his head. He had the soup-bowl cut worn by deranged men in the street.

"Not finished!" said Nuong, taking the mirror away. "Not to see yet!" she said, and began her hypnotic lifting and snipping.

"So tell me, Anything," Robert said after a moment. "How's Sarah?"

Anthony jerked his head and Nuong's scissors pierced his ear.

"Anything!" Nuong cried. "Sorry! Not move when cutting

hair!" She was nearly weeping with distress, frantically dabbing the side of Anthony's head with a towel.

"Nuong, get some bandages from the back," Robert said.

She ran off to do that. Robert folded the bloody towel into a pad, poured witch hazel on it, and put it against Anthony's ear. It stung wickedly. "It's nothing," Robert said. "A scratch. Problem is, this part of the ear is a fairly vascular area. Unlike the lobe. Have you ever considered an earring, by the way?"

"No."

"It might offset the disadvantage on top. Hold this for me, will you?"

Anthony held the towel against his ear. Slowly, lightly, Robert began massaging his shoulders.

"I have no idea how Sarah is, and you know it," Anthony said.

"I know nothing of the kind," Robert replied, amusement taking flight from his voice like the hawk that Anthony's film crew had startled off its prey. The bunny remained on the ground, mauled but alive. "You and Sarah aren't together anymore? When did that happen?"

"Two years ago."

"You stayed together that long!"

"A second ago you were surprised we weren't together now."

"Are you with somebody else?"

"I have dates."

"Dates!" Robert seemed to marvel over the concept. "But no Ms. Right?"

"Not yet," Anthony said. At the moment he had a bad crush on an assistant director he'd met doing a toothpaste commercial, a dirty-blonde from Santa Monica who wore denim shorts and hiking boots on the set and barked directions at everybody through a bullhorn. She could bark anything she wanted at Anthony, but all she'd ever told him was to get his shadow out of the shot.

His entire career consisted of concealing all evidence of himself. In a perfect job, Anthony was the man who wasn't there.

"So who left whom?" Robert asked.

"It wasn't that simple."

"Nonsense, Anything. Of course it was."

"She left me."

"For another guy?"

"As a matter of fact, yes. Happy now?"

"On the contrary. I'm sad. The leopard never changes her spots, does she?" He massaged more deeply. "She'd done that before, you know."

"I know, Robert."

Nuong returned with gauze and adhesive tape. She and her husband bandaged Anthony up. "You look like van Gogh now," Robert said when they were done. "Women will love that."

Nuong spun Anthony around. His right ear was a big white nodule on his head. The right shoulder of his cape was spattered with blood. His ponytail dangled from Robert's breast pocket like the tassel on a Shriner's fez. He looked into Robert's eyes. "I hope you're satisfied."

Nuong pulled her husband's sleeve. "I think Anything upset," she said.

Robert strolled calmly around the chair, musing upon his old lost friend, biting his lower lip reflectively. "The haircut's too bourgeois, isn't it?"

In protest, Anthony averted his face. His gaze fell upon the kid with the skates. The kid was in one of the shampooing chairs at the rear of the shop, having his head prepped behind a portable room divider. All Anthony could see were the Rollerbladed feet and the freaky ballooning pants. The feet wiggled like giant tropical fish to the jive on his CD machine.

Robert saw Anthony looking and ambled over for a look himself; then he returned, speaking more Vietnamese to Nuong. She answered with sounds like small birds escaping her mouth. They cackled like this for a minute—the male bird and the female bird tweeting and hopping and nipping each other's breasts.

This vignette of their coupling evoked one from Anthony's life, an incident that occurred not long before Sarah left him. He had come home late one night from a difficult shoot, and knocked over a table lamp as he entered their room. Sarah sprang up in bed and screamed, "I feel like a big onion!" and then fell back into deepest slumber. Anthony, who'd been exhausted, lay awake half the night. He never mentioned the remark, but after she left, it became the crucial detail, the emblematic, haunting thing. What had it meant? That her life with him was smelly? That it made her cry? That it consisted of layers? Layers of what?

"You like that?" Robert asked, jutting his chin to indicate the kid.

"Don't be absurd," Anthony said.

"I didn't think so." He stepped behind the chair. "Sit still this time."

The massage had relaxed Anthony, and now the relaxation climbed his spine and flowered in his head like fate or justice. He closed his eyes and sat still as Robert worked on his head with the clippers. With each buzzing pass of the tool, another extraneous onion layer fell away from his life. It felt good, like being loved by someone. After a long time, Robert spun Anthony around in the chair. "*Voilà*," he said.

Anthony opened his eyes. The rest of his hair was gone. In its place was a dark, lustrous nap—his under-fur shorn of the feeble growth it had struggled in vain to nourish. He touched it and felt a thrill. It was healthy and thick. He'd forgotten the basic shape of his head; now it bodied forth, all presence and strength, the cranium of a hero. Why had he walked around all these years with that dead straw hanging from his skull?

The answer echoed back—because he'd been fearful and vain.

Into the inviting pelt of his temples Robert had carved symbols, but not the chevrons and lightning bolts every teenager had. Instead, Anthony had mathematics—multiplication, subtraction, addition, division. He had equals and square root. He looked like a magician or a wizard from a book. He looked better than the guys in the ads for MTV. If this was his punishment, something had gone wrong. His newness and mystery canceled out the sting of reproof. How could it be atonement if it didn't hurt?

Nuong hovered nervously nearby, trying to assess Anthony's mood. "Easy haircut to have," she said hopefully. "Shampoo and go away."

"He's happy, Nuong," Robert said. "He likes it."

Anthony looked up into his old friend's eyes. "Math was my best subject."

"I know, Anything. You told me years ago, remember?"

"I wonder why I never followed up on it."

"Because you're a deeply flawed person."

At the register, Anthony offered Robert money from his wallet. "Pay the lady," Robert said. Anthony took another look at himself. It was like the old days on LSD, when you went to the bathroom at a party and your face melted in the medicine-cabinet mirror. "Can I ask you something?" he said to Nuong. "The first time I came here, you told me your husband was a lawyer. That was the only reason I never asked you out." He had discovered Nuong just after Sarah left. "You mean you weren't really married back then?"

"I always marry Robert," said Nuong.

Anthony turned to him. "You're supposed to be a lawyer."

"I am a lawyer," Robert said.

"How the hell did you get into cutting hair?"

"I just put up the money for the store. You're the first hair I've ever cut."

■

The plush passenger seat of Robert's Alfa was like a person in itself, and in this person's lap Anthony rode, in a car that was magical compared with his own old wreck of a thing, the same yellow hatchback he'd had eight years before. Coming out of Shear Satisfaction, Robert had seen the hatchback on the street and walked Anthony to it in disbelief. "How do you expect to get a new girlfriend driving a car like this?" he'd said, tapping the crumbling rocker panel with the toe of his tasseled loafer.

"The type of woman I like doesn't care about cars," Anthony said.

"Oh. And what type is that?"

"The alternative, nonmaterialistic type."

Robert snorted gleefully. "There's no such person, Anything! Women love cars. Yes, your women from Cambridge with their Ph.D.s. When they get together by themselves, what do you think they talk about? The kind of car a guy drives. Why do you think they're not making a commitment to you? They're waiting for a man with a decent automobile."

He steered the Alfa out of Cambridge and toward Boston's North End—Paul Revere's neighborhood in the olden days, but for most of this century a small working model of Italy. They were going to Caffè Vittoria, scene of the crime of their friendship, as Anthony thought of it now, located right around the corner from the building where Robert and Sarah had lived. They'd often hung out together there, the three of them. Robert claimed to have an appointment there today. Anthony had been back to the venerable café a few times in the past eight years, always against his better judgment, to make Sarah happy. She loved Caffè Vittoria, but it was the one place that twisted the knife in Anthony's brain, dispelled his Robert-amnesia until he found himself staring at the door, convinced that his double-crossed friend was about to walk in—Robert, who didn't even live in Boston anymore but who could, like the monster in *Frankenstein*, materialize instantly wherever Anthony was.

Robert was not Italian. He was a Presbyterian from flesh-colored Ohio, but his inner life had begun when he discovered the dusky peoples of Europe and the Levant. He adored everything about the North End, including its famous mistrust of anyone without an Italian name. Anthony, possessor of such a name, lived in Cambridge. He had always tried to acquaint his friend with the other side of the Old World, the noncharming side that screamed and beat you up and then smothered you after that. Robert only scolded him for failing to honor his heritage.

They were taking a route that Anthony didn't know—under the Expressway and down grubby streets across from the Boston Garden—and suddenly, before Anthony was ready, they were there. They parked and walked together up Hanover Street, aorta of the North End, past new espresso shops and restaurants Anthony didn't recognize. In the window of the world-famous Mike's Pastry, where life itself had a sweet cream filling, he caught their reflection—a male fashion model escorting a telephone installer from Mars. The old guys from Central Casting were in a cluster on the curb, hats and pinky rings and shouting mouths. They shouted at Robert, and he shouted back, and then they saw Anthony and fell ominously still. Out of the public eye, with Robert not around, they would have leaped on him like lions. Anthony knew this because he was virtually their son. But today they let him move on to the jewel of North End cafés, where he peered through the glass for a minute as though looking across time for his former self. Robert held the door and Anthony stepped inside.

A guy behind the counter was steaming milk for cappuccino, raising and lowering the metal pitcher with a flourish. Over his shoulder he saw Robert coming in. "Roberto!" he called out. *"Paisan!"* Then he saw Anthony and forgot what he was doing, and the hot milk foamed all over his hand.

"Nice haircut, huh, Rocco?" Robert asked, buffing Anthony's head with his palm as though caressing a large brown nut.

Rocco gripped his scalded hand in a towel. "Where do you find these birds?" he asked.

Robert laughed and walked Anthony into the room. It was all the way it had always been, an Italian spaceship parked on a knoll above Boston Harbor. The golden tin ceiling spread like daybreak over the marble-topped tables. Gilded wrought-iron railings bordered stairs down to the dungeonlike basement room and up to the mezzanine, where spotlights shone on the painted diorama of a painfully blue harbor rimmed by mountains. Sinatra was singing "They Can't Take That Away from Me" on a fluid-filled jukebox that bubbled and pulsed through the color spectrum like a giant

Lava lamp. He'd been singing "I've Got You Under My Skin" the last time Anthony was here; he sang many songs in Caffè Vittoria. The jukebox was actually an urn containing Sinatra's soul, along with the spiritual essence of Tony Bennett, Jerry Vale, and Vic Damone, all watched over by a black-robed Cardinal Law in a frame on the wall.

Several tables on the main floor were empty, but Robert liked the mezzanine. Anthony opened the small menu and stared at the categories of drinks—the coffees, digestifs, grappas, and cognacs. "*Paisan*, huh?" he said.

Robert poked him in the chest. "I've been inducted."

"Into what?"

The inductee's smile collapsed. "What do you mean, into what? Into the Order of the Sons of Italy."

"You're kidding me."

"No, Antonio, I am not."

"How the hell did you manage that?"

"I told you. I was inducted. The citizens of the North End have taken me to their breast."

A waitress appeared at the table, a fortyish woman from a long line of Mediterranean forebears. Her hair was dyed a black not found in nature, but neither was it the black of the Rollerblade boy. Extreme though it was, hers still meant to convey the idea of human hair. "Grappa," she said to Robert.

"Yes, Isabelle, thank you. And a Galliano for Antonio here."

"I don't drink sweet things like that," Anthony said.

"He forgets," Robert told Isabelle. "When his teeth were coming in, Dad would rub Galliano on his gums to ease the pain."

Anthony looked up in surprise. "When did I tell you that?"

"This was when he was a baby," Robert added.

"Oh, good," Isabelle said. "I thought you meant recently." She turned to Anthony. "Got a tooth coming in today?"

"No. I'll have a beer."

"In this hallowed place, Antonio?" Robert said. "A beer? Have a Galliano. For old times' sake. For back when Dad used to soothe your gums."

"You two are brothers?" Isabelle asked. "You don't look anything like each other. Who takes after Dad?"

"All right, I'll have a Galliano."

"You didn't put up much of a fight," Isabelle said.

"You should have seen him in the hair salon," Robert said.

"I wasn't gonna say anything." She wiggled Anthony's good ear. "You could use a little something here. Complete the look. Silver, maybe with a stone." The she slid her pencil behind her own ear and went away.

"That's Isabelle," Robert said. "Great lady."

Anthony asked, "Did you meet Nuong because she cut your hair?"

"Yeah, as a matter of fact I did. Isn't that great?"

It was so great that it struck Anthony dumb.

"What's the problem?" Robert said. "You don't like Nuong?"

"No. I've always liked her a lot. I didn't like her much today, though."

"Ha! Perfect. You always were a fickle person."

"I thought you always liked me."

"I did, Antonio. I still do. That's the point. I'm the rational, consistent one. You're the emotional loose hubcap. You're the runaway truck."

Anthony looked away. His eyes fell on Robert's handsome jacket. "That's an expensive suit, isn't it?" he said.

"Yes."

"You've done well for yourself. The suits, the car, a store for your wife."

"Most of my clients are prosperous people with a knack for major blunders. Those billable hours add right up." He tickled the addition sign on Anthony's head.

Down on the main floor, a tall, gray-haired man called up to Robert. He was at the foot of the mezzanine steps, honoring the jukebox with coin.

"Hi, Pasquale," Robert said, waving back. "That's Pasquale," he told Anthony.

Pasquale pushed some buttons on the throbbing machine. Sinatra's "Witchcraft" began to play.

Anthony breathed deeply and said, "I'm sorry I slept with Sarah."

"You slept with her?" Robert said. His lips twitched and fluttered on his face, independent of his other features. It was disturbing to see. Even Orson Welles didn't do that. "Were you tired?"

"I'm saying I'm sorry, Robert."

"Hey, can I ask you something? I'm just curious. Who seduced whom?"

"She seduced me, I guess."

"You guess? I always had the impression that Sarah intimidated you, Antonio. In fact, I had the distinct idea that she scared you to death. It must have been something when she came on to you. Fourth of July, huh?"

Isabelle arrived with their drinks. Anthony was playing dead, hoping the bear would go away. Robert raised his glass in a toast and sipped his grappa. "It was over between Sarah and me before you slipped in," he said.

"What?"

"Finished. Absolutely. Had been for some time."

"I didn't know that," Anthony said. "She never told me." His hand was trembling, but he got the Galliano to his lips.

Robert winked. "I didn't say she knew."

Once, this would have been the most fascinating information in the world. It was amazingly irrelevant now. "Are you saying you're not mad at me because I slept with her?"

"Sarah was a woman, you were a man. Should I be mad at nature? Besides, you behaved honorably toward Sarah. You practically married her, for God's sake."

"It's a great relief to hear this, Robert."

"Sure. Glad I could clear it up. One thing, though. You were not a man of honor with me, Antonio. Your closest friend. In relation to me, man to man, you behaved like a worm. No, you behaved lower than that. What's lower than worms?"

"Slime, I guess," Anthony said.

■

They fell silent in the blue light coming off the Amalfi Coast or whatever it was painted on the wall. Three or four tables away, a man's voice said, very slowly, "Your . . . personality . . . bums . . . me . . . out." No one said anything back. When Anthony lifted his face to see who these people were, a beautiful woman was looking down at his head.

"Check out the man's hair!" she cried.

"Hello, Celeste," Robert said. "You're late."

"I know, I know, I know!" she said.

"Celeste, this is Anything. Anything, Celeste."

"*Anything!*" she exclaimed. She was possibly the most exuberant person Anthony had ever met. "Really? That's great! What a great name! You mean, like, 'Whatever'? 'All options open'? 'Total potential'?"

"Yeah, I guess," Anthony said.

"He guesses!" she said. "He doesn't know!" She pulled out a chair and sat down. "Why do I feel I'm interrupting something?"

"I'm afraid I've been giving Anything a little scolding," Robert said.

"Welcome to the club, Anything," Celeste said, slapping Anthony on the back. She was wearing a dazzling vest with colorful yarns and bits of metal woven into it. Also a white silk blouse, a tiny red skirt, and the translucent black stockings women never wore anymore. The world's great religions could probably be traced to the feeling Anthony had upon seeing her legs.

"So what time is it?" she said, and reached for Robert's Rolex.

He pulled his arm away and hexed her with his fingers. "Whatever you do," he told Anthony, "don't let her near your watch." Then he looked at the Rolex himself. "It's three forty-five. You were supposed to be here at three."

"We weren't even here at three ourselves," Anthony said.

"I know that, Anything. Don't contradict me. I was allowing for Celeste's affliction."

"I can't wear watches," she explained, showing her wrists, each bereft of any timekeeping device. "My body stops them."

Anthony laughed.

"It's not a joke," Robert said. "She's afflicted."

"One in a thousand people has it," she said. "Our bodies put out a magnetic field or something."

"I've never heard of this," Anthony said.

"The old-time jewelers all knew about it. If you were one of these people, they didn't even try to sell you a watch. It wasn't gonna work, and that was that."

"Well, then, it must not apply to battery-powered watches," Anthony said. "Most watches today run on batteries. Just go get yourself one of those."

"Nope, it applies to them, too. I even tried one of those calculator-watch combinations—the thin little business-card type? Got it to balance my checkbook with. The calculator part kept working, but the clock stopped dead." She looked at Anthony's wrist. "I could stop your watch right now."

He took off his rubberized quartz chronograph, good to a hundred meters below the surface of the sea, and held it out by its strap.

"What did I just get finished saying?" Robert said.

Celeste extended her wrist. "You have to put it on me."

"That's part of it?"

"Sometimes."

He fastened his watch to her wrist. If the jolt he got when he touched her skin didn't stop the thing, nothing ever would. He looked. The second hand was still going.

Celeste leaned back to look Anthony over. "So what kind of trouble are you in, Anything? Besides wardrobe trouble, I mean."

"Who said I was in any?"

"You're getting scolded by Roberto here. That means you're in trouble. Big trouble, probably. Believe me, I know. So what did you do, snuff somebody?"

"It was personal," Robert said. "Anything is an old friend of mine."

"Robert!" she said. "You have an old friend like Anything and you never even mention him?"

"He's been away. He just got back."

"Where did you get back from, Anything? Pluto?"

"The really funny thing," Robert went on, "is that Nuong has been his stylist for years, and I didn't even know it."

"I love stuff like that!" Celeste exclaimed. She returned to Anthony's head. "So what's all this you got up here? Addition? Subtraction? What's this one?"

"That's infinity," Robert said. "When did you drop out of school? Kindergarten?"

"Math was never my best subject. Wow, infinity," she marveled, touching Anthony's buzzed temple. She turned to Robert. "Nuong knows how to do all this? That little slip of a thing? What else does she know how to do?"

Robert and Celeste laughed naughtily through their noses.

"Don't worry about Nuong," Anthony said. "She knows plenty."

"I'll bet, Anything, if she's been working on you."

"Our country dropped bombs on her hut when she was growing up. She lived through that."

Robert and Celeste sat there frozen for a moment. "She grew up in an apartment building," Robert said finally.

"O.K., we bombed her apartment building," Anthony said. To Celeste he said, "Robert helped."

"The hell I did."

"I meant with my hair."

"Oh, that. Yes, I did help with that."

Celeste leaned close to Anthony on her elbows and traced his multiplication sign with a fingertip. "If you really, you know, *liked* a girl . . . would you put her initials on your head?"

"Of course he would," said Robert. "The pity is, there's no one special in his life right now." He drew closer to Celeste. "Anything has recently undergone a terrible heartbreak."

"Not that recently," Anthony said.

"Recently enough," said Robert. "The pain is fresh."

"I'm so sorry," said Celeste. She put her hand on Anthony's hand. "A disappointment like that can make a person brittle."

"I'm not brittle."

She laughed. "You're reliving the goddamn war in Vietnam."

Isabelle arrived to serve Celeste a drink she hadn't ordered—Sambuca poured over three black espresso beans.

Celeste sipped this beverage. "I guess you've been told you look like Vincent van Gogh," she said.

"He has," said Robert.

"It's a cruel look. Interesting, but cruel."

"Anything in a nutshell."

"He wasn't a cruel person, though. I've read up on this. He was a sweet guy who just happened to look cruel by accident. That was his tragedy."

"He was insane," Anthony said.

"So goes the rap. You believe whatever you read, Anything? I love van Gogh's paintings. I think his paintings are, like, the epitome of everything."

"There you have it, folks," Robert said.

Celeste laughed and punched him in the chest.

"Let's see your stuff," he said.

She had an oversized black leather bag, which she hoisted to her lap and opened to produce a pile of fabric swatches—rich, colorful fabrics with exotic patterns woven into them.

"Celeste owns a wonderful boutique up the street," Robert said. "I buy all my clothes from her. See these?" he said, fingering the swatches. "These are the *most choice* fabrics"—he kissed his fingertips—"the newest weaves from the best Italian textile designers. You'll never see these anywhere else in America. Celeste has a connection for these things."

They were gorgeous fabrics, even Anthony could see that. "Are you having a suit made?" he asked Robert.

Celeste gaped at him. "You'd make a suit out of these?" She touched some of the pieces and turned to Robert. "Maybe he has something?"

"No, he does not have something. These are fabrics for draperies and sofas, Anything. Nuong and I are redecorating Shear Satisfaction. Celeste's helping us."

"Oh," Anthony said. He watched as they leafed through the samples. "The blue one's my favorite," he threw in after a while.

Celeste backhanded him in the biceps. "That's my favorite, too! I wasn't gonna tell him till the end, see what he said."

"The blue's nice," said Robert. "A little bright. I tend to favor the grays."

"Tell me," Celeste said, smoothing Robert's padded shoulder. "Everything's gray with this guy," she told Anthony.

"Roberto!" a man's voice called out.

At the foot of the mezzanine steps a middle-aged man with a big gut was beckoning Robert with his arm. His pants seemed to defy gravity, staying up despite being worn far below whatever could be considered his waist. The men in Anthony's family wore their pants this way, too. Celeste looked to see who it was. The man winked and waved hello to her. Then he saw Anthony's head and his smile disappeared. He squinted and craned his neck at their table. Anthony looked away.

"What are you doing with that goombah?" Celeste asked Robert.

"Don't say that around here!" Anthony whispered.

"Oh, I know that guy," she said.

Robert extricated himself from beneath the small café table. "Anthony, this is my man," he said. "I gotta go."

Anthony pointed to Celeste. "I thought this was your man."

"Oh, thanks a lot," Celeste said. *"Anthony."*

"Give him a lift home, O.K., sweetheart?" Robert said, kissing Celeste's cheek. He gave her a business envelope and shook Anthony's hand. "Great to see you, pal. Call me, O.K.?" He put the fabric samples under his arm and went down to meet the man. They walked to the front door and out to the street.

The envelope had a window through which Anthony saw his ponytail. Celeste put it in her bag without looking at it.

"*Anthony*," she said again, and stroked his engraved temple once with her palm. "So that's the name your mama gave you, huh? Never suspecting you'd do things like this to yourself."

"Yeah, that's the name she gave me."

Celeste shook her head. "We go through so much for you bums."

Contrition with women came easily to Anthony, because of the nuns. He hung his head the way he used to as an altar boy. He had an overwhelming urge to tell Celeste something true about his life. He said, "Would you like to know something? I went to Woodstock."

She looked as though he'd started speaking Vietnamese. "No kidding. Recently? The movie? The town? What? What are you telling me?"

"The event. The thing. Woodstock. I was there."

"You were there."

"Yeah."

"And you feel I should know this."

"I thought you might find it interesting."

"You're telling me you're an older man."

"No! That's not what I meant at all."

"Woodstock," Celeste said. "I think I saw the movie. Maybe I just dreamed I saw it. Hey! You mean if I saw the movie *Woodstock*, you'd be in there?"

"I might be. I don't know. I've never seen it."

"You were *at* the freaking thing, and you've never seen the movie?" She shook her head. "You're a wonder, Anthony. A real wonder. Anthony what, by the way?"

He told her his family name. It was a long, complicated one. His people were the only people in the whole United States with that particular name.

"Jesus, Mary, and Joseph!" Celeste said. "That's gorgeous! *That's* your name? You have to do something with that name, Anthony! When you have a name like that you're supposed to pass it on! Give it to babies!"

Anthony laughed. "You should talk to my mother."

"Don't say that, buster, 'cause I might. I might look up her number and give her a little report on you."

Isabelle brought the bill. She and Celeste wiggled fingers at each other.

"You don't have to give me a lift," Anthony said. "I can get a cab."

"I don't mind. For some weird reason, I trust you. Are you from another planet?"

Anthony thought about it. "No."

"You can tell me. I believe in that stuff."

"I'm not."

"Well, I'll still give you a lift. But it'll have to be to my store, down the street. I don't have a car. Wish I did. I love cars. You have a car?"

"Yeah, but it's in Cambridge. I'll just get a taxi, thanks."

"Oh, no, you gotta come back to my store. I want you to try a few things on. I have some new things I think would look great on you. This isn't a sales number. I just wanna see. You have the physique for nice clothes, Anthony."

"Celeste. I'm not really into stuff like Robert wears."

"No, no, no, Anthony! I'm talking about *clothes*, fashionable clothes. The newest things from Milano! You think I'd put you in Robert's suits? He's a . . . *suit*, for God's sake. The man is, like, *so straight*. I do what I can do, but he's all business. 'Lighten up!' I tell Robert, but it does no good. He won't even wear, like, an adventurous *tie*."

"Did you meet Robert because he shopped in your store?"

"Not exactly."

"You live here in the North End, too, I guess?"

"Do I live here in the North End? I grew up across the street,

Anthony. Hey, know what? I have a VCR, and some eggplant parm in the fridge. Why don't we rent *Woodstock* and see if we can find you in it? Wouldn't that be a riot? Plus, we'd get to hear all that weird old music again."

"I still think a lot of that music's pretty great."

"Oh, brother. Sorry, no offense."

Anthony paid the bill, tipping Isabelle exorbitantly, and they got up to leave. From the edge of the mezzanine he surveyed the ancient spectacle of Caffè Vittoria spread out below him. At this moment it captured the whole point of human life. Celeste's arm appeared in front of his face. She was showing him her wrist. His watch had stopped—the second hand was not moving.

Her pleasure in this was a stunning thing. "Now you believe," she said.

"Yes, I do," Anthony answered, and he did, in something, though he wasn't completely clear on what. "Hey, hold on," he said. "I just had a thought. When a person such as yourself—"

"An afflicted person."

"When an afflicted person gives a watch back to a person like me—"

"A normal person." She snorted and cracked up.

He stared at her for a minute. "Does it start working again?"

She took his arm and led him onto the stairs. "Who said I was giving it back?"

HEAVY LIFTING

■

Dwight Jr. has uttered his first intelligible word—"Da," his name for Dwight Sr. The elder Dwight is predictably proud, but he's also a great believer in the perfectibility of man, and feels there's room for improvement. He's been playing Bob Marley albums nonstop at home, trying to get Dwight Jr. to change it to "Jah"—God's Rastafarian name. Dwight believes that children need a strong transcendental figure early in life, and what better choice than Dad? So far, young Dwight is sticking with the earthly "Da," though he dances to reggae like a born Rasta. "If you can do 'Da,' 'Jah' should be easy, right?" Dwight asked me the other day. " 'Jah' should be a pretty small step, don't you think?"

One small step for Dwight Jr. One giant leap for Da.

Dwight Jr.'s day-care provider is indisposed today, so the little guy is here at Paradise Productions with Anita and me, helping us with the video crisis we're in. I'm holding him on my lap so he can't crawl under the table and pull the plug for the computer I'm writing this videoscript on. He can't be on Anita's lap because she needs both hands to work the editing console, plus he pulls up her blouse to nuzzle her breasts. He tried that on Susie, our receptionist, so she won't watch him anymore. He tried it on me, too, but my nipples just cracked him up. My belly button was also good for a few snorts. If I hold Dwight Jr.'s ankles with one hand and his body with my upper arm, I can type fairly well for a minute, until he squirms free enough to grab the computer mouse, trying to activate the painting program he uses on Dwight Sr.'s machine at home. At ten months of age, Dwight Jr. is bigger than most two-year-olds, and he fools you into thinking he's a rational being. I started the day calmly explaining to him that computers can't paint till they have software to eat, and Da's computer at home is like the piggy that ate roast beef, whereas this computer here is the piggy that ate none. I've stopped explaining that. We're down to physical restraint and "No paint."

Dwight Sr. is supposed to be here, too, but he was spirited away by Marco Tempesto, laser-light artist and star of *Commando Cuisine*, the weekly cooking program produced by Dwight and Anita for public-access cable TV. Tempesto is catering tonight's banquet at the Cambridge Marriott, where God knows what version of this video will be shown to an audience of space freaks and skeptical millionaires. Tempesto also created the computer animations in the tape itself. Actually, he got Paradise Productions this gig in the first place. He and our client, Vernon DeCloud, go way back.

Vern's video belongs to a sales sub-genre called, by Dwight, "Brie-TV" because such tapes are almost always shown during lavish cocktail parties. Brie-TV is basically expensive PR for luring investors to large business ventures. In these parlous times it has become a Paradise Productions specialty. The budgets are big, your client takes all the risk, and you get to do fun things like helicopter shots, computer animation, and hanging out with the blown-away-but-still-famous-enough actor you've hired to narrate it. Then your client stages a gala function, the guests graze and drink, you roll the tape. If the potential investors come away feeling they've just seen the client's venture on the nightly news, you're aces.

The problem this time . . . Well, there are many problems, but for starters the client's venture is not taking place on the planet Earth, so we're targeting a special breed of investor. Besides that, investment videos are, by their very nature, slick salesmanship, yet Vernon DeCloud instructed us that slick salesmanship was all wrong. "We're asking people to join the most monumental undertaking of all time," he declared when we began the project. "The greatest expedition ever conceived by humankind. We're going to make it sound like Boston Harborfront condominiums?"—a snide reference to a recent Paradise Productions success. But the ultimate problem is that Vern is Mr. Venture Capital—the financier who helped launch the computer companies that turned Boston into Silicon Valley East—and he can change his mind about anything any time he feels like it.

In retrospect, we should have seen it coming; clients often start out wanting the wild, chancy, ground-breaking presentation, only to chicken out later on. Vern told us of his long-standing interest in Zen Buddhism, so we decided our angle would be capitalism crossed with Zen. Except we didn't exactly know what Zen was. We brainstormed for a couple of weeks, watched time-shifted episodes of *Star Trek: The Next Generation*, sent out for a lot of sashimi. Then Dwight and Anita flew around the country interviewing astronauts and scientists, while I stayed home writing mystical voice-over narration. Tempesto came up with some amazing computer-simulations of outer space. And though it's a Paradise Productions policy to avoid client input whenever possible, Vern was invited to see several cuts along the way. He pronounced each of them fine. Anita called him daily for approval of every little tweak, and Vern was that soul-soothing thing: the happy wealthy client.

But yesterday, with no warning, Vernon DeCloud lost his nerve, which partly, but not completely, explains why Dwight woke me up at 5:50 a.m. today with a phone call to my girlfriend's apartment.

"I just had a terrible dream about Walter!" he exclaimed when Rebecca grabbed the receiver. "Is he O.K.? He's not dead, is he?"

She flopped over in bed to look. I was sleeping with my mouth open because I have one of Dwight Jr.'s colds, and in the dim predawn light, with the suggestion of death in her groggy head, she took me for a corpse. She screamed. I sprang up at the waist like a zombie and she clobbered me with the phone.

"Walter, you're alive!" Dwight said when I got on. "I looked for you an hour ago and you weren't there."

"That's because I'm here, Dwight."

He was calling from the main editing suite at Paradise Productions, directly above the first-floor apartment I sublet from them. "Then I fell asleep and had this awful dream. I dreamed you died, Walter."

Rebecca peeked out from under the comforter. "Dwight dreamed I died," I told her. She put a pillow over her head and laughed, or at least her body quaked like a person laughing. "Dwight, I'm not dying. I'm just moving in with my girlfriend."

"You're doing it?" Dwight said. "You've decided? You're leaving us, Walter?"

"Well, I mean, that's the issue at hand. No, I haven't decided. But you'd still see me every day. Unless I'm fired." It was 6 a.m., the time Rebecca's clock radio goes off. The man in the helicopter came on. "Dwight, why were you looking for me at five in the morning?"

"So we could work on Vern's tape, what else? We got you big-time money to write this script, and now in the clutch you're not there. What if Watson had been shacked up when Alexander Graham Bell called *him*? We wouldn't even have the telephone today."

"You haven't been to bed, have you?"

"I fell asleep with my head on the tape controller and I had that dream. My face has all these marks on it."

"Why do you do this to yourself, Dwight? Why do you work this way? Is it because this is the only way the poetry happens?"

"It's because Vern has rejected our video, Walter."

"Nonsense, Dwight. He loves it."

"No, he called yesterday to say it's too weird for the big investors. They're not gonna get it. It has to be real straight and obvious, and no politics or philosophy. I couldn't talk him out of it. Didn't Anita tell you?"

"No."

"We have to do something about our communication in this company," Dwight said. "Walter! Come here! I need you!"

■

I met Vernon DeCloud several months ago during an Indian lunch in the town of Waltham—a topological oddity that seems to abut or actually contain every other town in the Boston area; whenever people give you directions to somewhere, they ask if you're coming from Waltham. Much of the unseen technological life of the Northeast takes place there, in long, low-lying buildings with black slits for windows or no windows at all. Vernon DeCloud's offices are somewhere in those miles of industrial park where asphalt seeks its own level like marshland. But for this meeting he'd summoned us to Taste of Calcutta—Dwight and Anita, their partner the Doctor, Tempesto, and me. Dwight likes the Doctor to attend all meetings, because his Harvard Ph.D. comforts clients. I'm never invited to meetings, or even told they've taken place. I had no idea what this project was about. But Vern had insisted that the proposed scriptwriter be there. All the magic begins with the writer, he told Anita. Obviously, he was no ordinary client.

"I've seen your demo reel," Vern said after I'd shaken his hand and sat down. "Very competent, very professional."

"Thank you, sir."

"Don't call me 'sir,' Walter. That was the problem with your reel. Respectful, safe, boring."

"Oh."

"But I sensed something more—some greatness within you that wasn't being expressed. I understand you're an actor. You've done Shakespeare."

"Right."

"The greatest dramatic mind of all time," Vern said, jabbing at the air with a pappadum, "and you've strutted his words upon the stage! That's what we're looking for, Walter! The human soul in flight!"

"I see."

"Don't say you see if you don't see."

"I think I see."

"All right. Now, you may not be aware of it, but there's a whole subculture of people, heavy scientists included, who are thoroughly disgusted with the way our government has botched space exploration."

"We don't even *have* space exploration!" Tempesto exclaimed across the table. "Remember how you felt in the Mercury days? Remember Apollo? We were like gods! Now we just fly around in that glorified airplane. We could have been on Venus already!"

Fragrant, steaming dishes of food arrived. "My daughter's a sophomore in college," Vern said, ripping open a plump poori, "and she doesn't believe men really walked on the moon. She thinks it was actors on a set."

"We're not leaving our descendants any great mythic frontier," said the Doctor.

"The point being," I said, "that these alienated space people want to blast off on their own."

"Right," said Vern. "And they know how. They have a detailed ten-year plan, starting with a space station, and then a colony on the moon, and finally a city on Mars."

"A Martian city in ten years, Walter!" the Doctor said.

"The government's gonna let you do all this?"

"Our government wants out of the space business," said Vern. "They don't know how to run a business. They can't even deliver the mail right anymore. They'd like nothing better than to get NASA's budget back, but they don't know how to extricate themselves. Someone has to help them."

"Isn't this the coolest thing you've ever heard?" Anita asked me.

"How about it, Walter?" Vern said. "Are you psyched? We only want people who are psyched."

"He's psyched," said Dwight, hefting the tandoori chicken. "His rate is three hundred a day."

Mr. Venture Capital reached across the table to shake my hand, and then served himself some basmati rice.

I nudged Dwight in the ribs. "Thanks, pal!" I whispered.

"You get one-fifty," he whispered back.

The lamb vindaloo came around to me, and its fumes cleared my head. "Stupid question," I said. "How are you planning to get up there?"

"Hardly stupid, Walter," said Vern. "Of the essence. Marco?"

"You know how they keep telling us the Cold War is over?" Tempesto said. "Well, thousands of missiles are sitting in silos, ready to go, and the most imagination our leaders can muster is to dismantle the things. After they bled us for the taxes to build them! This government kills me! There's your heavy lifting."

"Those aren't for going into space, Tempesto. They fly sideways."

"We change their trajectories, Walter."

"They'll reach that far?"

"Far enough for the space station, which is our staging area for the lunar colony."

I turned to Vern. "So what's the lure for these investors you're trying to round up? What do they get? The chance to send up their experiments? Find out if they can make their macaroni and cheese work in the weightlessness of space?"

"We'll put in some boring short-term stuff for them," said Vern. "Most investors aren't philosophers, are they? But before money, there's existence. Before existence, survival. That's the other part of the picture."

"The other part."

"The exodus, Walter. Look around you, my friend. No, not the restaurant. The world. Don't you see what's going on? I know it's hard to contemplate, but let's face facts. Sooner or later, we must leave this planet."

I glanced at my colleagues, busy spooning out saucy entrées. This wasn't news to them, apparently. "Everybody?"

Vern slapped the table. "Excellent! He pierces to the crux! No, not everybody. Everybody won't be able to, though I'm afraid in the end everybody will want to. I'm not surprised you haven't thought about it. Most people haven't. Most people have been brainwashed into a deadly lethargy. But let me assure you, you'll think about it soon enough. It's going to get pretty slimy down here before long."

"Pollution?" I said.

"No, Walter," said Vern. "Class warfare."

■

I resigned in Dwight's Bonneville on the way back to Paradise Productions. That is, I tendered my resignation verbally. It was not accepted.

"*Now* what's the problem?" said Dwight, looking at me in the rearview mirror.

"This guy is one bizarre Republican and you know it, Dwight."

"Vern's a great guy!" said Tempesto from the passenger seat.

"Yeah, a great guy who wants to privatize outer space for himself and his rich pals, and leave everybody else to rot on the doomed planet."

"He never said that," Anita said.

"He's a kook, Anita. He wants to fly into outer space with military-surplus war missiles."

"Perfectly feasible," said Tempesto. "Great idea."

"What's next? Gaffer's tape? Parts from Radio Shack?"

"Never mind gaffer's tape!" said the Doctor. "What an epic moment in human history this is! Think of it, Walter! People leaving their birth planet! Extending human life into the heavens!"

"Without me."

"But Vernon *wants* you," said Anita. "You auditioned and got the job."

"Vern's touchy about personalities," said Tempesto. "He has mystical ideas about teams. A team is a very specific group of people."

"A genius financier personally tapped you as scriptwriter," Dwight said.

"Then why don't I get the three hundred?"

"All right, you can have two. That's good money, Walter. Twice your usual rate."

"I want the whole three."

"Walter, when an employer quotes a rate on a subcontractor, it includes all kinds of hidden expenses. We have to pay all your benefits—your health, unemployment, Social Security, pension and welfare."

"You pay all that on me?"

"Starting now," Anita said.

Back at Paradise Productions, Dwight and the Doctor sat me down in the coffee lounge. "Don't you watch *MacNeil/Lehrer?*" Dwight said. "We're in the middle of this very weird reversal. American capitalism is a pitiful retarded giant nobody wants to be seen with. Our businessmen want to be anything but who they are. They want to be like the witty Germans, the stylish Italians, the swashbuckling Aussies."

"They'd be African," said the Doctor, "if you told them that was the coming thing."

"But more than anything else," Dwight continued, "they want to be Japanese. They want to *think* Japanese, but they have no idea what that is. They talk about being hip and radical and cutting edge, but it sounds like something on a civil-service exam. It's bizarre, Walter, but we're to the point now where investors are actually *afraid* of ideas that make sense to them. If they understand a business deal, that's terrifying, because everything they understand is wrong. Right off the bat, they're not thinking Japanese. But if they don't understand it, that's terrifying, too, because maybe it's just freaky bullshit. How would you describe a situation like that?"

"Pathetic?"

"No! Fluid! It's a fluid situation. We've talked about those. What happens in fluid situations?"

"Us little piggies have roast beef?"

"Yes, Walter!"

■

"You know what?" Anita says. "I don't want to do this anymore. I quit."

"You can't quit. You're the producer."

She takes a small video camera from a shelf and points it at me. The red light starts blinking. "Tell me how you feel about moving in with Rebecca," she says. "Talk about that."

"Da!" says Dwight Jr., pointing at the camera.

"See that? He sees the camera and says 'Da.' Is that adorable or what?"

"Anita, could you turn that off?"

"People pay good money for this, Walter. Video therapy. You talk about your problems on camera, and it helps you work through them."

"It's not helping me. It's making me upset."

Dwight Jr. stands on my lap with his killer Stride-Rites, then flings his head back and swooshes down the front of me, pretending I'm a slide. He hits the floor with a squeal and climbs back up to do it again.

"You're an actor, you can't get nervous in front of cameras. Plus, therapy doesn't always feel better at first. Lots of times it feels crummy for quite a while. So what about moving in with Rebecca?"

"First of all, I might not do it. I'm leaning against it, in fact."

"Don't listen to Dwight, Walter. He acts so hard-boiled, but deep down he's incredibly romantic."

"Really. What about Tempesto and the Doctor? They're against it, too."

"Tempesto and the Doctor. Men who think women should be dragged around by their hair."

I was eating dinner at Rebecca's a few weeks ago, when, out of the blue, she said, "Isn't it about time you moved in?"

The tableau shimmers in my mind like one of Tempesto's holograms: the oakey Chardonnay like gold in my upraised glass, Rebecca's homemade chicken pie on my plate, Rebecca herself across the table with her dark hair in a red ribbon and her steaming fork poised in the air. "Moved in what?" I replied innocently.

"Moved in *here*," she said, her eyes hard and moist. *"Moved in with me."*

For some reason, I suddenly remembered the story of a famous jazz critic who suggested to Miles Davis that he, Miles, drop by the next time he was in the jazz critic's neighborhood. "What for?" Miles reportedly said. "What for?" I blurted to Rebecca.

It took a night and a day to make up with her, and then I negotiated for more time, and sometime after that I mentioned the episode to Anita—seeking, I suppose, impartial womanly guidance, though what could I have been thinking?—and soon people were stopping me in the hallways of Paradise Productions to clap me upon the shoulder and say, "Things are getting serious, Walter!"

Not Dwight, however. He's opposed to it. Men shouldn't do things like move in with women, he told me. Men have their freedom to think about.

"Freedom to do what?" I asked.

"To sleep with other women, for one thing."

"Dwight, how could I do that?"

"Easy!"

"What else?" I asked, but he couldn't think of anything. Anita lets Dwight do whatever he wants, except that one thing.

"Dwight, you yourself moved in with a woman," I pointed out.

"So?" he said.

Anita drops down on one knee for a different angle with the camera. Dwight Jr., the most videotaped child in history, hams it up by wrapping an arm around my neck and taking a bow as though we're doing some old biplane stunt.

"Anita, we're getting punchy. I'm gonna make fresh coffee."

"Just tell me your gut feelings. Not what everybody else says. Tell me what you, Walter, personally feel."

"I feel it's an awfully big step."

"But you want to do it."

"That's the problem."

"Talk about how you feel with that cute little boy on your lap. Isn't he a doll? How would you like a little boy of your own?"

"I want a little girl."

"A girl! Wonderful! Tell me."

"Well, if I had a girl, I wouldn't have to get symbolically killed or kicked in the crotch all the time. She'd worship me and love me forever."

"No, eventually she'd nail you."

"You think?"

"It's part of human development. Dada gets it in the coconuts."

Susie's voice comes over the intercom. *"Dwight for Anita on 3. Anita, pick up 3."*

Anita punches the button for the speakerphone. "Where the hell are you?" she says at her husband, but it's Tempesto's voice that comes out.

"Captain's log, Stardate 4217. We have established contact with the space colony. But something has gone terribly wrong. The men are no longer in charge. The slave women have taken over."

"Yay!" Anita says at the phone.

Dwight's voice comes on. *"Anita? What's going on? Where's Walter?"*

"We're doing video therapy. I'm taping Walter talking about moving in with Rebecca. We're getting some really great, heartfelt stuff. His anxiety level is dropping dramatically."

"I happen to know Walter has decided against that. Nothing personal about Rebecca. Lovely girl. But Walter needs to be near his work."

"When did I say that?"

"Is that you, Walter? Your voice sounds funny."

"Your son has his finger up my nose."

"Well, take it out. Hi, Dwight Jr. It's Jah speaking. Jah."

"I never said I decided, Dwight."

"You said words to that effect."

"I said I couldn't make up my mind."

"That's not how it sounded to me. What kind of shape is the tape in?"

"The way you left it," I say. "The sound of outer space clapping."

We've spent the morning staring at Dwight's all-night samurai recut of Vernon's tape—talking heads answering questions no one has asked, narration that doesn't go with the pictures, ten-second black holes, all in the structure, more or less, of our Harborfront condominium video. When Dwight left with Tempesto, he told us to fill in the holes and polish it up.

"You haven't done anything to it?"

"We have some ideas," Anita says.

"Wonderful. Say goodbye to Walter and we'll talk about it."

"Dwight, no!" she says. "I need him!"

"Well, we need some help over here, too."

"Help doing what?" I say.

"Walter, bring little Dwight with you. Dwight Jr., leave Mommy alone now. Come to Jah."

The door swings open and the Doctor comes in. "Ready?" he asks me.

"Ready for what?"

"To venture into the field. Didn't Dwight call you?"

"Yes, I called him," says the speakerphone.

■

When the Doctor got his Ph.D. in anthropology years ago, he was all set for a big academic career, and then he signed up to work for a summer on an ethnographic documentary. Somewhere out in the bush he went cinematically native. He's been in the film business ever since, where there's more raw anthro than in any tribal village. At some point in the Doctor's barefoot wanderings with the 16 millimeter, he was promised to a chieftain's daughter, and he's theoretically next in line to become king of an obscure

South Pacific island. Among the principals of Paradise Productions, he is the most genuinely excited about Vernon DeCloud's delusions. The Doctor, it turns out, has some unfinished personal business with the academy, and Vern's project is how he plans to finish it—by becoming the first anthropologist to live in space, where he will undertake a trail-blazing scholarly study of private-sector space cowboys, combined with documentaries for public TV and a two- or three-volume coffee-table book tie-in.

The Doctor is also an amateur folk musician, and in this capacity he composed the anthem "Hardware Dude," theme song of Marco Tempesto's *Commando Cuisine*. The show is taped each week in the home-ec labs of a local high school, to which the Doctor has now driven us in his bottle-green Austin-Healey. The taping is done on Thursday nights, not Saturday afternoon, but since Tempesto was cooking anyway, he wanted to get a special episode out of it—catering the large banquet event. Dwight Jr. refuses to walk, so I'm conveying him piggyback down the wide school hallway, spurred on by the Stride-Rites. My adolescence is flooding back to me. We pass countless padlocked student lockers filled, I presume, with weapons and drugs. "This is where you'll be spending your days, Dwight Jr.," I say. He slaps the metal doors as we lumber by.

I've never been here, but the Doctor knows where he's going. He hangs a left and pushes open a set of double doors to reveal Tempesto under movie lights in the center of a vast lab room, standing at a worktable in an achingly white jumpsuit with COMMANDO CUISINE stitched across his chest in glossy red script—the name of his catering service as well as of the program. He breaks eggs one-handed into a bowl and fluffs them with a whisk.

Dwight directs, standing off to one side and pointing to things he wants his camera operator to shoot. He sees us, and wheels over a stainless-steel table piled with large net bags of onions. Dwight Jr. climbs down my body to be with Da. "Have you ever had Tempesto's onion tart?" Dwight asks me. "No? You're in for a treat." He takes a whopping chef's knife from a wooden tableside holder, flicks its edge with his thumb, and hands it to me.

"I'm chopping onions instead of working on the video?"

"Sometimes the only thing to do is to leave Anita alone, and then she pulls it together. Plus, we have to think of the big picture. What if the video's a bust? We want to make sure there's plenty of good food, right?"

"Maybe Tempesto could do one of his laser-light shows."

"Good thinking, Walter. We're going to get it right now. That's why you're taking over for us."

"This reminds me of a wonderful feast I once filmed in New Guinea," the Doctor says.

Tempesto beckons him over into the camera's purview. "We have a world-renowned anthropologist in our studios today, ladies and gentlemen. Doctor, any little-known culinary lore you'd like to share with us?"

"Well, Marco, did you know that the natives of Coney Island have more than one hundred words for Sno-Kones?"

■

Marco Tempesto got his start as Vernon DeCloud's technical wizard. Back in the days when Vern was doing his first big venture-capital deals, the young Tempesto was pulling cable through Vern's ceilings, installing phone systems, configuring computers, maintaining databases. Tempesto even wrote software back then, though he won't type one line of code today. Language is a quagmire, he says. He works only on machines themselves now, machines and food, and then only if he's made them himself.

His real heart is in gargantuan visual art. Not the thousand-mile serpentine trenches you've seen in travel magazines, the ones requiring a bulldozer and a bullheaded grant-recipient. Tempesto doesn't work with dirt. He doesn't work with brute force. He works with light. Though hardware is his mistress, Tempesto's deepest passion is for the immaterial, for things you can't take apart with a screw gun, things that don't really exist outside the concatenating powers of the mind. You wouldn't know it from the lather he can get into over gigabytes and megaflops, but the physical world, for Tempesto, is merely a doorway into the metaphysical.

More than anything, he would like to turn the nighttime sky into 3-D color TV. That would be the most incredible hack of all, he says, and he claims to know how to do it, but it would cost a lot of money, even for a few seconds, and so far the funding has been elusive. He pitched the idea to his old friend Vernon DeCloud—financing celestial television by selling some sky-time for advertising—and though Vern would be perfectly happy to go down in history as the man who turned the stratosphere into a Coke commercial, he said no. Vern didn't believe Tempesto could do it. He thought it was just techie hand-waving, and that's what hurt the most. In desperation, and though he considered it an ugly idea, Tempesto submitted a proposal for turning the new moon into a Gulf Oil sign. The Gulf people said his idea wouldn't work and sent it back.

Meanwhile, another laser artist beat him to a synthetic aurora borealis, and Tempesto still smarts over that, though by all reports it was less colorful and shorter-lived than his own would have been. And a holographic northern lights was pretty obvious anyway. Tempesto envisions art videos viewable from one-third of the earth's surface at a time. Why? For the transformation and unification of human consciousness.

■

Tempesto's staff went to the Marriott in two panel trucks full of food and drink, leaving the Doctor and me to button things up in the laboratories of American culinary education. Dwight Jr. got to use the big boys' urinal in the high-school bathroom because it was the kind that goes all the way down to the floor, and that seemed to be the high point of his day, if not of his life. While the Doctor helped him, I washed my hands three times with the anti-bacterial soap from the pump dispenser, but they still smell like onions. My eyes continue to cry, too, here in the passenger seat of the Doctor's Lilliputian car, with Dwight Jr. sitting on my lap and the seat belt around the two of us.

We corkscrew down into the garage beneath the Marriott, where the Doctor unfurls himself from the Austin-Healey, lifts Dwight Jr. out, and then pulls me from the car like a vet birthing a calf. We ride a mahogany-lined elevator up a few flights, and when the doors slide open we're in a lobby with scores of people milling around, name tags plastered to their shirts and jackets saying, HELLO! MY NAME IS, followed by their names in red Magic Marker. A cloth banner spans a wall, saying, in two-foot-high letters, WELCOME INTERNATIONAL SOCIETY FOR PRIVATE SPACE EXPLORA-TION.

We sidle around the edges of the room, me clutching Dwight Jr.'s jersey so he won't disappear. "There's a society for this?" I ask the Doctor. "Nobody told me that. I thought we were showing a tape to a bunch of investors."

"Yup. We're doing that."

"These are all people who think they're personally going to outer space?"

"The investors are here, too. The society is a bunch of space-junkie anarchists who've been E-mailing each other for years and getting all charged up about the government. Vern just stepped in with the idea of organizing their first meeting and letting some money people see the talent and energy."

I bump into a paunchy guy in his thirties with a plastic cup of beer in his hand. He has that rumpled software-engineer look. "Where are you on this space stuff?" I ask him. "The bleachers or the field?"

"I'm on the first rocket off this ball of dirt!" he says.

"The field." I wink and give him the thumbs-up.

Soon we come to the entrance of the hotel cocktail lounge. "Karaoke!" says the Doctor, leading us inside. The dim bar is populated largely by men cheering one of their brothers onstage as he turns in a grisly rendition of "The Impossible Dream." There's a smattering of women with the same crazed techie look in their eye as the guys, but if they're drunk on space exploration or anything else, at least they're not singing about it.

"Da!" says Dwight Jr.

"You have to love karaoke," the Doctor says.

"No, I don't."

"Men never used to be able to do things like this in public."

"Those were the days."

I leave him to his study of lounge behavior, and carry Dwight Jr. up another flight to the grand ballroom. The dinner program doesn't begin for a half hour yet, but most of the tables are occupied by people snarfing appetizers and arguing about outer space beneath massive chandeliers and three large mirrored disco balls that seem to be left over from the nineteen-seventies.

One nice thing about a big gig like this is that the video people get to bring a guest to the ball, and I see mine now at a table with Anita. When I get there, Dwight Jr. stops slapping my head and climbs down to root around in his mother's leather satchel. Rebecca rises to kiss me. "You reek of onions!" she says.

"It's bad, isn't it? I can't get it off. Make sure you try the onion tart. I was a human sacrifice to it."

"Rebecca came over to Paradise to hang out with me," Anita says. "We worked on the tape together!"

"I helped find stuff to fill the holes," Rebecca says. "We had to lose a lot of your voice-over. Sorry."

"I hate voice-over anyway," Anita says.

"Then why do you always hire me to write it?" I ask.

"Oh, voice-over's important."

I chew on the logic of this, but my brain spits it out. "What did you think?" I ask Rebecca.

"Reminded me of the condominium one. Condominiums in outer space. Why did they need a video in the first place? They've got all these loonies in the flesh."

"Don't say that too loud," Anita says.

Tempesto's helpers have changed into their serving clothes, black slacks and blousy white T-shirts that say COMMANDO CUISINE below a picture of a hungry-looking computer chip holding a knife and fork. They circulate with platters of spicy fried calamari, boiled Gulf shrimp, giant stuffed mushroom caps, baked Brie on baguette. The commando himself is working on the ballroom stage in a fresh white jumpsuit, hooking up his laser guns and racks of electronics gear.

Dwight materializes with a glass in his hand. "Cheers, Earthlings."

"What are you drinking?" Anita asks. "Give it to me."

"Vodka tonic. Nature's perfect beverage."

"Remember when they used to say that about eggs?" Anita says, taking a sip. "That eggs were nature's perfect food? They don't say that anymore."

"I think they might find out a few things about vodka tonics, too," Rebecca says.

"I'm getting mine in before they do," says Dwight.

I watch Vernon DeCloud schmooze around the ballroom, and in this way I figure out who some of the investors are. They're basically guys in expensive suits, human beings like you or me, except different. Vern arrives at our table and shakes everybody's hand.

"This is Rebecca!" Anita says. "Walter's moving in with her!"

"Well, I might be," I say, putting my arm around Rebecca's shoulders. "We're talking about it."

"Look before you leap," Vern says.

"Who are you telling that to?" Rebecca asks.

"Everybody!" says Vern. He looks apprehensive. "There's a billion dollars here looking for a place to park," he tells Dwight.

"They're gonna love it, Vern. Don't worry."

"I realize this was an unusual assignment," Vern says.

"No it wasn't," Rebecca says. "They do all the outer-space people."

To his everlasting credit, Vern has a snort with us over this.

"Trust us," Dwight tells Vern. "We understand the mentality. We *are* the mentality."

We join a line to have our plates filled with Tempesto's stuffed loin of pork and piquant trimmings. My onion tart—I think of it as mine—seems to be a big hit as well; I suspect we have quite a few vegetarians on hand. In the minute or two that Dwight and I are alone, back at the table, I say, "You really think we're looking at class warfare down here, Dwight? I've been trying to decide if I'd want to bring a kid into this world."

"You see any haves giving their stuff to the have-nots?"

"Not exactly."

"Me neither. On the other hand, there's always a chance our children will reject our rotten act and start living right. It's worth hoping for, I guess. If you had a kid, you'd probably move out, though."

"Yeah, probably."

"I'd say hold off, then."

When most people are well into the food and wine, Vern introduces the keynote speaker, a famous scientist who appears in our tape. Vern says not one word about class warfare or planetary exodus. He sticks to the usual stuff about capitalism on a new frontier, the rock-solid investment of it all. The scientist is well known for his desire to leave this planet, and his speech is easy to understand—Mars or bust. I observe the reaction of a few investors: they don't look too impressed. Tempesto's staff serves coffee and dessert—zabaglione for a group this large! Tempesto! —and then the room lights go dim, a large silver screen scrolls down the wall above the stage, and our tape begins to roll.

The new cut of the video is as predictable and dull as I-80 through Nebraska. True, extolling the glories of boldly going where no one has gone before would be preaching to the converted here, but the converted would have enjoyed a little preaching, and the investors would have enjoyed seeing them hoot and holler about it. Instead, it's all about commercial applications and short-term yields, things the space people think are stupid and which must look, to the investors, like the hand-waving they see every day in their part of the world. All in all, we have succeeded in cryogenically freezing the whole audience by remote control. If I were in charge of this show, I'd say spoon out large second helpings of zabaglione to anybody wearing a good suit, but I'm not in charge, and the zabaglione's probably gone anyway. I look at Dwight. He holds up a finger to say *Wait*.

Suddenly the ballroom goes dark—the vast cavern of it absolutely black except for the red glow of the "Exit" lights at the edges. The whole room audibly draws a breath. Trance music starts to shimmer on the PA. Then just as suddenly it's light again, but not the way it was before. Three bright colored beams are shooting from Tempesto's laser guns, each of them hitting one of the now-spinning disco balls on the high ceiling. The open space between the balls goes luminous with the whirling, commingling refractions of the beams, and the resulting mishmash does look, at first, like the northern lights, a vague conglomeration of colored radiance suspended in the air. But soon shapes assert themselves in the welter of foggy colors, the shapes of a gigantic human face—an ear, a nose, a mouth with moving lips. The face has three-dimensional substance, but you can see through it, too. I hear startled cries from the tables around me, every conference-goer staring up in astonishment at the moving holographic visage. A disembodied woman's voice booms from the loudspeakers on the walls. *"Tell me how you feel about moving in with Rebecca,"* the voice says.

"I feel it's an awfully big step," replies the gigantic face in the air, and the amazed ballroom begins to laugh. My table is the only non-laughing one.

"What the hell is he doing up there?" Dwight croaks to Anita.

I stand up and stumble backward among the tables to get some distance on the unholy spirit-head hanging in the air above us. Goddamn if it's not me. *"I might not do it,"* my giant face says. Then a humongous Dwight Jr. crawls into view and slides down the front of me, so palpably real that the audience cringes and covers its collective head.

"Da!" says Dwight Jr., pointing up at himself in the air.

This may sound odd coming from an actor, even one who scarcely acts anymore, but every time I see myself on tape, I wonder, *Is this a man anyone would care about? Is this a person someone could love?* And often I have my doubts. But not this time. This time I think I'm a knockout. Brando, DeNiro, and Pacino put together never had a gig this good.

Tempesto arrives. He's laughing like a person in shock. "Where's my moon animation!" he exclaims.

"This is supposed to be a low-altitude lunar fly-by!" Dwight says.

"I thought this was it!" says Anita. "Dwight Jr. was playing with the cassettes before I gave them to Tempesto. This is something I was doing as a wedding present!"

"What wedding?" I say.

"*I want a little girl,*" my monstrous mouth declares, a gleaming chandelier between my translucent teeth. "*If I had a girl, she'd worship me and love me forever.*"

I look around and see that it scarcely matters what tape is playing. It could be anything up there. The audience is reeling with technique, the pure technique of an outlandish trick, for Tempesto has succeeded where all others have failed—he has somehow projected real-time full-motion video into a massive hologram floating in open air. He leaps onto the stage, his hands clasped in victory above his jumpsuited form. Here in the very birthplace of astounding hardware hacks, surrounded by the buildings of MIT, a ballroom's worth of technology junkies is giving him a standing ovation. "This is only a demo!" he screams to the convention. "I can do this in the sky! A whole continent at a time! All I need is some up-front capital!"

The investors are on their feet in ecstasy. If this isn't thinking Japanese, they don't know what is. They've got Sony by the short ones now. Vernon DeCloud appears onstage. "Let's hear it for Marco Tempesto!" he shouts into the microphone. "One minute of paid ads in the sky every night and we can go look for other solar systems!"

The crowd goes wild, and then a woman's voice says over the loudspeakers, "*What's the problem with men, anyway?*" When I look up, Rebecca's giant 3-D face has replaced mine in the air. "*What's the big deal about living together?*" her hologram goes on. "*He's at my place every night anyway.*"

It looks amazingly like her, and it's strangely enchanting to experience her features thirty feet tall. That's her smile exactly, big as a queen-sized bed. Her eyes are really pools. Those dark, curly cables are the hairs on her head. I've never seen her in detail like this.

Here on the ground, she's out of her chair and standing beside me, our mortal faces turned up to the numina we've become.

"It's them!" somebody exclaims. "They're here! The guy and the girl!"

The audience turns to look at us.

"Move in with her, you bum!" somebody shouts.

"He's not a bum!" Rebecca says.

"You're too good for him, sweetheart!" a man calls out.

"He doesn't look that bad to me," a woman says.

Anita stands on her chair and cups her hands around her mouth. "Let's put it to a vote! Should they move in together?"

The ayes come in like Niagara Falls.

"*I can't help it,*" Rebecca's tremendous mouth is saying. "*I love the big dope. I know we'd be happy,*" and suddenly I realize that I'm nuts about this monumental woman. And another thing: with her face as big as it is, she looks a lot like my mom.

"Jah!" cries a little voice nearby. Dwight Jr. is jumping on his father's lap and waving at Rebecca's face above us.

I turn to my flesh-and-blood girlfriend. "I'm crazy about you, you big goddess! All right, I'll move in!"

"You will?" she exclaims, and then she leaps into my arms. I stagger around, trying to find my balance beneath her weight. The ovation from the ballroom is deafening. I have the idea that I'm a rocket shuddering with its payload on a pad, that the sound I'm hearing is my own incredible motor. In my eccentric circuit of the floor, I catch a blurry glimpse of Tempesto surrounded by men in expensive suits. The Doctor is flashing us with the strobe of his Nikon. We're going down in anthropology. Finally I stabilize and come to a teetering halt beneath the unearthly glow of the first-ever demonstration of celestial TV. "Now what do I do?" I gasp to Rebecca.

"Fly me to the moon."